I0667115

THE GOOD WORLDS ARE ALL TAKEN

DAVID GIONFRIDDO

APOPHENIA

This book is a work of fiction. The characters and incidents portrayed in it are all drawn from the author's imagination. Any resemblance to real persons, living or dead, events or localities is purely coincidental.

"Statement Of David P. Gionfriddo," "Venus In Rags," "Who's Afraid Of Tobias Wolff?" and "Rodger Pidgeon Is Dead" first appeared in *Paraphilia Magazine*.

"Just Punishments" first appeared in *Antique Children: Revolt of the Underdogs*.

Cover Image: William Blake, *Christ in the Sepulchre, Guarded By Angels,* Victoria & Albert Museum

ACKNOWLEDGEMENTS

First and foremost, I must thank Díre McCain and Dave Mitchell from *Paraphilia Magazine* and Apophenia/Oneiros Books, whose support and encouragement were most directly responsible for the pieces in this volume. *Paraphilia* got me writing again in 2008, and the voices and visions Díre and Dave brought together in that project continue to be a source of inspiration. Thanks also to Jim Lopez of *Antique Children* for giving me my first hardcopy publication when he selected "Just Punishments" for his excellent *Revolt of the Underdogs* issue in 2011. I also have to acknowledge Rick Moody, a genius writer and a great and generous teacher, who taught me that a story can take many forms and encouraged me to explore them all; and flash fiction queen Meg Pokrass, an insightful artist whose online writing challenges provided many shots of literary adrenaline. For general support, friendship and encouragement, the list becomes unmanageably long. But I offer a word of humble appreciation to the many sick and disabled friends I have met in the social media community, who continue, with their strength, perseverance and dignity, to keep me plodding forward. Most of all, this book is for them.

STATEMENT OF DAVID P. GIONFRIDDO OF VIRGINIA, NOMINEE TO BE AN ASSOCIATE JUSTICE OF THE SUPREME COURT, TO THE SENATE JUDICIARY COMMITTEE, 126th Congress, June 30, 2024

Judge GIONFRIDDO: Thank you, Chairman Marquardt, Ranking Member Dinwiddie and all of the members of this Committee, for giving me the opportunity to testify here today. I would also like to take this opportunity to thank you for your selfless, tireless work on behalf of the American people and our judicial system.

At the outset, let me say that being nominated as an Associate Justice of the Supreme Court by President Masters is one of the greatest and most unexpected honors I have ever received in a 50-year legal career that has spanned all facets of public and private practice. It is an awesome responsibility and, consequently, carries a great deal of public scrutiny. However, a free and robust "Fourth Estate" is one of the glories of our republic. Not in a spirit of rancor, but, rather, to dispel the air of suspicion and innuendo, I would like to discuss some of the

1

matters the press has raised. My life is, as it must be, an open book, albeit one with a few creased and tattered pages. Some of the more senior members of the panel will know what I mean by "book" and "pages."

It is true that the advent of "net culture," commencing during the early-to-mid-1990s has preserved and broadcast heretofore private aspects of life in a way never anticipated by the Founding Fathers, but, again, I say that no public servant should have cause to fear the sanitizing effects of sunlight. I certainly do not.

This observation is a good lead-in to the so-called "Melrose Missives" of 1995-96. During this time, as a senior associate at the Boston law firm of Belding & Hammersmith, I became, as, indeed, did millions of Americans, a devotee of the television drama *Melrose Place*. At this time, I was also receiving my introduction to online culture, courtesy of my first computer, an old Dell with a couple hundred megs' [sp?] hard drive and a 256K modem the size of a transistor radio. [Laughter]

Sen. FIBULA: Remember the racket those suckers used to make?

Judge GIONFRIDDO: I know. I believe one like it currently sits on exhibition at the Smithsonian's Twitter Pavillion. [Laughter] At the urging of several "friends" (please note that I never met any of these individuals personally, or had the opportunity to discuss their motives with them at any length), I

2

began disseminating episode summaries in what I believed to be a humorous vein. I did perhaps half-a-dozen of these during the spring and summer of 1995. I now understand, as *CharlotteObserver.net* has pointed out, that some of the turns of phrase contained therein, particularly references to actress Marcia Cross as a "flame-tressed floozy," or oft-repeated comparisons of Loni Anderson's physical features to common household appliances and breakfast foods, were neither clever nor particularly humorous.

I accept full responsibility for the public opprobrium caused by these communiqués, and ask the Committee to consider my youth, the giddy freedom of "email," and the timing of these messages, most of which were written in the wee small hours, after long days spent advancing American commerce and doing *pro bono* legal work on behalf of indigent Death Row inmates. They most certainly are not representative of the man I am today, or the service I will render to the Court.

But these messages were lost in the ether, or so we thought, and had no consequences. They were like a joke told among friends in a country-club locker room. This sense of false security and collegiality could help explain the rather lengthy and detailed discussion of Penelope Spheeris' 1988 documentary film *The Decline of Western Civilization, Part II: The Metal Years*, which I unwisely penned for the naively-transgressive website *rocktillyoupuke.com* in the fall of 1999. Editor Tom Tollefson's blog *Consensus Working Overtime*, a fine publication I consult often, has dissected this piece at some length and, I might say, with a somewhat untoward and mean-spirited relish, particularly my disapproving references to what I call the "muff" scenes featuring the hard-rock band Odin, and the use of W.A.S.P.'s controversial anthem "Animal ([expletive deleted] Like A Beast)." These quotations were taken out of context from a longer, and considerably more-thoughtful-than-implied, piece, in which I took pains to warn of the chiropractic dangers of hair-whipping, and noted the strong anti-alcoholism statement made by Blackie Lawless' aimless vodka-chugging in an otherwise-empty swimming pool. A fuller and more sensitive reading of this article might be said to reveal the first public stirrings of a social conscience, one which I have taken great pains to develop over my career.

The reasons for, and my contrition over, the rather ill-fated and tasteless decision to select former President Jimmy Carter as the next decedent in the *deadpool.net* contest of later that year were discussed at great length with Special Agents Morin and Finley of the United States Secret Service during an exhaustive October 1999 interview, transcripts of which were provided to this Committee. For that reason, and on advice of my counsel, Mr. O'Shea, I will forego further elaboration at this time.

I would have liked to say that this incident "scared me straight," and that I could close the book on the relatively harmless shenanigans of a young, work-hard, play-hard attorney enjoying the fullness of life in a major metropolis. This I surely would

4

have done if not for the unfortunate and – I predict – legally corrosive lawsuit[1] brought by *Vanity Fair* to obtain copies of my Netflix and Amazon transaction records from the American Bar Association and the Office of White House Counsel. It goes without saying that such an act, and the publication of the information thus obtained, strikes at the very heart of citizens' rights to privacy.[2] But since, as it were, that particular horse is "out of the barn," I feel compelled to offer a few words on my own behalf.

I make no apologies for my love of films of the so-called "horror" and "fantasy" genres. These represent some of our nation's most treasured cultural achievements. Our grandparents thrilled to the terrors of *Frankenstein* and *Dracula*. Our parents shrieked at James Arness as *The Thing From Another World*. And, in our younger years, we gazed in rapt attention at *Poltergeist* and *Nightmare on Elm Street*. As many of you know from reviewing the current Medicare reform proposals offered by the CBO, there is nothing as cathartic as a good scare. [Laughter]

---

[1] *Conde Nast Publications, Inc. v. Pickering*, Civ. Action No. 24-CV-1658 (S.D.N.Y., slip opinion filed March 3, 2024) ("there can be no overriding privacy interest where the information is imminently likely to become part of the public record").

[2] *See, e.g., Griswold v. Connecticut*, 381 U.S. 479 (1965). The Committee should note that my citing of *Griswold* for its application of constitutional penumbra theory to "the sacred precincts of marital bedrooms," *id.* at 486, should not be construed to imply any sexual misconduct by the author or any other person or persons of his acquaintance.

But, seriously... As many writers have remarked, horror is often a way of discussing, through metaphor and allusion, social issues deemed "too hot to handle." In the 1950s, *Invasion of the Body Snatchers* served as a metaphor for McCarthyism, and the original *The Day the Earth Stood Still* (which I still prefer to the Keanu Reeves version – no offense, Sen. Nakanaela!) explored fears of nuclear annihilation. *Rosemary's Baby* was a veiled discussion of emerging female reproductive rights. And so on. Viewed in this light, the events depicted in that tawdry and sensationalistic *Vanity Fair* article can be seen as nothing less than a young law partner's exploration of important historical and social currents.

I put it to this Committee that a film like *Chopping Mall* (Jim Wynorski, U.S., 1986), lampooned for its "infantile *mise-en-scene* and execution," has much to say about American consumerism and its impact on the value of human life, things that anyone who has read my opinions in the "Baby For Sale" cases knows concern me deeply. A philistine might see *Nazi Love Camp 7* (Lee Frost, U.S., 1969) as "a C-grade orgy of titillation," in one pundit's formulation, but I defy cable commentator Michael Wigham to make such a statement to a family touched by the Holocaust. *Sex Creatures From Beyond* (Cyntha Grossnickle, Canada, 2019) …mere B-grade nonsense or a brave effort to combine environmental activism with a profound sensitivity to violence against women? My own vacation home is not that far from the Everglades, Mr. Chairman, and, were such a toxic spill to really happen, I would certainly fear for the consequences on my darling daughters Dixie and Evangeline. Flesh-eating arthropods or simply a higher incidence of psoriasis and asthma...*forewarned is forearmed.* I know that none of you would begrudge any father this vigilance, although my detractors have wasted no time at all in spinning it into evidence of "unfitness to serve."

My 2012 elevation to the federal bench in the Eastern District of Virginia did not force me to cloister myself. Rather, it occasioned in me a renewed desire to experience the life of the people, particularly the young people who will comprise our nation's future.

It was in that spirit that I "signed on" to Facebook in the fall of that year. I found many interesting features – or "apps," as they were then called – that put me in touch with forums on green energy, fair trade, climate change, and other stimulating and vital issues. Clearly, I could not have enjoyed the free and unfettered exchanges I had with my many young friends in the guise of a recently-appointed federal district judge! Despite the bewildering whisper campaign launched by *ascend.org*, this and this alone was the reason for my use of a *nom de Net*, and a profile photo of Spanish matador Francisco Ordonez. It turns out there is little that the young won't share with such a face.

Which brings me, inevitably as the dawn, to yet another of the misconstrued, and perhaps unwise, pranks seized upon by *Vanity Fair* and other opportunistic opponents of my nomination. Had I known of the awesome trust that was to be vested in me today, there is simply no chance that I would have used the LivingSocial Facebook utility to post "Five Teen Actresses With Whom I Would Like A Session 'In Camera.'" It was uncalled-for, and best viewed as an overabundance of enthusiasm for my research on young people's hopes and struggles. I would particularly like to apologize to Mses. Bynes and Paxton for some of the unsolicited comments added to this post, and to Ms. Cosgrove for the very poor judgment I showed in mailing her – or, more accurately, her "people," I would guess -- a sound file of W.A.S.P.'s "Animal ([expletive deleted] Like A Beast)." And now, I seek simply to let my and my family's wounds begin to heal, and to move on a wiser and more prudent jurist.

Let me step back for a moment at this time to remind this panel that one possible reason for my high-spiritedness at this time was that millions of people the world over – myself included – believed that the world as we know it was due to end on December 21 of 2012, as foretold by the prophet Isaiah, certain once-in-a-century celestial alignments and the termination of the Mayan solar calendar. No doubt many of you have had your own "nothing to lose" moments that prompted various thoughtless behaviors.

As for the books that have crept into the discussion, *The Anarchist Cookbook* (William Powell; Barricade Books, 1989) and *How to Disappear Completely and Never Be Found* (Fin Kennedy; Nick Hern Books, 2008) were what we like to call "gag" gifts for a friend retiring from a supervisory position at the Department of Homeland Security in 2016. I can only recall opening either volume once, to write appropriate inscriptions.

One's ability to read, watch and listen to what he pleases is, I feel, central to the American experience, as is the right to freely practice one's religion, although this might be news to the staff of *undergod.org*, who have recently raised, in quite unflattering terms and against all manner of historical and legal precedent, my attendance in support of Evangeline at the recent Wiccan Beltane observances in Charles County, Maryland. For this, I make no apology. George Washington was a Freemason, Richard Nixon a Quaker and Nancy Reagan attended séances. Although it is rarely discussed, it is well known among presidential historians that Theodore Roosevelt was an Elk and that, during his Senate years, Lyndon Baines Johnson often attended – in his own cape – conventions of the Order of Demolay. And neither my dispensing of ceremonial corn cakes from the pentacle plate, nor my invocation of Sekhmet the Lioness and Cerridwen, Keeper of the Cauldron, should give this Committee a moment's pause as to my allegiance to the Constitution, my support of American heartland values, or my ardor to defend basic freedoms.

Without unduly emphasizing the negative this afternoon, I find it unsettling and somewhat disheartening that I should be called upon to answer for a series of innocent, miscast or downright laudable events by muckrakers who would seek to impede my own destiny and to deprive the

9

American people of the labor of a dedicated public servant. Our most cherished rights and institutions are at risk, a fact driven home to me by my recent correspondences with a Latvian dental assistant and a Filipina seamstress who wrote me of their lifelong quests to share freedom in America with a respectable, successful gentleman who owns his own home. I trust this panel to protect that dream. Goddess bless the Supreme Court of the United States and Goddess bless America.

I will now be happy to respond to your questions.

JUST PUNISHMENTS

It was the great day, the anniversary of the founding martyr's burning, and for at least an hour, the church, like the greening world, had begun to revive.

— *It's a symbol, an offering. A climax to a glorious pilgrimage!* Senior Prelate Macomber waved his hand grandly, like a conductor, to sweep in all of the new Motherchurch's airy interior spaces. *And more than all of this, it is our home.*

One could feel the larger-than-average congregation, from the best-dressed members of Needle's Eye, adorned in their crimson and indigo finery, to the Inheritors huddled together in a lively back-bench scrum, squelching a great inner rising, a collective ovation of cheers, wolfwhistles and Tonguespeak. It was beyond dispute that Granite Macomber knew every curse, every whisper, every shaken fist it would take to turn a crowd to his advantage. He could, it was said, charm the pitchfork right out of old Belial's claw, and get it spit-shined, to boot. On good Sundays like this, one could still recall the glory days of jam-packed masses and raw throats.

Macomber's tone reminded Ed Czarnecki-Whaley of the fiery rhetoric that had roiled around the launch of the great Building Mission six years earlier. Old Elder Dignan, in his measured, trembly voice, had quoted from ArchProtector Keane's 2030's epistles warning of waste and ostentation and "the suffocating vainglory of the material." The

11

Savonarolans should, Dignan pleaded, be models of simplicity, piety and thrift, meeting on the web ring, in the storefronts and the mobile tent services, leaving the gaudy display and ceremony to those hangers-on who stuck with the Church of Rome or the wealthy Protestant denominations. But little could stand under the onslaught of Macomber's lacerating broadsides. *Man is a frivolous and concupiscent animal,* he had glowered. *God sees through his pretenses and facades, and shame on us for trying to hide our base nature behind such transparent ploys. Best to accept that men are a communal species who need a meeting place and who draw strength from numbers and rite and fellowship, and to humbly accept the opprobrium that flows from these facts! Anything else would be an attempt to outsmart the Lord your God,* he had warned, *and would trigger even harsher consequences.* Everyone already knew about Dignan's frailties, and there were rumblings that his relations had fallen hopelessly behind in their district enjoyment taxes. Soon enough, they might be classified res-transient. He hardly seemed to be reveling in God's favor. The whispers grew louder and the legal tender flowed by the tens of thousands into Macomber's Building Fund. And stone by stone, his monument rose.

And the end result was The Haven, this marvelous edifice, its translucent quartzite and fiberglass dome a source of the wondrous multicolored light that flowed through Chatelet's angel and archangel panels. Ed was marveling at the way Uriel's wings glittered as he petitioned God to judge mankind, his ears filling with the ragged, soulful notes of Hymn 18, "A Kingdom Lost and Found":

A paragon of all the Earth
With holy censure bound
A fallen race
We ask God's grace
A kingdom lost and found

Ed was so overwhelmed by the sweet terror of contrition every time he walked the Hall of Penitents, past the life-size bronzes of Adam, the wrathful Cain, Herod, and, finally, a downtrodden Judas clutching his pieces of silver, that he didn't even mind when the ushers wheeled the brass urns down the aisle for the Unburdenings. Along the pew, people dug into pockets and purses for folding money, credit vouchers, wristwatches and loose jewelry. With a beatific smile, Ed's daughter Lorra reached below the stone kneeler and produced the ancient oil portrait of Grandfather Czarnecki that had hung in the dining room as long as Ed could remember. In its ornate gold frame, it had the look of a museum piece, and Ed could see the envy tattooed on the faces of the other Rebuilders as they clutched their coins and sparkly baubles. As he passed, Usher Blanton leaned in and whispered:

— *Can you stop by Macomber's office after mass? He wants a word.*

Ed could not help feeling grand and important and necessary as the congregation finished its

13

admissions of unworthiness and Macomber ascended to the pulpit, the spotlight picking out the gold thread that rimmed the flames on the scarlet robe commemorating May 22, the Feast of the Founder. He had heard the traditional Founder's sermon so many times he could practically recite it by heart:

> *Man, wrought to preside over Creation, has been the perpetrator of an endless series of wrongs, betrayals, disappointments, conspiracies, intrigues, backslidings, peccadilloes, dawdlings, ditherings and general failings. Adam and Eve partook of forbidden fruit. Cain slew Abel. Why, the world grew so rotten and tainted that God had to flush it clean with flood. And still, the Lord forgave, sending his only Son to redeem the race. And how, my friends, my cousins, was He repaid? St. Peter denied Him, Judas betrayed Him, the Romans scourged and crucified Him. What father among you could forgive such things? And still, man proceeds along an infinite, unbroken thoroughfare of sin, war, genocide, dispossession, a vast and varied menagerie of smaller, yet equally bitter wrongs. When disaster strikes, when the earth moves, when children suffer, we wring our hands and ask "Why?" I would challenge them and say "Why not?" Why should He not wash his hands of man, turn his attention to other societies, other worlds? For I tell you today that it is our duty, our sacred travail, to atone, to expunge, to reclaim with our suffering the holy favor of the Lord.*

All around him, female parishioners pricked themselves with their golden Penitence Pins, and the men sandpapered arms or ran their hands over flames snaking from crimson-colored lighters, the tang of seared skin mingling with woodsmoke from the burning Gauntlet of Flame that linked the church gate and the Sander Street parking lot. Soon, they were all chanting the recessional apologies, and marching out to the great pipe organ blaring "How Sweet The Lash." As Lorra and her friends from the ecumenical school squealed with gleeful fright beneath a rain of embers from the canopy of fire, Ed squeezed his wife's hand and stroked the bristly fur on the inside of his vestment.

— Why don't you catch a ride with the Fletchers, babe? I have to see the Prelate on...church business.

******

— Ah, enter and harken, Gatherer Willing!

At times like this, Ed would reflect on the mad, serpentine course his adult life had taken. For most of his 20s, he had knocked around the education mills of West Puissant, doing distance- and sleep-learning classes in a variety of disciplines – Sexwork Management, Information Retrieval, Parapsych Services. He had been lured in by the holodeck ads of all the biggest and wealthiest ed companies, and was sure he was onto a winner with CareerStar Megaversity's Synthetic Real Estate Creation Certificate Program, but ran out of tuition funds before the final exams. He had been reduced to street crime and cell donation when he wandered into the Maxie Park Lost Cause Center and prostrated himself to the Savs. From day one, the other Inheritors had called him *cousin*, and included him in the neighborhood lashings. Buzz Joy from the roundball league had even squared the wheels on his old ice-blue Remora free of charge. The church took him off the street and found him a fourth-floor walk-up in the Rubber District, paid for with his wages from the Kurlin Street Reclamation Center. And it was at one of the Savonarolans' starvation suppers that he first locked eyes with Carmen, smiling nervously in her mold-flecked sackcloth at the too-loud rumblings in her precious tummy. Her little pout was like a flaming arrow through Ed's heaving ventricles. They were joined as Fellow-Travellers after a whirlwind six weeks, their foreswearing attended by the whole Puissant assembly. Kazzie came two years later, little Lorra a year after that. The Center made him an assistant manager, and then, just last year, he realized the greatest triumph of all. In a small, private investiture ceremony, the Prelate conveyed unto him his church-name, Dirrt Willing, and elevated him to the rank of Seed-Gatherer. He was substantial. He had assignment and purpose.

The Prelate's sanctuary was dark and warm and filled with the smells of things old and neglected. Once there had been a Croatian girl who would come in and flick a feather duster at the spare furnishings, but Macomber had cashiered her after some of the Trustees complained of the expense. Ed

16

ran a finger over the arm of a sofa and exposed a line of dark wood. He wondered if this was some sort of passive aggression, a way of punishing the church for its pettiness by letting things go to pot.

— *Don't be put off by dust, Gatherer. It's your beginning and your end.*

— *The very same,* Ed agreed. *What service can I do for you and our church? Are we having another door-to-door vanity purge?*

Macomber silently looked down at his clasped hands.

— *It has been months. And, just between us, I know where we can find a pair of obsidian earrings and a lynx stole.*

Macomber looked up and smiled a smile that was fond and stern, gently twisting the ring that was his only outward ornament: a silver signet bearing the order's motto: *Patentia Dei Lassus Est.* The old man had let him hold it once and read it under the light and, without being asked, had patted Ed on the small of his spine and offered a translation: *God is getting peeved...* It was a small moment of intimacy that made Ed feel like a biblical titan.

— *Good son, there is a matter I mean to discuss with you.* Macomber blew a wisp of dust from the cover of an old volume of philosophy. *It's the monthly Plaints of the Forsaken. I'm afraid I am sensing of late a certain lack of intensity...*

The Plaints! Ed's sacred and particular trust! From the minute one stepped into a sanctuary, the Pillars of the Orthodoxy were drilled into you, and principal among them was the Blessedness of the

17

Forsaken. Because the suffering of the sick, the poor, the anguished, the damaged, purged their innate corruption, they were always closer to God. And because they were so sanctified, they had God's ear. Their petitions and intercessions flew past the muffled prayers of the fit and prosperous, and commanded the immediate attention of the Creator. It was Ed's charge to harvest for the congregation lost, forgotten, and broken demi-saints and willworkers to pray for the church's needs at the monthly Feasts of the Forsaken. There was no more sacred duty entrusted to the Savs. And with a wife who was a hospital volunteer, a brother in Residential Displacement, and a niece who served as a dispensary aide on the mobile mental health caravan, he was in a rosy position to locate new *sanctus paupers* for the Savs' unworthy. He had been admitted into the Society of the Abject after securing for Macomber an armless expeditionary ranger who claimed to be possessed by six discrete, identifiable demoniac figures. The church had been packed to the rafters that memorable day, and three days later, Caretaker Yazback had uncovered a cache of 21st century gold ingots while reinforcing the anti-wildlife moat. The trove had funded that season's entire Flagellants' Progress – the longest and best-attended ever – with enough left over to reglaze Borowski's famous Holocaust Window. But it was no secret that two years of peace, coupled with recent advances in nanorobotics and neuroscience, had really made it slim pickings out there, and the last twelve months of club feet and dermatitis and Lagos

18

Belly had really let the air out of the penitential balloon. The last fest, which featured the mom of an Intermittent Anger Syndrome (IAS) toddler, found the church barely a quarter full, with a 64% plunge in the Unburdening take. If Tabulator Breitling hadn't thrown in an antique railroad watch and a 1920s sapphire Freemasons tie pin, they would have barely made enough to publish the monthly *Transgressions*.

— *The Northeast is getting fat and lazy*, Macomber said. *Everybody is working, eating. The borders are quiet. It's the Devil's Peace. The Happy Lie.*

Ed hid has face and nervously fingered some broken glass he kept in his coat pocket for moments like this.

— *The blame is all mine, Prelate*, he said. *I've been working longer hours. And we took a family vacation to the Aliquippa Coal Fire. I can dig deeper. Try my contacts.*

Macomber smiled and put his hands on Ed's shoulders. Ed could feel Macomber's poisonous contempt at his failings, and the sting of self-reproof made him tingle with pain and the joyful expectation of pain. It was no wonder, he thought, that his herd would follow Macomber anywhere. He already felt brighter and cleaner.

— *No matter, acolyte*, Macomber said, reaching in his pocket for a handkerchief. *Here, clean up your hand before you bleed on the Kleiber. Let us pray together for diligence and resourcefulness:*

Needles of pain
Scarrings of fire
Keep our throats parched

Our hearts drowned with desire
Make us pure in the flame
Pull us free from the mire!

   — *Gatherer, we must collect our seed for the coming famine. I shall trust none more than thee to find us a clear channel to the shriving heart. I confide that things are at something of a tipping point. We cannot fail in our revival.* He clasped Ed's raw hand in a firm grip, and Ed could feel the powerful smarting of the sea salt his mentor had hidden in his palm.

   — *So shall it be.* Ed's brain screamed in wild, sweet insult. He would surmount any obstacle to please his holy warder and to strengthen Motherchurch.

******

   Carmen, as always, had come through like a champ and proven her worth as a helpmeet. Together, they had inventoried all the new patients at the Longevity Centre and separated out the best candidates. From the great undifferentiated mass of recharging prosthetics, cerebral stimulus realignments, and nanoprophylactic device insertions – cases too routine to win the church significant favor – they had settled on three: a child born with Remar's Palsy, an older woman severed at the hip in an AquaRay accident, and a recent tourist in Caucasia who had returned with the beginnings of hemophaegic fever. Ed's eyes had widened over that one. A plasma-drinker was serious – methane-shroud serious,

20

continental-shelf-eruption serious – and this one, a certain Denys Landesmann from one of the outlying favelas, was, according to Carm, strong enough to hang on for a while and no longer contagious. Since the paralytic boy was having trouble forming words and the accident lady was unable to properly kneel as the rites required, it looked like Denys was their guy. Dirrt would make a pastoral visit tomorrow. The administrators didn't like it, but the Supreme Court had upheld the Savs' solicitation rights, "in furtherance of paramount spiritual objectives." They made Ed wear that embarrassing identifying collar, and restricted him to two hours in the morning, when most of the patients were still a little foggy, but they could never keep him out entirely.

Ed made sure to put on a good front the next morning. He trimmed and waxed his Vandyke to a razor point, pulled back his hair with some styling cream and shined up his black Nehru duster. He was every inch the holy man as he walked through the virtual door of the St. Eponymous Longevity Center. A small mob jostled for position at the Diagnostikon™ self-serve kiosk, scrambling for the various medicinal lichens and mosses, Omnium poultices and shock stix it doled out for their tokens. He felt like he knew these people, the long-haired merlins, the unshaven downsiders, the bespectacled university types, who felt sure enough about their alternative fixes that they could no longer justify expensive, time-consuming professional treatment. He caught a few condescending glances and a sharpish shoulder to the sternum, but he kept his bearings and advanced toward the elevators. A tall woman with stylish periwinkle hair, factory-perfect breasts shrink-wrapped in the folds of a tiger-striped jumpsuit, handed out sample infusion packs of the new sex drugs – Fervistat, Propulsia – and slipped Ed a glance he read as embarrassed. On the third floor, at General Registration, he approached an officious-looking nurse who scanned his clothes up-and-down with the sort of distaste a Border Conflict veteran might have for an Unfit-to-Serve. It was all right. He was accustomed, and had learned to relax and enjoy the scorn.

– *Landesmann*, she mumbled, flipping virtual pages in the register, *that's Epidemiology, Room 1224. Please observe the posted time limits.*

Of all the various departments, Ed found Epi the most dispiriting, with its calming sea-foam green walls, its pervasive odor of disinfectant, the constant whine of the glove and gown shredder. It all made him feel unclean. 1224 was a double, the mod near the door covered with an iso-tent, inside which curled a small, elderly person of indeterminate gender. Ed peeked behind the sani-mesh curtain at the far mod and tapped on the safety rail in lieu of knocking. In these matters, he had learned, refined manners always made things easier.

He was shocked by what he saw. There, before him, lay a youngish woman – Denyse, not Denys – black-haired, broad-shouldered as an ex-athlete, hollow cheeks bracketing piercing turquoise eyes that hunger had pulled gently back into dark orbital shadows. Her hand floated in the air as if

22

remembering something it had once clung to. Most unnerving of all, she had an inquisitive expression, as if she had been waiting for him with prepared questions.

— *A visitor. And a tall, dark stranger to boot. I would have liked to look a little more...together...*

Ed hated being put in a position to dispense compliments. Saying led to feeling and feeling to believing, and then, to wanting.

— *Oh, you look wonderful. Fact is, I was expecting to see some sickly little man. It was a little startling.*

— *Bennie of having a man's name. The boys are always pleasantly surprised. Mother's way of giving the raw-boned child a leg up.*

So there would be a little extra tonight, Ed thought. Maybe some penalty stones under his side of the mattress. Denys had nervous, fluid features that changed with tricks of the shifting sunlight. Ed imagined that her moment of perfection had been fleeting, and when she stared thoughtfully out at the starlings on Reconciliation Square, he imagined she was trying to recreate in her imagination that transient moment, before care and illness had begun to weather her. Against every instinct, Ed found himself shaken, moved.

— *Ms. Landesmann*, he sputtered, *I guess it's fairly clear from the...*, he showily fingered the crimson religious visitor's yoke, *that I am here in a...representative capacity.*

— *Here to save my soul?* Denys smiled in a way that was not altogether friendly.

– *Uh, well, no,* Ed sputtered, *we were rather hoping you would deign to help us with ours.* The farther he got into his pitch, the more momentum he gathered, the more welcoming the terrain became. He explained the nature of Man as Holy Experiment, the series of miscues that began at Eden (a tale he softened to avoid misogynistic overtones) and continued through all the wars, crimes and unconsummated schemes of the race. Denys seemed to be searching for interstices in his exegesis as he described the great obstacle course of the world, dotted with beauty and harmony and pleasure on which sojourners could stumble on the way from trial to trial, and how history's most pious and godly men (*people,* he corrected) were gifted with the keenest and most clarifying pain – privations, martyrdom, stigmata, and the like – and how the Savonarolans turned over every stone in search of those who held the Bitter Gift, those megaphones through whom man's requests for forgiveness could be more clearly sounded before the Lord.

– *Just out of curiosity,* she asked in a voice without quarrel, *would it be the suffering that made a saint holy, or the holiness that amplified the suffering?*

– *You're a sharp one. It's a yin-yang, chicken-egg kind of deal, one of the great mysteries. They're each interwoven, shot through, and strengthening the other all the time. See what I mean?* He knew he lacked Macomber's gift of speaking from faith, trampling doubts and objections with the rhetoric of ironclad conviction. He hoped his answer would contrive a bridge between the charming set-pieces he had so carefully rehearsed.

She let out a sigh.

– *It's just that I don't seem to be having much luck with the Old Fellow. If I can't get him to do for me...?*

Ed reached over and tenderly clutched her arm, as he had been taught by the men from the Mission Office. *Hold the candidate's arm as you would hold an injured sparrow,* they had said. *Impress, don't oppress.*

Ed knew just what came next.

– *Oh no, child, you mustn't wish away the pain. Yours is a wondrous process, a purifying, a great spiritual scrubbing that eats away the dross and fault. It's a holy torment. St. Theresa of Avila. Saul on the road to Damascus. Find the sweetness at the heart of the horror.*

She met his stare and smiled just a little. *I don't know, uh, Dirrt... This sounds like the pitch the Leatherettes down in District J give the weekenders' Citibusses. Kinky. Whips and shockers for the alter kockers, you know, like the jingle.*

In the hallway, a hovercart led by a pair of dispensary aides hummed by, loaded with tinctures, psychotropic waters and neural feedback slates. When he turned back to Denys, Ed saw she had turned on her side, and nervously nibbled the moisture sensor on her ring finger. She had been taken by a new mood, one of powerlessness and anger.

– *Sir, have you ever been really sick? Have you ever thought there might be no "better"? That the person you were, the life you led, might be just...gone, fled from the world? And that all you had was...this?* She stretched out her arms and clawed nervously at the bedrails. *That this would be your world?*

— *No better than we deserve. Each has his Hell.*

— *Sounds like maybe you need some Leatherette time,* she said. She quietly went on humming the Warm Leatherettes' holovision theme, but it went ever more slowly and mournfully, like a torch song from a dead era.

Ed felt his face redden a little. *Punishment delivered in a sensual context foments its own new sin.*

— *You sound like you're reading from a book.*

— *Several,* he corrected.

Ed took the opening and went on describing the Savonarolans' rites, the Foreswearing, the Admissions of the Wicked, the Festivals of Abasement – as large as the Flagellants' Parade, as quiet and intimate as the Nightly Ablution of the Flame and, lastly, the most joyous celebration of the liturgical calendar, the Feast of the Forsaken. He fixed his eyes on her eyes and began describing the power of the community, yearning toward reunion with the divine, and held in his mind the coaching of the trainers – *blaze, blaze, don't let her attention wander from the outpouring of holy joy!* The sweet, selfless petitioner set aside her burdens and was temporarily released, as she lifted the sinners in her wake. *The love and gratitude of our community will be the most powerful bliss you've ever felt,* Ed protested. *And you'll be doing a spiritual service available only to an anointed few.*

She stroked her hair and, at last, looked away, for what seemed like a long while. She ran a finger along the bedsheet, reacquainting herself with her physical shell, glancing down at her legs as if they were blind auction items, as if she were thinking about nervously parting with some once-unappreciated part of herself.

— So, are you asking...me...to do this thing?

Ed nodded his head, just a little.

— I don't know...Look at me...I sometimes ask things of Him, and He seems so...random. Not like he doesn't care, but like he turns it off and on. She delicately traced the line that filled her withered glands with Hemifane. *There's no cause and effect. Bad comes from good. It's like He doesn't exist, or He does and hates us, or He does and he's...indifferent. Doesn't care, or not too much.*

For a moment, Ed was the Fisher Supreme. He worked the hook in tightly and inched her toward the net. But now, the line had broken and she was drifting away, taking with her his own esteemed place in the congregation. A little too ardently, perhaps, in a voice that ran a step ahead of his own true belief, he assured her that what she took for indifference was a diamond love, unbreakable and pure and filled with mineral fire. God brooked no halfway measures, no muttered pretty-pleases. He spurred us toward ultimates, but was always there at the breaking point, ready to shine a smile and welcome us into his Everlasting Manor.

— I'm sorry. I didn't really mean that. I'm full-born Fourth Assembly. It's just there's so much soul-saving goes on in these wards. Seriously. Last week it was Pentecostals, yesterday, a Jehovah's Witness with a face like a bowl of baby owls, and last night this Baha'i man who made us listen to Seals and Crofts songs. She chuckled. *It's exhausting, is all.*

In her smile, Ed saw the barest wind-ripple of shy gratitude.

— *Let me think it over for a day or so, Mr. Willing.* She held out a pink Archivette for Ed to tap with his own. *Tap me your codes?*

She was in. Ed knew it.

******

— *Eddie, will you get the lights?*

As lovely as she was under the sun, or under the freon wands of the local commercial center, Carmen was, Ed thought, prettiest of all in candlelight — the round cheeks, the doll's eyes rolling in and out of the flame's subtly-painted *chiaroscuro,* her downy copper hair shining like an autumn solar stormhalo. Her thumb delicately skimmed the pages of her leatherbound Faith Diary; after a moment she settled on a page, nodded in silent agreement and walked into the bathroom, returning with plastic bottles of alcohol and rosewater in one hand, two razor blades cradled in the palm of the other.

— *The Cuts tonight?* Ed asked.

Carmen unwrapped the blades and lightly doused them with the precious liquids. In matters of faith, Carmen ruled the roost and Ed was glad to let her lead the domestic sacraments. There was nothing more loving that a wife could do for her hub, and at times like this, Ed was so full of devotion he wanted to shriek. Together, they purred the familiar prayers:

These blades are vessels of Thy will
The flesh to scourge and blood to spill
These wounds are windows for Thy light
To cleanse the spirit in Thy sight

Ed went first, passing his blade through the flame and over the loose flesh of her exposed arm. He tried to empty his mind of intention and let his hand be guided. The point gently made contact and dimpled the skin as his hand fluttered in a gentle, sketching motion, swooping in the recognizable profile of a dove's wing. He felt her pull back, then exhale a little as the wave-edge of pain traversed her and the track of his line sprouted red.

— *My turn,* she said. *I bring you closer to the Wellhead.*

Over years, Ed had learned to love that first touch of localized heat, and to relish what was to come, the delicate scoring, followed by the sting and the little risings of blood. He closed his eyes and pictured a quiet, humble baby-martyrdom, and was filled with an emotion so embracing he found himself speaking his thoughts aloud.

— *Sweet saving blood,* he said.

Carmen wiped her blade on a white felt cloth. *It's not the blood that saves,* she said. *Only Christ's can do that. What saves us is what brings the blood, and the scar that remains.*

Her confidence, her mastery of the rites, filled Ed with pride. Some of the Ablutions – the Cuts included – were a delicate balancing act. In order for the rituals to have the desired effects, the correct response was one of pious, remorseful gratitude, rueful fondness. Some of the parish had come to associate the cutting and scourging with a kind of pleasure, and that was its own unique sin. Some, through intensive counseling, had broken the downward spiral, but others became Unfit, and were forced to leave, presumably for lives of sordid pleasure-addiction: the Itch Without Respite. Ed silently gave thanks for his continuing freedom as he leaned forward and traced Carmen's delicate wounds with his lips. The day had been so long, so involving. Even as he imagined those sky-blue jewels peering out over an ocean of fear, he knew to his core that the rich, familiar pain now had a beautiful, unfamiliar face, a face that filled him with comfort.

The Ablutions done, they shared the moment Ed liked best, patting each other down with paper towels, rubbing each other with aloe salve and calmly embracing, whispering verses of quiet solace. The calendar on the wall showed the date in electric blue, so, sharing an admiring smile, Ed pulled closed the privacy barrier sealing off the children's rooms while Carmen reached on tiptoe toward the high shelf in their bedcell where her copy of *Permissible Pleasures* was hidden.

— *Your turn to pick, Magic Man*, she purred.

He'd been forced to abandon some of his favorites – the Porch Swing, the Paint-Shaker, Aftershock, Labrador Luge – but it was a small price to pay. *Pleasures* wasn't the world's thickest tome, but it still gave them a pretty fair range of options. He collected himself and pulled taut the slack in his features as he spun around the open book and indicated the page.

      – Stockbridge Sleighride, I think, Kitty.

      – Easy on the coccyx, Angel Eyes.

The small house always got him thinking about his kids, straining to hear through the thin composite walls, but Carmen's surprisingly punishing shoulder massage relaxed him and ushered him back into the moment. It was a hundred shades of nice, the simple sleeping platform covered by a crisp linen sheet, the air filled with the scent of burnt orange and the quiet tones of his Rubaiyat Rainbow sonofile, ringing like dying echoes. He was so relaxed as he let slide his nightwrap, he could already feel a thickening, but he still happily accepted the shotglass of Maxador – preferred by Motherchurch for its strength and brevity of effect – Carmen offered. He wished Marburg-Taedong, S.A., could do something about the aftertaste, which reminded him of dental epoxy and cheap rye whiskey strained through a dryer sheet.

*Stewardship Husbandry Succor Faith Stewardship Husbandry Succor Faith...*Ed repeated to himself the Man's Matrimonial Duties as Carmen emerged from behind her dressing screen and straddled him. He had donned his blindfold, but he could still feel his body wracked with a light tremble, fast as the beating of a finch's heart, the moist medallions of flesh on her back thrilling clutching fingers. He tried to stay poised just at the last foothold before the Slide to Desire, to enjoy the heat, the modulations and hidden vocalizations in her breathing, the sweet berry and pine of her hair cleanser, as one might a bite of smoky venison or a panoramic seaview, as a puremind would. He held to this safe and sanctified contemplation as her gyrations increased in depth and power, as the lifeseed crawled toward freedom. And then it was gone, her breaths long and languorous, her muscles soft and drained of tension, his brain awash in fading stars and lightning.

—*What?* she asked. *Are you trying to fly to Heaven, King Raptor?*

As he slowly consented to let the room surround him again, Ed wiggled his fingers and realized he had been reaching to grip a pair of phantom bedrails.

—*Just trying to get my arms around all that goodwifeliness*, he said, hiding the surprise in his voice at the elsewhere quality of his own thoughts.

******

The Council of Censurers had always told Ed he had the gift of reading people and, sure enough, just a few days after his initial visit, Denys had notified the priory staff of her interest in helping Motherchurch. So in order to keep the dark and beastly forces from dissuading her, and to ensure she understood the intercession process, he arranged for a week of daily hospital sessions, during which he walked her through the most elementary catechism and answered the confusions that he knew would arise.

—*Make this right*, the Prelate had said, *and I foresee an elevation…Cultivator Willing…*

32

Cultivator. Cultivator! Motherchurch had only eight of these, and Cultivator Galey's death in February had left an opening. Beyond that were just the three Harvesters, who had the Prelate's ear and helped him puzzle through thorny ethical issues. It was like being a prince, and you got a piece of the Unburdenings, for the expansion of the flock.

Ed still felt like a bit of an intruder, and reintroduced himself with an apology, but the warmth in his face and the needles along the spine reminded him of how glad he was to see Denys again. And he imagined she was glad to see him, too. Propped up by a cloudbank of pillows, scanning fashion photos of bronze-tinted models reenacting the first Olympics on her broadsheet omni-mag, she seemed sharper and more engaged than before. Her hair shone and smelled like Castile soap, and he could swear that she had thrown some silicate gauzer on her laugh lines and forehead. He took the lid off a cup of Rancipur Red from the canteen, and the smell immediately brought baby rosebuds to her cheeks.

– *Thought you could use a wake-up*, he said.

She smiled, and everything felt proper.

Together, they went through the major topics in the Book of Learning. As the hours went on, he found himself watching those eyes, not for the questions they asked, but for the insights they provided, the way they tested the forcefulness of arguments, wandered away to consider a passage with really stark or ecstatic imagery. Was he teaching her, or vice versa? Outside, he could hear the

33

faraway, steely sounds of the local visionary-school gamelan, serenading the passing infocrats with some crowd-pleasing 20th century worldbeat.

– *"Soul Makossa,"* Denys observed.

Ed stroked his beard. *Not bad. I would have said something by War.* The workers from Foresight Cartel circled the musicians contentedly, in patterns, like metal filings elucidating the fields that swam around their Great, Eternal and All Powerful Bar Magnet, the Always and Everywhere. He could recognize that his faith had made everything so special and meaningful and dazzling as reflections of the ineffable that nothing really amazed him anymore.

– *Now, let's talk for a moment about the Parable of the Mouse.* He was still a little distracted, now that he had noticed the distant song. *This is important stuff.*

The Book of Eldon, unearthed during the drilling of a water well in the desert of En Gedi back in 2021, was like the C4 that had blasted away the deadweight of Catholic dogma. It collected he teachings of Eldon, a descendant of the House of Cain, living in the time of Noah. He travelled the land that is present-day Jordan, observing the tarnished state of man, urging repentance and foretelling a grave calamity that was to come. It had never been embraced as part of the *Codex Vaticanus,* it was presumed, for various theological reasons, including its impingement upon the traditional Flood story and its unsympathetic view of mankind. But the Savonarolans embraced it, considered it a centerpiece of their belief. Ed had broken down the first time he had read its closing verses, a climax worthy of a classic novel:

Ch. 122:

1 And clouds replaced the heavens, and a thunder like a father's reproof tumbled from horizon to horizon, and the first of an endless, purifying rain began to fall through daggers of godly fire. 2 I feel in my marrow I will not see its end. 3 Let you who read: repent, rebuild.

The Parable of the Mouse was a bedrock teaching that all converts were required to learn and embrace. While travelling in Gilead, Eldon came upon an agitated crowd in a small settlement in the region of Gad. A merchant, Epithalius, convicted of stealing, was to have his hand severed in punishment. But the man had many friends among the people, and they argued for mercy. Faced with this quandary, the judges asked Eldon's counsel. He insisted that the sentence be carried out. If a mouse and a man stole crusts of bread, he reasoned, whose guilt should be greater? The mouse had merely acted according to the dictates of its Creator, but the man, through his gift of free will, freely chose to offend. This teaching was the foundation of both the Church's Doctrine of Perpetual Contrition – the great Turning Back – and the Doctrine of Native Grace that shielded the plants and animals from sin.

For is it not he, to whom was given the strongest seed, the richest soil, from whom the most plentiful harvest is expected? And if he cannot feed his house, then who shall his servants' hunger accuse? (18: 5-6)

Ed could tell from the way Denys fixedly twisted a chewed-on sani-straw in her hands that she was unsettled.

— You look vexed, he said. *Is there something I can…clarify? Harmonize?*

She measured her words.

— It's just that it seems – I don't really know that there's a word for it – unloving? Disloving? Deloving? Just so hard and harsh.

— Well, actually –

— No, please, let me finish. Let me get this out before I forget how to say it. My grandparents were old-line Christians – revivalists, host on the tongue, meatless Friday, the works. I was always comforted by the fact that man had some kind of spark…

— Spark?

— Some special potential, some capacity. Something perfectable, like a window…

— Or a keyhole.

— To God. Something we could reach, a power. That could always replenish itself.

Ed thought for a second. Truth was, most people he gathered were already converted before he opened his mouth. He rarely had to work this hard.

— Glad you brought that up. Man, of course, was gifted with a soul that separated him from the animals, and animated his…higher faculties. But as his potentialities were greater, so much greater was the betrayal, the Shortfall in which he dwelled on Earth. So much given, so much asked.

Ed dug for a passage in his book.

— I think the key is found here, in Chapter 39: the Parable of the Goat.

— The Goat?

— It addresses God's love for the animals. And the burden of man.

36

He tapped the side of his head twice to engage his Focushift:

12 And Eldon cast his hand toward Jeptha's livestock and spake: "The goat provides milk and meat, and thrives as a blessing on this house. But the beast needs be fed and nurtured and nursed when sick. In the state of nature, he lives and thrives without the care of men. But give the beast over to men and it relies on men's toil or it perishes. 13 Just so is the soul of man. 14 In the joy of the Garden, man wanted for nothing. Grace alone sustained him. But outside the vale of God's creation, his spirit has become troubled by passions, wants, the poisons of pride and rage. 15 When man ceases to strive toward God's law, when he no longer retraces his path to the Garden, the soul withers and suffereth neglect.

— *But the soul is something more, something incorruptible. It's not like a bad heart or a bad liver.*

Ed thought for a second. *It's strong, and hard to get at, for sure, and it's protected by everything a man has and is, and all of human history's good works. But it's not inviolable. There are sins so bad, choices so impure, that they can turn it sick and raw. That's the truth those other faiths could never face. You can't murder the Son of God and get a do-over. You've got to work to earn that second chance, and I don't mean some water on the head or some bread in the belly. It's got to hurt. It's got to.*

He could see her face was lined with worry.

— *It's not a sales pitch. There's no other way.* The naiveté was touching.

— *Love?*, she asked, in a pleading sort of voice.

— The Teachings tell us that Love without Penance is…deceit…A sin that feeds on sin.

Ed grasped her hand and tried to lead her in quiet song, to bridge the little fissure that had erupted between them and threatened to pull them apart.

— Why not go off and live in the woods? Back to nature? He delicately cautioned her against simple readings of deeply profound texts whose meanings had been parsed by scholars. And, he went on, Motherchurch did sponsor Eldine Retreats like the Dead Mountain Forage and the Lost Forest Walkabout, whose ceremonial value was vital to the life of the flock.

— Literalism is, after all, inserting oneself into the role of God, Ed said. *He allows us only…intimations of Truth. But ours are better than theirs. Of that I am sure.*

The hour came for Ed to go, and, smiling, he packed away his book and his array of laminated verses and illustrations. It had been a productive session, and he felt her leaning slowly toward the corrections of the Stern Word. But still, there was something in her long silences that made him wonder about the persuasiveness of his presentation.

— In order to be a worthy petitioner, he said, *you've got to believe. You've got to accept the doctrine. Should I come back tomorrow?*

She nodded sadly.

— I believe in the reason, the purpose, that brought us together.

— That's good. Very good.

— Yes, it is.

******

38

For the next three days, Ed returned, taking Denys through the prerequisites to the Pauper's Service: the Admissions of the Base, the Renunciations of Pleasure, the Acceptance of Wrongs. With the supervision of the duty nurses, he administered the purges of wind and water. Doctors prevented the purges of blood and bowel, but he was able to substitute an earthen masque and a reading of the Cycle of Longing, accompanied by sonofiles of St. Job's Choir. On the Thursday before Sunday service, she was at last sufficiently prepared. Ed looked down at her, weak but placid, her eyes as sad and lovely as the first day he saw them. Sunday, he would, with the help of handpicked church attendants, deliver her, and secure for himself a richer post than even Carmen had ever dreamed for him.

    — *Loving Cousin, is there any favor you wish before Sunday?*

She turned away sadly, as one who asks an impossible thing.

    — *You're a good man*, she said. *Get out. Get you and your family out.*

******

From the foyer of the Executive Residence, the Prelate could see the festival that the service had become. News of Denys' appearance had triumphantly reversed the trend of dwindling attendance at the special observances. The grounds outside the church steps were full of eager parishioners dressed in their finest hair shirts, thorn crowns, and barbed wire belts and jewelry, who had bought up service tickets like 20th century teens at a rock music show. Some of the zealous had rigged up a fire pit filled with charcoal, and pranced and frolicked across in bare feet, singing in high, unintelligible voices, while others painted friends with the ash. The air was full of thick butterscotch light from an Ozone Event, and the happy sound of vigorous lamentations, the carnival chime of the jezebells that swayed on the wrists and ankles of the adulteresses, divorcees and the wanton. It filled Macomber's heart with hope as he walked into the dressing room where Ed sat, watching his star supplicant being groomed for the celebration. The attendants were Graziella, her coalblack hair rudely slashed in jagged lines, as if by broken glass, and JoElla, a cheery pepperpot with the body of an Iron Age statuette and a sweet voice that hummed holovision themes as she streamed hot wax on Denys' neck and shoulders like Christmas tinsel.

    — *Marvelous*, Macomber said. *I think it's a sell-out. And the pouches are filled with baubles for the Unburdening.*

    Graziella Flees-the-Snows, a reformed streetwalker from District J, was the arresting offspring of an Ogunquit tribal elder and a Eurasian casino whore from the Splendid Earth Gaming Facility up in the Airy Concession. The Ushers and Tabulators doted on her because her defiant eyes and sculpted jawline put a savage, stunning face on Motherchurch's mission, but also because she spoke for one of the

Savs' strongest growth sectors. In 2080, Prelate Modicum Chase published the first of his *Revealed Gospels*, including the testimony of Amagin'aa, Flower of the Wild Glade, a Native American princess rescued from Hades during Christ's post-Crucifixion uprising. The cult had become so popular that the church now counted some 18,000 Natives and their descendants among its members. *Good channeling, great marketing*, Macomber once privately joked over what Ed had guessed was one too many cups of nettlestalk wine.

— *It's good to see the fervor again*, Graziella said, gently tracing a mud cross on Denys' cream eggshell forehead. *And we owe it all to you.* Even under the shapeless chain mail, the men could see the slide and sway of a body that radiated heat and danger. Macomber's eyes lingered a little too long, fascinated by the perfect play of the chemical sun over the futurist sculpture the links had made of her impeccable rump and thigh. He considered her a special project, a "blessed reclamation," and insisted she be the beneficiary of his generous personal attentions. Ed could see from the way he touched her shoulder, cross-hatched in faint scars, as he excused himself, that their relationship had achieved an exciting new level of spiritual mentorship.

— *See what I did?*, she asked, holding up a tiara of wilted white lilies.

— *Exceptional*, Macomber said. *All the beauty and transience the sacrament demands.*

The three of them – Ed, Macomber, and Denys, her hoverchair gliding three steps ahead in an envelope of contemplative isolation – moved through the freshly-trimmed Anomie Garden. The Prelate clasped Ed's shoulder and pressed a purple voucher – he had seen pinks and blues, but never an actual purple – into his palm.

– *Your share of the ticketing, … Cultivator Willing.*

Ed tried to suppress his pride and excitement, diverting his eyes toward Denys, positively luminescent in her floral crown and the special, plasticene vestment reserved for the Feast's honoree. When she stood, the straight vertical lines gave no hint of the drawn but still provocative body it sheathed, but the delicate flame designs, in overlapping hues of garnet, crimson, canary and tangelo, led the eye toward the starved and holy shadows of her face, the still-lucid eyes. He had to admit, she would be a sight walking down the aisle. She motored soundlessly past the obsidian image of Black Edgar, the self-immolated anchorite, pausing to touch the clump of briars that had been left in tribute by the schoolkids. At the top of the mound that served as a sort of makeshift levee, she stopped and looked out over the glassy jade safety moat.

– *A little seedy,* the Prelate apologized. *It accrues a little algae during the hot months. I'll have Shinji add some clarifier in the morning.* He could see that she was fascinated, and a little put off, by the trays of butcher scraps and offal on the other side, between the moat's stone bank and the thickening woods of the wild zone beyond.

– *It's something that we do,* Macomber said, *for our animal friends.*

The real estate up in the Dales, on the edge of the Reclaimed Wilderness, was cheap and less restrictively regulated, perfect for a project like The Haven, and they had done well to carve out their oasis of peace, but there were always problems with the ferals – discarded housepets, migrating coyotes and bobcats, strange hybrids of wild and tame. All the stakeholders out here had scare stories about nervous standoffs, frightened children, raided trashpiles. The church kept its moat to protect the daycare kids and the outdoor festivals, and left food for the outcast beasts it excluded.

– *During storm season, the hail and electrical disturbances send the poor creatures into all the local basements for shelter. We have little ones about,* Macomber explained, *but still we do what we can to look out for the nobles, to keep them whole.*

Denys seemed to take that in for a second and spun to face the men.

– *So they can die with a full belly.*

Ed was tiring of the preliminaries. He wanted to get to the glorious consummation, the beautiful rite that would seal his success, his advancement, in the warm salt of the Wastrels' Tears.

– *Something like that,* Macomber said. *Something along those lines.*

******

The church was filled with the moans and whispers of the faithful, half-amazed at the sight of jam-packed pews, as Rhona, on the reproduction

43

vintage Bavarian pipe organ, burst into the opening chords of Hedda Stahl-Drescher's *Symphonie Armlich*, Macomber's preferred introduction to the Plaints of the Forsaken. One by one, the celebrants, faces shrouded in ceremonial hoods, started up the gray limestone aisle. Then came the Prelate, looking heroic in his wax wings, and the little attendants, Hero and Ava Krstic, age 5, looking like mischievous cherubs in their ragged white gowns, showering the ground in sharp-edged pebbles of chert and rose quartz that gently pierced the bare feet of Denys, the Selfless, the Ruined, supported by a stout male usher at each elbow. Heads swiveled in unison as she nestled in her place of honor at the simple iron altar rail, and Cree Walther's lilting soprano made the music almost too poignant to bear:

O let me live just long enough
To ask a boon of Thee
To just redeem
The fever dream
Of man's ignominy

Macomber, Ed thought, looked a little straighter, more assured, than he had seen him in recent months as he ascended the splendid porphyry pulpit, carved by Tabulator Monreale – son of a son of a son of a Carrara quarryman – in scenes from Christ's descent into limbo and the inspiring Harrowing of Hell. Carmen grabbed Ed's hand, digging her nail into his palm, just short of drawing blood.

The Prelate paused a moment for effect, letting the buzz go quiet. *Mothers, fathers, brothers, cousins!* he thundered. *We gather today, filled with roth and regret, but also hope, for our monthly Plaints, summoned by that ingrained messenger of God, conscience, to survey from a distance the burnished western gates through which we were so roughly cast, and the grudges, the slights, the thoughtless hurts that, stone by stone, construct the modern mortal prison. Today, we remember the vows abandoned, the promises and obligations neglected, and the hundred thousand ripples that each sends out into human society. What is it that dogs us? Spite? Wrath? Fear? Fear of the crushing burdens of righteousness? Today, we set aside our fear, for we are led by Sister Willworker, a cousin with the bloodthirst who has consented to take our cases to the Lord from the brink of the chasm of Death, that place where end all fears and desires. And we know by virtue of our faith that from such a platform, our spokesman will have a straight shot – like a tin can on a string – to the ear of the Almighty, who views such cries with solicitude and tenderness. For this, we thank Sister and cry unto the seat of judgment in the familiar words:*

Celebrant: Light of the World, we come in contrition

Congregants: Hope of the World, we come in belief

Celebrant: Light of the World, be our pillow of respite

Congregants: Hope of the World, be our font of relief

Ed marveled at the boundless fountain of words that could be found to describe a basic idea: that man could never be good enough to deserve the bliss that had been prepared for him.

This was not the standard service, Ed thought, full of haughty rhetoric and insincere, lifeless participation. Every responsorial was delivered in a loud, sonorous rumble, and the Unburdening urns overflowed with a wild cornucopia of luxury goods and vanities. The choral interludes, often abridged, were expanded to include multiple lustily-intoned verses. And the Acknowledgements of Blame, usually two or three rote admissions, went on for thirty minutes, the faithful rising *sua sponte* to add more and more cracks in the world traceable back to their and their loved ones' follies:

Shengana Fever deaths in Little Haven public schools!
Hardd Keever bankruptcy suicide!
Teenage foraging diet fads!
Recreational beatings of the residentially displaced!
Psychic high-school dream-bullies!
Rampant price speculation in polar ice floes!
Breeding of Dreadnought Fighting Wasps and Spitting Beetles!
Home animal customizing!
Pride!

– *Yes! Yes! Pride!* they all agreed, murmuring and shifting rambunctiously, until Macomber, fearing a loss of control, rang the gilt Herald's Bell to quiet the parish again. He motioned to Denys, who

46

with great effort, hoisted herself to her feet and accepted the elaborately-illustrated parchment on which was written the church's secret prayers for human reconciliation. With nervous fingers, she folded the paper, placed it in the belly of the magnificent alabaster dove and offered it to the cheering crowd. With a subtle motion that all but the most intent would have missed, she slid a small folded sheet of her own inside, then hooked the bird to the specially-rigged pulley line. Shinji the arthritic Okinawan caretaker, looking a little uncomfortable in the golden ringlets and flowing cassock of an archangel, hoisted the bird without complaint toward the high, glistening gold leaf, carnelian, lapis and mother-of-pearl *Salvator Mundi* reredos that was all that remained from Cagniolosi's original Tuscan Savonarola shrine, while Cree's wordless musical ecstasies brought the worshippers near to a sweet, stinging climax Theresa of Avila herself would instantly recognize as the love-arrows of the Holy Spirit. Just as the bird was about to kiss the Lamb in a breath of cinnamon and clove incense, Denys, turned, extended her hand over the congregation, and unexpectedly spoke, in a voice as thin, pure and penetrating as the sound of a tuning fork:

The prayers I make are not for all, but each;
Don't loath but love, don't taunt but teach.
My life is spent, but from here, I see
What God condemns makes mortals free.
Discovery and expression guide
You to the holy place inside.

She executed a deep and pious curtsey to the people, bowed to the Prelate, and staggered out past the stunned, scandalized directors, worthies and aspirants. Over the objections of his wife, who grabbed at his arm, Tabulator Erstwhile slid out of his pew and put his arm around their sacrilegious servant's waist, turning her uncertain gait into something insultingly straight and dignified. For a long time, the Prelate stood, stunned by what had happened, then motioned the Ushers forward again, and all was forgotten in the normalcy of the supplemental Unburdening for the recruitment of unwed mothers. Ed looked back toward the west end foyer, but they had gone, who knew where. The ominous and jarring improvisation, which Ed attributed to the deleterious effects of hemophaegia and the side effects of the psychotropic medications that fought late-stage bloodurge, had evaporated like the smell of the incense, leaving only the clean and nourishing daydream of answered prayers.

******

Canonical law barred Ed from seeing Denys after service; Carmen heard around the hospital halls that she passed two weeks after mass, her illness entering omega phase just 36 hours before the end. Ed sent a handsome bouquet of seasonal wildflowers to the burial, a small service attended only by a hospital Visitor, a nephew and a pair of elderly ex-coworkers. In the following days, he waited and watched for the imminent blessings to manifest. It did not take long for unusual, and quite unexpected, things to happen. Rorimer Quast, the church controller, was killed in an elevator accident, and, more calamitously, a midnight strike of Garbus' Static set off a fire that gutted The Haven, roaring up the nave like a river of flame, engulfing the transept and its celebrated terracotta apostates, and turning the altar and apse into blackened ruins. The reassurance investigators who paid the claim had contractual audit rights over the church books and records, and without Quast to keep out the prying eyes, they discovered several serious deviations from the district building code's materials prescriptions. Squaring off these cut corners in a series of tense closed-door sessions, the investigators, a fire marshal and a warden of the public safety magistery exhumed an untidy number of unexplained payments to a holodisc producer in SkinCity and a runaway rent-to-own candyboy named Ruud Gibney. The civil prefecture steered clear of religious matters, but the holocasts had no such scruples, and soon the steaming skin of The Haven was familiar b-roll for stop-presses like *Coot, Cudgel and Crumpet* and *Lash Tango in Parish*. Attendance at SubPrelate Lopes-Isenheim's jerry-rigged "services" (usually little more than half-heard rants belted from under a plastic tarpaulin, drowned in the mad buzz of destruction equipment) fell like the Walls of Jericho, and when a broken-hearted Macomber was found dead, an empty vial of Decelerase at his wrist, it was only left for the trustees to padlock what was left of the edifice and send the vestments and movables to public auction.

As a Gatherer, it fell to Ed to participate in the gloomy final walk-through and clean-up. In the charred wood and stone, he found the alabaster dove, and inside, a folded sheet of paper with large, nervous writing: *Punish the Wicked Reward the Good Humble the Strong...* The rest of the sheet had been burned away. This must have been Denys' prayer, for the broadness of its invocations violated the late Prelate's teaching that God's time was infinitely too valuable to waste on generalities. Ed rolled the paper in his fingers, watching the charred edges fall away like cigarette ash or crumbs or gravedust.

In late October, they set up the rail guns and demo towers and turned the church campus into a field of jagged timbers, melted glass composite and broken masonry. The next days and weeks had the weightless, unhinged orientation of those that immediately followed a loved one's unexpected death. Ed knew the moves to make: sleep, eat, shit, cleanse, dress, but he felt like some sort of data avatar, a ghostly figure being moved through manufactured space by unseen minds and hands. An upscale gallery had taken over the Reclamation Center, and once the transfer was recorded, Ed started the soul-gnawing process of interviewing for jobs, trying to explain away the church scandals while the personnel wranglers stared uncomfortably into space, past the deviant. Sundays were the hardest. At first, he fielded three or four calls a day from slammers offering him slots in the mainstream faiths, but now he had fallen off the radar, and spent his Sabbaths aimlessly surfing cyberspace and building scale-model moon-colony shuttlecraft. Every now and then, they were visited by old church friends who had caught on with the Planet Wardens or the Vessels of Prophecy, and he and Carmen would politely pretend to hear the Voice of Elijah or fly with extinct egret flocks, but nothing really took hold. It was worse on Carmen, who, on still nights, tried zestlessly to lead him through the old Ablutions. Her blade, which once swirled and dove in strokes of invention, now just dully flicked parallel cuts that Ed could hardly stand to exhibit. The barefoot sin-walks that once took them through all the town's richer districts, now were little more than lazy lopes up and down the driveway. Only the kids seemed to be making a good transition, the rigors of religious life giving way to early-morning holocasts and animations, games of stunball, and long computer chats with WonderVale players in Malaysia and the leftover –Stans.

Without the church's directives to give spiritual meaning to their couplings, Carmen lost interest in sex, letting her hair grow greasy and straight, spending more and more time distractedly rearranging her collection of acrylic Eldine statuettes, devising elaborate intrigues for the lovely Amagin'aa and her father Kalimbaré. Ed felt more and more like a curator than a father or husband, and by the New Year, he found himself typing out a prescheduled electronic home-alert explaining his growing sense of remoteness, his inklings of impending shipwreck. Then, he was in the Remora, heading out of town toward the Public Possessions, where the hurt, the out-of-fashion and other in-betweeners went to reboot and reconfigure. He found a furnished flop at the Alhambra, a rundown cement-and-stucco rambler once trimmed out in Spanish Muslim ornament, now blasted by hail and sandstorm into a state of accelerating decline. Drowned in the contents of a plastic flask of Glasstine, Ed lay back on his dormition mat and waited for the night-curtain to fall.

In his dream, Ed was back in the woods behind his boyhood home in Ohio. At the edge of the feeder stream that cooled the county windfarm, he bent in quiet amazement at a real bullfrog, and cupped his hands in a vain attempt to catch it. On the wind was the turbine-whirr of the cicadas, who thanks to the blurring of the seasons, stayed aboveground all year long. Ed felt that time had ceased moving in a straight line, and that he had taken up a safe, permanent place in this landscape. From behind a rustling of birch limbs, he saw a familiar form, the fleshly wave of Graziella. In her lovely brown skin, her dark eyes seemed windows to some undiscovered, negative space. Her chocolate shoulders were smooth and unmarked; her hair, no longer hacked in unflattering planes, had grown wild, luxuriant and windblown. She was dressed in the loose buckskin, flame-licked at the margins, of Amagin'aa, as she strode toward the water's edge, her footfalls sending up sprays of white and gold sparks. As she walked, Ed watched her step through her body, which she discarded like a rumpled caramel snakeskin, and emerge as smoky glass, light as vapor, beckoning. He awoke in a volley of heartbeats and a mist of cool sweat, his hand feeling an old familiar tightness at the loins. He breathed soulfully and walked over to the soot-dappled picture window.

Moon-brushed curls of high thunderhead were rolling in from the Near Plains, like the holocasts had foreseen. Ed could never before remember wishing for a nightlong, soaking rain. But now, he wanted to stand in it, drink it down. That would make the lay and roll of the world feel right again. Maybe that could work.

VENUS IN RAGS

— *Timido ergo sum*, Renzo Caliari laughed, scanning the newsbytes streaming across the Demarest Building's electronic ticker. *Sorry. Timeo, timeo. Call me next week and let me know how he does. And don't overdo the spiders and snakes.* On the corner, a gangly barker in an old NASA space helmet bounced a dancing tin marionette on the end of a wooden paddle. As he got closer, Renzo could see the puppet was a caricature of President-Elect Cervantes, dressed as a Mexican *bandito. Make me a big fat Wynne Godchaux and you've got yourself a sale*, he told the man, leaning to drop a plastic Vend-All™ token into an empty Mason jar. All up and down the avenue, people breathed deeply the cool spring gusts, laughing, singing lazily, punching the air. It made it that much harder to think about sitting across the conference table from Gunshy Godchaux and his ticky-tack pissboys.

He was already eight minutes late for the meeting at Kinetix, and that would make his news that much harder to break. They had hired Gestalt Media to work with Mil Krenzel, a hot new hypertext writer with a string of big sellers. His trips appealed to young and old alike, but on the holocasts, his gelatinous form, his darting eyes lost in folds of splotchy skin, made the test audiences recoil. And he did not possess what Renzo would call a ready wit. The labored maneuverings of his mind, which resulted in delicately structured drafts needing almost no editing, came off, in a conversational setting, as something approaching pugilistic dementia. Gestalt was the expert at hyping the hardcases, and Renzo had dispatched Gareth Heiss, their top neurotrainer, to help Krenzel develop a functional agoraphobia. Heiss had already unloaded the big stuff – car crashes, natural disasters, violent crimes – and was now fine-tuning, drilling Mil on the smaller hazards – wasp's nests, ambient infections, snakebites. But the conditioning took time, more time than a cheapskate like Godchaux was willing to fund. By the end of next week, Renzo would assure them, Heiss would have their cash cow so jittery about airborne fungi and UV rays that he would be a full-blown recluse. *That*, he thought, *they could work with.*

Kinetix was founded in 2018 to market the *Total War* games. The state-of-the-art multi-player environments had sold tens of millions of units worldwide, in the process changing fashion and language. Players striving to enslave the planet began dressing and speaking like its avatars, even forming residential communes and surgically adding "Khaled al-Masri" forehead scars or amputating ears to replicate "Lt. de Peyster's" Zimbabwe insurgency wounds. By the mid-2020s, Congressional hearings on the so-called "Ragnarok" school gassings and a series of state parental-consent laws regulating cosmetic mutilation caused the company to branch out into infant conditioning programs, young-adult cannibal romances and hypertext self-help packages like *Loving Your Parasites* and Ichi Obata's *Do*

Nothing! Get Everything! The firm merged with pharmaceutical conglomerate Paulus GMBH in 2026, catapulting famous cost-cutter Godchaux into the corner office and completing the transformation of Kinetix from hacker hobby to corporate jungle. As he walked into the majestic lobby, Renzo couldn't help but notice the vintage PowerMac behind safety plexiglass, a small nod to the conglomerate's homespun beginnings.

Godchaux's 8th-floor conference room, all bamboo and ivory with a great segmented ebony conference table that must have cost an imam's ransom, was the picture of elegance and taste, arranged in the Eastern Dynastic Revival style that all the multis courting the exploding Asian markets rushed to adopt. The glass wall, centered by a stained glass panel of the Green Dragon, faced east, and caught the rays of the morning sun. With the flip of a switch, the halves of the table would slide apart, revealing a carefully-recreated mountain stream, fed by pumps beneath the bamboo flooring, that ended in a stand of artificial sawgrass whose motion coyly led the eye to a costly-looking Han Dynasty screen. It was all so tasteful. The only clutter disrupting the carefully-crafted *feng shui* was Godchaux himself, hands clasped behind his back, staring out over his city, and the trio of black-clad yes-men that made up his movable geek chorus.

— *Sorry I'm late, all*, Renzo said. *Hung up in the Nervous Pride parade.*

— *Perish the thought, prof*, Godchaux intoned. *A little good news will make it better, eh? All things in time.*

— *That's nice*, Renzo said. *Wordsworth?*

— *No*, Godchaux said, signaling one of his assistants to fetch a mask of fresh Oxy, *Lou Rawls, I believe.*

Renzo smiled, opening his iScreen. *So very, very underrated.*

OK, magic time, he thought. Renzo had done this dog-and-pony show so many times, it was almost reflex. He even amazed himself as his pointer nimbly moved across the screen, highlighting and expanding charts tracing Krenzel's rise from nervenet non-entity to up-and-comer to phenom to the very edge of saturation. He dipped in and out of a canned video clip of the Ottmar Ramedge holocast on Self-Salvage, mixing close-ups of the host and audience members with AboutFace™ instanalysis of muscle movements and facial tics that connoted tedium, aggravation, drifting attention. It was an easy segue into Heiss' background and conditioning theory, and status reports on the "boot camp" and its progress, the growing fear of Outside in the brain of their artist.

— *Beautifully done*, Godchaux said, leaning in on his elbows, *but tell me some stuff I don't know.*

— *Spoken like a leader.* Renzo described the man that Mil would become, his energies funneled into the production of more and better works, his mind undistracted by the world outside his door, a beautiful, lustrous shell accreting around him, making him an object of, in turn, fascination, passion, obsession. Once Heiss would pack up, Phase Two would begin. They tagged it the Salinger

Plan. Darnell and Spinoza, ex-Main Justice who worked with Witness Protection, would disappear Krenzel, arranging semi-annual relocations, scrambling phone signals, bouncing IP addresses through Australasian relays, and arranging appearance-altering polymer implants for face and body. If sales lagged, any number of fabricated deaths, accompanied by leaked burial video and autopsy reports, could be arranged.

— *We're going to make Miss American Pie his bitch,* Renzo crowed. *Boy won't be able to find his face in the shaving mirror. He'll be a ghost haunting himself.*

— *Positively crystalline,* Godchaux said. *Think you can disappear his lawyer and his CPA, for real?*

— *We don't get into actual physical death. Cops, probate, imposters. Too many...variables...But we do refer...*

******

— *The new AmbiGauge™ is on your desk,* Sadie called to him as he strode past main reception at the Gestalt, Ltd. HQ. *Video buys on Scrambled Eggs have topped out, but Gilly Wave is upped from murmur to commotion.*

He stopped for an instant to read the digitab Sadie handed him. *Between Friends was the high water mark for insemcoms, but our little treasure could turn into something yet, mistress. Anything else on tap?*

— *Lord Sweetwater videoconference at 3. Won't say what about.*

— *Without surprises,* Renzo mumbled offhandedly, *we'd all expire, like wind-up toys.*

By 2050, media promotion had become so sophisticated that the biggest film idols, the greatest pop icons were virtually unknown. It seemed to defy logic, but as his mentor Sweetwater used to say, *logic is for bores and peasants; ours is the realm of the irrational.* And none could know better. Gestalt's CEO had been humble Gervais Sweetwater, a promotional assistant at EMI, when he began to climb the industry ladder. He had seen the satin jackets, the gold records, the private jets, drug flame-outs and tabloid romances, and he ascended the rubble as the internet became a worldwide distraction and trickled valuable product to the masses for free. With the mainline of public demand running dry, profits could only be sustained by cutting costs: movies became shaky hand-held pseudo-docs; television, a rookery of home-videos and cheaply-made stunt- and game-shows; music, a net of narrowcast, homemade tunes cobbled together on laptops. Nothing was worth seeing or hearing. The media combines became dinosaurs, shedding artists and staff, while they frantically persecuted their own fans and searched for an inroad back to the Eden of public imagination. One night in the endless winter of 2016, Gervais was reviewing the anemic PPV numbers for *Tourette's Family Reunion!: Unrated,* when Newton's apple struck him on the crown. And nothing would be the same.

All at once, he knew, the old models, the ballyhoo and spectacle, were a flash limousine careering toward a beckoning gorge. Saturation, not moderation, was the enemy. He would take things underground, play the game of whispers and implications. He would be the wallflower in a roomful of whores. His canvas would not be the tin ear or the bleary eye, but the relatively neglected slate of individual invention, where consumers could conjure their own stars.

Jacaranda Kindall was the first to benefit, and for her Lord Sweetwater always harbored a fondness that only grew after her untimely suicide by poison at 22. Hers had been a crude and unassuming demo, just her lovely, punishing voice moving from trill to dirge, accompanied by Rajiv, her tabla player, and the old aborigine Harkora on didgeridoo, a hard red sun setting on Uluru in the background. No production values to speak of, but Sweetwater always had a gut, and there was something in the careless way she handled a tiger snake, the unusual lyric about the snake goddess ushering tribal boys into adulthood, that spoke to him, that stirred a kind of chaste passion. All his genius would be spent making her a success. First, old Muslim riot film, carefully damaged and leaked to the web, fueled blind gossip items and passing newsmagazine references to an Indonesian music event so sexually suggestive it had set off civil demonstrations where, of course, all video and audio recordings were burned. These rumblings embellished House of Commons debates on public anti-burqa laws, and Kindall testified from behind a screen to the volatility of Islamic temperament. Her song was "reconstructed" for several late-night spins on the World Service, and some art photos, her golden hair surrounding vague features rising from a plume of geyser steam, had pride of place in a Hans Rittger show at the Tate Modern. A tour was cancelled, as was a rumored cameo as Joan of Arc in a Terence Blodgett musical comedy whose financing fell through on the eve of principal photography, and a star was incubated. The public could not get enough. In fact, they could not get any, which was the whole point.

But there would be no happy ending for "Little Randi." Sweetwater had not yet perfected his techniques and, with no counselor at her side, Jacaranda was driven deeper and deeper into depression by her seclusion and secrecy. On the eve of *Forgiven Sins'* much anticipated ECD release, she ordered a showing of *Diva* from her suite at the Mayfair Hotel, swallowed two dozen Seconal tabs, and washed them down with half a bottle of plum wine left over from the launch party. The funeral was a secret operation, for she yet had months of commitments to break, and she was buried in a country churchyard in New South Wales, beneath a headstone whose epitaph Sweetwater had personally chosen:

Who will hear the final song/That flutters up like steam/On bird-proud wings, a refugee/From hustler's giddy dream/What madrigal will lead us on/Through countryside and town/'Til, flower-like, we touch the dirt/And bed the nightmare down

It was Juvenal Hartline, but when asked by the newscasts later, he claimed to have penned it

61

himself. The young girls ate it up. Gervais quit the company, went into seclusion with a psychologist, a neurosurgeon, and an ex-*Times* city editor, and in March 2019, opened Gestalt in a former Soho leather shop. The rest, as they said, was herstory. Renzo was chilled and excited to see the next chapter he would write.

When he entered, the conference room was already full. There was his assistant Magdalena; Desmond Quarles from Metrics; Odalys Siempre, the new Internet person; Chief Scheduler Rainer Hutt; and Arky Hedgepeth, Sweetwater's unctuous, brilliantined proxy, whose task seemed to be to skulk around making unwanted recommendations about things he barely understood. And hovering above the holo-cone at the center of the long glass table was Lord Sweetwater, all three dimensions and 24 inches of him, a silk dressing gown loosely wrapped to give everyone a gander at the 30 pounds he had chemically melted. Of course, no one with Sweetwater's money ever had to age, but the anti-mutability team at the Dworsky Clinic had given him their finest work and, as a result, he looked barely half of his 72 years, something he considered essential to the scouting of sexy young singers.

—*Where were you on holiday, your Lordship?* Renzo asked. Sweetwater and his peers were pioneers in the new *louche* tourism, which scoured the Third World for cheap, unexplored pockets of crumbling grandeur.

—*Lovely little spa just outside of Mitú. Colombia. Along the Vaupes. They have a marvelous little clinic there – all expats, of course – where they do this very smart curare infusion. 30% metabolic reduction.*

Hedgepeth wasted no time in chiming in. *You do seem rather more relaxed, Lordship.*

– Still the odd mortar fire to keep the rebs at bay, but it does prevent the place from being overrun by your Rodeo Drive housewives.

– Can't make an omelet, et cetera, et cetera, Rainer droned, as if to put a period to the digression. Only he and Renzo could talk to Sweetwater this way; Renzo had his history and only Rainer could master the subtle web of concerts, interviews, travel and appearances/disappearances on which their profitability depended. *I'm anxious to see this new –* he paused for effect – *presence…*

– Fine thought, the tiny image said, waving his hand and remotely dimming the lights. *Then, je presente… The Ayoreo Angel…*

As Sweetwater's image faded, it was supplanted by a vision of deep, sea-green jungle night, dappled by needles of pearl equatorial moonlight that pierced the heavy rainforest canopy. Over a dim rustle of footfalls moving along the fern-carpet, they could discern a gaunt, graceful figure emerging, cautious, limbs full of feline instinct. It was a girl, on whom hung the torn remnants of a cotton blouse and a summery linen skirt. Her hair was black and straight and swooped around her face and down her back like a comet's tail. Her body was moist with rain as the shadow subsided and she revealed a face hungry, lost, yet as structurally precise as a Nautilus shell. Her hazel eyes, almost Asian in their casual

63

wisdom, shone with some *sub rosa* unrest that smoldered like a coal fire. Her lovely mouth moved in words of silent need, and Stillwater filled the absence with his distressingly affectless narration.

— *Las mendigas, the staff would call them. Unfortunate byproducts of the coupling between the medical tourists and the homegrown hostesses. Many of them are turned out for reasons of economic necessity, and form little encampments from which they subsist by begging, foraging, what have you.*

— *So sad*, Odalys added superfluously.

— *Indeed. Poor urchins, rife for exploitation. Damn shame, really. But this one had…a quality.*

— *Clearly*, Arky added. The video image swirled and changed direction to let the room absorb 360° of her. She bent to pick up a handful of coins, her brow as defiant as a runway model's.

— *Lady S., who has always taken quite an active interest in this aspect of the work, took rather a shine to this one, and managed to somehow convey an invitation to our lodge. Although language divided us, she seemed fascinated with our collection of soundcards. Yma Sumac and Miriam Makeba and the like. Well, long story short, she had somehow, through mimicry, most likely, developed this fantastically unique vocal style.* In an instant, the room was filled with a field recording of what seemed to be three voices at once, a sinuous line that carried a simple folk melody into a rhythm break like the clicking of forest insects, and then exploded into a starburst of sweet, incanted songbird notes, before finding the melody again in a shower of mysterious, aboriginal phrases. Even Odalys, clinical behind her tortoise-shell microfocals, seemed shaken and emotionally displaced. The overall effect was like being in the presence of a lovely, anomalous natural event, a sunshower or a springtime flurry. For several long minutes, nobody spoke. Desmond threw in first.

— *A young Barbara Carrera. With a little Isabella Cantu. Claro Que Si era. But not medicated.*

— *An angrier Hope Sandoval, with a little criminal edge. Like the carhop girl from Cocalero. Blanqui...*

— *Blanca Donaire. But more inviting. More available. Post-Darna. I'm thinking a virginal Talisa Soto.*

— *Or a wiser, more weathered Selena. But not a sound like hers.*

— *Oh, no, no,* Odalys said. *A sound like nobody's. And a bearing like a more natural Luz De La Luna. Luz without the stylist or the eelskin bodice or the cliff-diving boyfriends.*

— *Does she have a name?* Rainer finally asked.

Sweetwater breathed a little sigh at his end of the connection. *Damned if I know. Goes without saying, I think, that recordkeeping is not the locals' forte.* The windowglass lightened, and the Amazon vision faded to smoke.

— *Needless to say, this project is all upside. And none of the usual industry baggage the strivers tote along. Pure modeling clay for us to shape as we may.*

— *Within permissible ethical bounds,* Renzo offered. Everything was recorded, after all, and these sorts of statements had a way of returning to haunt.

— *Nearly goes without saying.*

Renzo's thoughts had drifted. He wondered if Gonsalves in Mexico City West could scare up some material that might show their young charge's talents to good effect. *Maybe get Canciones de Luz thinking along the lines of Zulema's soundtrack work?*

Bit by bit, Renzo found himself checking out, lulled to insentience by the usual brainstorming blather. Something about positioning this nameless waif, probably rendered defenseless by culture shock, as an avenging spirit of the vanquished forest, duets with the usual coterie of social-issue scolds, globecast benefits for Colombian orphans, blessed by South American crusaders-for-hire. From the silence and the rhythmless finger-tapping on the other end of the line, Renzo imagined Sweetwater's impatience at this conventional thinking rising to dangerous levels. By day's end, he would be tasked with devising the antipromotional strategy, and Mags and he would be on the magnarail south. He was already kicking around some strategies, little pulses of sheet-lightning for Sweetwater's ears only.

— *A fashion spread...Lilypads, leopards and Lepidoptera. Fer-de-lance body armor. Volcanic ash and tourmaline crystals. A cape of bird-of-paradise feathers. Shot by Raisa or Creg LaCreg, on every commercial digiwall.* Hedgepeth could be tiresome, but he was adept at leaving his detractors too bewildered to profit.

— *Mr. Caliari,* Sweetwater concluded, *see that the brains in Branding Module start working on a name. And let's touch base again after the evening 'Gauge is in.*

******

Gervais Sweetwater was calculating, visionary, passionate in the way that a former generation of gentry were allowed to be, before everything had been reduced to debits and credits. As befit a man in the business of reshaping the human mind, he was imaginative in ways that, to the ordinary world, closely resembled madness. Not only did it make him a subject of public fascination, Renzo reflected, it also left him refreshingly open to sideways strategies. Renzo was a very large fan, and loved the semi-annual sojourns to WildWind, Sweetwater's Calatrava-revival fortress on Isla Nueva in New Cuba. Renzo tipped some cane sugar into a demitasse of Turkish coffee thick as cake frosting and counted the volumes on the shelves of WildWind's library, one of the nation's biggest. But it was a library with a difference. The tens of thousands of vintage volumes were shrink-wrapped in clear plastic, their covers sealed in individual combination locks whose digits Sweetwater's archivist Moraine transcribed on slips of paper and immediately burned. They were never read or loaned, and only rarely seen by outsiders.

— *I love them,* Sweetwater said, *but I have always been afraid to open and read them, as if their contents, the tripping verses, the dusky vistas, would fly away like Pandora's devils.* He seemed not a bit sad about the allure of their forbidden contents. *Beauty and wisdom,* he said, *they don't abide. As I'm sure you've observed.*

— *Like a private zoo,* Renzo said, *or a prison.*

— *More like a reliquary. A repository of some sort of spiritual energy. The remains of the race's soul. Never to be dissipated.*

Across the room, Magdalena, demurely dressed in a high-necked blouson and grey cotton skirt, tailored in the chic suffragette style, gazed into a glass case filled with 19th-century miniatures, and scratched sketches in an antique moleskin notebook. Renzo respected the care she took with her style and accessories, but sometimes felt she tried too hard. She could be off-putting, like a theme-store assistant, but she was diligent, punctual, and never lost her composure. And he had to admit that her vintage ink tattoo, a gold and eggshell rendering of Klimt's *Water Serpents* that swam from wrist to clavicle, and an ass-length ponytail barber-poled in rust-red and umber, were cool icebreakers with the arts caste. She had her own money, pollution credits from a sulfur leak that killed her dad, and that meant she didn't have to hound him for raises and supplemental bennies. They had a nice understanding.

Never one to overlook a pretty woman, Sweetwater sidled over and let a hand flutter onto her hip.

— *Interested in enamel-work?*

She delicately cross-hatched a background and lowered her book for Sweetwater to see. *I'm more attracted to your cameos. Italian?*

— *Volterra, to be exact. You have a keen eye.* He turned back to Renzo. *I love these small objects. To me, they've always been emblems of what we do, plucking beauty out of the air and crystallizing it in lovely little souvenirs.*

From far down the hallway, D'Uberville's heels clacked on the marble floor. He materialized at the threshold, holding his master's snifter of Armagnac.

— *Will there be anything else, sir?*

— I'll bet Magdalena is hot and tired after the long trip. Why don't you get her a bathing suit and turn on the poolside lights? Nothing like a nightswim. She gave Renzo a look and waited for the nod, then, with a blushing smile to their host, she let the valet lead her away. Sweetwater watched her move, buffing fingerprints from the surface of his display case with the end of his robe's satin belt.

— She has quite a sturdy build, he said finally. *Could be quite attractive, in a certain light.* He looked at Renzo in a way that was mischievous without intimacy. *I don't suppose you ever...dallied...?*

— Not at all. That's for clowns and amateurs. No good can come. Remembering \Sweetwater's sweet tooth for ingénues, he instantly regretted his tone. Wasn't this, after all, the guy rumored to be the inspiration for Countess' *Love the Way You Hate Me*, and La Gioconde's *Little Boy Lost*? The sign-on tones of his holo-deck reminded him daily of the wreckage his boss had left in his wake.

— Stout lad, he smiled. *There's plenty of the other once the workday's done. Let's take our drinks out by the pool.*

Sweetwater slid a fader switch and the helium lamps along his great oblong pool began to glow with a gauzy, rose light, picking out the sleek Himmelfarb sculpture, sticks of Pacific Modern patio furniture, the green-and-lapis tiles that framed the water's edge. As he made his way to the great marble bench, Renzo saw a shadowshape pushing wave patterns toward the steps that led out of the shallow end. Bronze hands clutched the steel ladder and, bit by bit, the water surrendered the glistening hair, the smooth neck, the gently rippling shoulders of a woman, unapologetic in her nakedness, oblivious to the eyes that studied her. Without a thought of covering up, she turned, expressionless, and walked, erect and balletic, toward them.

    — *First impressions are lasting impressions, eh?*

She moved like mist on riverwater, Renzo thought. He feared that any greeting, any sort of touch or acknowledgement, would demystify her, trivialize her, drag her into the world of slaves. He made a mental note to avoid this at any cost. Her eyes were unreadable, ice-perfect as gemstones, but the tight line of her mouth held the potential for conflict. She was a strong animal, waiting for a rival to decide on a submissive posture. Part of him wanted to tangle, and it unnerved him. He nodded gently to her, letting his eyes go where they would. The girl looked for an instant to Sweetwater for direction, then walked on, unconcerned.

    — *She has a wonderful lack of engagement*, Renzo said. *We can really use that. Takes months to drill it into most people. But she'll need to establish rapport with her…handlers…*

Sweetwater swirled the cubes in his blood-red tumbler. *Oh, not to worry, lad. Dr. Katie is coming next week. Mexican, I think. Forensic ethnolinguist from the University of Miami. She's going to patch together something we can use.* He drifted for a moment. *Charming woman.*

    — *Ha. There's a surprise*, Renzo said. His eyes were drawn by the sight of Mags, emerging from the changing room in a gold sealskin maillot, towel slung over a pale shoulder, frozen in place before the figure of the naked woman, who silently, carefully approached, laying delicate fingers on Magdalena's decorated shoulderblade, tracing along her arm the eggshell line of a woman's back, buttock, thigh.

— *Very good,* Sweetwater clucked. *We may already be well on the way.*

So Magdalena received a battlefield commission, detailed to help guide this new discovery along the path to wealth and influence, a path that few could understand and even fewer could hew through the impenetrable underbrush of sensation, intention and analysis. It was a great deal more subtle and sensitive than the work she had done for Renzo, but she took to it with an alacrity and verve that made him despair of ever reclaiming her services. Lord Sweetwater sequestered them all – Mags, the girl now called Vyasha, Dr. Kathryn Licht, Jonas the record producer, a handful of field recordists and a team of stylists – in a wing of Wildwind, scheming how to prepare the public for their new phenomenon, and vice versa. Renzo watched the team gel for a fortnight, then resolved to pack his bags.

— *Yes,* Sweetwater nodded. *Now we need you to make straight a path through the wilderness. To prepare the way, as only you know how.* Renzo fidgeted with an obsidian paperweight in a Native American firebird design and remembered the way Mags would lick her lips in concentration when she thought no one could see. *Demand and desire. Too important to be left to the consumer. Haven't I always said so?*

– *Repeatedly,* Renzo said.

*****

Renzo rubbed the sleep from his eyes and looked out from his floor-to-ceiling windows at the pale-rose new-summer city morning. It had been three weeks since he left Wildwind and, while Mags had been huddling with her team, Renzo had been working the phones, talking to promoters and market-conditioners, doing the spade work to launch a full-on ghost campaign. Magdalena had just hyperstreamed him some test recordings they had made with a local tabla/ kora backing duo and there was enough trembling animal life in them to support the next phase of his project. Renzo would clean himself up, call in to Sadie for messages and take a *plein air* stroll down to his accomplices in the Rising, that West Side neighborhood that was stirring from the ashes of the Shelter Riots. Poxx Magid and the rest of the Have-Nots danced on the edge of the law, and Renzo's corporate colleagues wanted nothing to do with them, but Renzo knew they had a feel for the streets, and would stunt for a few hundred credits. They could be very useful and, in a business like his, it never hurt to have some secret weapons. They could help him get "Panoptica" and "Malacuna" into the mix of sounds and symbols that comprised the City's swirling info-ocean.

He wasn't one of those executives at the Schoneberg who feared the rays of the sun, who rode the climate-controlled walkways to the uptown office blocks. On days like this, when the mercury hung below 110°, he loved to spread on the zinc oxide paste and parade in the open air, relishing the sights and sounds of the tattered city. From the street, the sidewalks and storefronts had a well-worn look that reassured him, made him feel like he was part of something living and durable. The upscale porno shops and self-enhancement clinics of the West 70s gave way to cheap food stalls and sidewalk peddlers, their blankets crammed with bootleg software and counterfeit handbags. From a street corner came the crazy chatter of two dozen caged finches and parakeets, some of whom trilled phrases in obscure Eastern dialects.

The Saffir Building at 36th and 8th marked the entrance to the Rising, a barren stretch of smoke-stained storefronts and half-wrecked apartment buildings strewn with glass and shattered masonry. Aside from a pair of dazed-looking streetwalkers and a nervous adrenochrome pusher spastically spinning a yo-yo, there was nothing above ground. But the muffled rockabilly music leaking up from underfoot told Renzo that the Cellars were already alive with action. On the next long block, from beneath a cluster of burned-out Ocelot chassis, the sound of a Saint-Saens sarabande percolated skyward. He knew he was nearing the street entrance to Cappadocia, the favored hangout of Poxx and the Have-Nots.

The six-year rule of the Christian Reclamation from 2024-2030 had changed America in ways no one had foreseen. Under President Highsmith and the Congress he controlled, abortion and contraception had been criminalized, with a new division of Justice devoted to eradicating the practices in the areas still under federal control. Nobody knew how many of the 3.3 million babies born in 2026 were accidental, but for years, the estimate had hovered around 750,000. Suddenly, America had an army of dispossessed children, a legion the pundits had dubbed the Unwanted, or, more poetically, the Forsaken. By the early 2040s, there were half a million runaway kids, meeting up in every major U.S. city. New York had a bunch of these makeshift gangs – the Naked and the Dead, the March Hares, La Cliqua – but a chance meeting with an East Village public defender at an after-hours Omnivox party had led Renzo to the Have-Nots. They were mostly teenaged squatters, less interested in big-time crime than aggressive mischief, anything to vex the status quo. They were perfect partners for Gestalt, and Renzo was not one to ignore such found bounty. The gang's members were fearless, had a taste for the outrageous, and loved diverting the cultural currents. Renzo could always count on them for a little late-night tagging or to start a commotion around some budding infostar. Jail was no big deal, just some hot meals and a mattress, a good deal.

In the corner of the room, beneath the great oval mirror, sat Poxx, fanned by Jezzie Garside and a younger girl Renzo did not recognize, a hard-eyed rail of a kid whose shoulder bore the raw-pink snowshoe of the Have-Nots brand, the tip of an ob-gyn's forceps.

— *Ha ha, Daddy C!* Poxx laughed. *Siddown and clue us in. What manner of dirty work you need now?*

Renzo smiled. *Trying to hustle me out the door? You're going to make me feel unwanted.*

The new girl cast a wary eye and swiveled in her chair, giving Renzo only the back of her magenta ducktail to stare at. Stam the enforcer, perched at the bar, threw her a reassuring glance.

— *Far from it,* Poxx said. *Don't want you taking your trade to the Little Wanderers. Two more,* he said, waving Jez over to the coffee station. Saint-Saens gave way to the desolate pleading of the Rolling Stones' "Salt of the Earth." It made everything seem smaller, sadder.

Renzo pulled a microdeck from his jacket pocket and laid it on the table. *A stunt. A seizure job. One of your guys auditions my girl's tracks in the heart of Times Square, and gets his mind blown.*

— *How bad?*

— *Just a little grand mal. A picturesque swoon, couple ecstatic moans, glassy eyes, enough to draw a crowd. An ambulance job.*

— *Maybe Moda. He did a little acting. Needs to make the grade.*

— *Nice initiation.*

— *Hey, Big Papa. Gotta earn the burn.*

Stam clicked off the envirosound, by now some obscure turntable gymnastics from the millennium's infancy, and slipped in Renzo's microdisc. The tabla was forest canopy rain, animal heartbeat, capillary pulse, and the kora danced in angles all around the wordless throatsong. Jez looked at Poxx with a desolate, lonely kind of amazement, like one enjoying the imprisonment of rain over a strange landscape. Poxx stared into his cup with dark intention, as if to hide his face from the others. *The back of my neck is all a-tingle*, he joked. *You may have some real sweet poison there.*

— *Music to seize to*, Renzo smiled. He imagined a lovely bit of stunting, a scrum of tourists, street thieves, beggars and omnicast junior honchos pawing to get a look at the fallen scruff, his body spasming quietly, his eyes intent on some mesmeric inner thrill of bushsounds. He heard the whispers and read the here-then-gone crawl-items asking about the source of this pure and vaguely perilous entertainment. He felt the mystery ripening in the deepminds of the millions, fighting toward the sun, to be born as curiosity, then love, then, if they all did their jobs right, soft dependency.

— *Thanks for the mud*, Renzo said. *Sure the new guy can sell it?*

Poxx took a long sip. *He's uberscale. Ran away from a prep on the island. The good side. You bought yourself a real Hella Hayes.*

— *You're still the goods*, Renzo said, slipping out into the sooty air. It was a good morning

*****

— *You'll want to scope this*, Mr. C. Sadie brandished a tablet in front of Renzo's face. He paused to look down at the brilliant green screen, dotted with newsblast icons. *Check Soundz To Die For.* He pressed the icon and there it was, as promised, a full-fledged hullabaloo on the sidewalk outside Haddix Worldwide. Moda, a bit thicker around the middle than he had guessed (mommy issues – he had seen it before) lay flat on his back, the steel knuckle-spikes scoring the synthetic paving. A news hostess, thin enough to cause concern, narrated the tale: the boy stricken, gagging, eyes rolling in his head, whisked to the District Triage Center, his personal possessions yielding an unlabelled home-cooked microdisc filled with strange sounds, sounds whose alien nature was magnified as rumors passed from nurse to doctor to administrator to newshawk. By now, the disc had vanished and was reported to contain ritual music dedicated to some little-known ancestral nature demons. Police, emergency and psychic hygiene officials were combing the area for the disc or information regarding its contents. A linkscreen at blast's end showed the story being picked up by a dozen screens, sites and casts, and YourVoice™ was full of worried bystanders hypothesizing about the sounds, their origins, and the nefarious aims behind them. It was swelling into a micropanic. *God, you are good*, Renzo thought. By tomorrow, sidewalk mics all over the city would be intercepting bits and pieces of hushed and fearful predictions, a sky filled with psychoactive sound. It was a perfect precursor to his status call with Magdalena and her team.

He preferred holding remote conferences in Hedgepeth's office. Renzo loved the form-fitting durafoam chairs, the rich assortment of legal and semi-legal liqueurs, the big, vivid holoscreen. And it

77

was always worthwhile to grab a peek at Maren, Arky's wonderfully exaggerated Queen Bee, the only assistant on the floor who could return the boys' strafing glances with an equally virulent hunger.

— *Arky back from the driving range?* Renzo asked.

Maren smiled. *From the look of him, he's still perfecting his fade.*

— *As are we all, Ms. Parvenu*, Renzo said. *As are we all.*

Arky seemed a little jittery as he swirled his Pisco on ice. There was no record company to foot the bill; this was Sweetwater's project and Gestalt would have to fund the R&D. If they were onto a winner, Lord S. could play Col. Parker for decades. If their Galatea tanked, the loss would be all his. Bad for everybody. Arky switched on the holodeck and the office was filled with staticky ghosts.

— *Fucking ozone scrambles the signal on hot days*, Arky said. *Seems like technology is always trading one set of gremlins for another.*

Like my career, Renzo thought, adjusting his spine to Arky's guest chair. Placing pop songs in teenage titty flicks and candy commercials made a lot more sense than disintegrating identities for fun and profit. Arky waved his tuner around like some kind of colicky Toscanini, and one by one, the figures of Magadelena and her cadre of experts swarmed into focus. As she did the introductions, Renzo thought he heard a note of distaste in her voice. She sounded like a foodco lobbyist that had just gotten a few more rat hairs into the punters' NutraSpread.

— *Gentlemen*, she said. *I think you'll be happy. We're creating something special. Something very special.*

She turned to Vyasha with a look of contrition that was indescribable. One that Renzo had never seen before. One by one, Mags introduced the digital figures whose shades filled the room: Syreeta, the Sri Lankan runway model; Dr. Licht; Jonas; Akili St. Loire, the dj and arranger; trainer Ed Trautwein and, finally, the designer Dayanarah, who seemed to control the room, her graceful body draped in garnet and yellow silk, embracing a kelly-green divan.

One by one, the creative team, assembled at a prohibitive cost known to only a handful of insiders, explained their aims and their student's progress. Syreeta discussed grace of posture and motion, and showed the repertoire of walks she had taught Vyasha: the crowded party cat-stalk, the Sunday promenade, the red-carpet strut, all drilled into her without sacrificing the native grace born on the forest floor. Licht untangled the previously-indecipherable strands of her tribal song-language, so organic to her music-making, and clued them all in on the romance roots that enabled her to engage in charmingly broken Italian-French-Spanish/Catalan. Jonas and St. Loire played important, subtly colored sound-visions they had freshly recorded with string quartets, Carpathian choral singers, harmonium, flamenco guitar, bandoneon, oud and tape samples from the length and breadth of human expression. And then Dayanarah, ageless and weightless, rose from her perch, and, with a wave of her hand, called in a march of models wearing elegant ensembles in yellow-green snakeskin, bird-of-paradise feathers, satin, lynx and lioness, set off with belts, anklets and breastplates inlaid with amber, chrysocolla, jasper, mother of pearl, carnelian and petrified wood. At the end of the train was a series of duster coats in chameleon skin that shimmered and changed colors and let the wearers sink into walls, the folds of curtains. Even through the broadcast-snow, the collection sent a sweet and thrilling eyeshock along Renzo's nerves, filling him with excitement. Shimmering under Vyasha's angelface, over the gently rolling muscles of her new, gym-sculpted form, the effects would be staggering. And what was most killing was that fans would never be able to get more than glimpses and glances. Arky looked at Renzo as if to say *money well spent.*

Already, "Zona da Mata," a swirling trance of organ, bass and sleigh bells, with vocal counterpoint from a Dade gospel choir, was ready to be streamed and pressed on micros for the mail order houses and the City's Minutes of Pleasure multishops. The AmbiGauge and Gestalt's national spiderweb of ambient mics told the story: the Times Square incident lived like a dormant virus in the urban music fans, who still ached to unlock a mystery that had grown tendrils of urban legend. Subliminals had been tucked into the quiet parts of the biggest and darkest independent films. The popular self-cutting artist Jack Antic had even made a "killer song" reference while hosting the Sexwork Awards two nights earlier at the Bardo Plane.

    – *The iron is hot*, Renzo said.
    – *White hot*, Arky nodded.

As the team faded behind masks of self-satisfaction, Renzo realized that the only one who had nothing to say was Vyasha herself. But they were accustomed to doing it all for their clients. "Overnight sensation," once a phenomenon, had been reduced to a business plan. With computer holofex, Audiofix™ for off-key singing, and state-of-the-art surgical modifications, there was no one that could not be made an object of envy, admiration. With Vyasha's beauty and skill, their work would be simple. Renzo felt a sort of satisfaction as he sat in the silence of the afterhours office, debriefing a Magdalena that had grown wearier and more put-upon than he had ever seen.

– *We have made straight the way*, he told Magdalena.

– *Ever thought about what we do*, she said. *I mean, really thought?*

– *Those with talents are God's jewels*, he replied. *We simply create the settings, carve and polish the facets, to make them shine. To make them eternal. After all, making stars is easy; they're only fire. The art is ensuring their light lives after the fire burns out.*

– *I meant*, she said, *what we do to ourselves.*

For this, Renzo had no answer. Just a self-deceiving scowl.

*****

The program lurched forward, with an inexorability Renzo had come to view with pride. The soft launch of Vyasha's new music was a week away, and much groundwork had been laid. But he still had some calls to make, some wagons to circle. Any good fader knew that nothing succeeded like excess, and that nothing whetted the public appetite like prohibition. Or, at least, condemnation. Man's secret desire was to become invisible, to erase himself from the world, so anything that promised self-effacement, paralysis, oblivion, was at some level deeply prized. Every hallmark of society – religion, war, politics – had reduced the importance of men to trembling penitents, points on a map, clicks on a voting screen. Neurochemical science had shrunk the most complex processes to tiny chemical secretions, Art had worked for a while as a celebration of skill and craft, but now it was largely viewed as a function of cerebral abnormality. Man wanted to fade into a great dirty, beckoning unknown. In the marketplace of ideas, damnation was readily available, and quite affordable on a variety of payment plans.

– *Renzo Caliari. I think I'm expected.* The guard at the reception desk squinted at his screen, as Renzo assayed the commotion in the lobby of Pastor Farshore's Church of Perpetual Longing. Men with headsets barked technical instructions for the evening holocasts. Tradesmen loaded cartons filled with balloons and bunting, and crates full of provisions for the post-service supper. Three backup singers for the Scars of Grace, tucked into teasingly snug lace bodices, signed missals as they assembled a trail of admirers. The guard nodded, and Renzo turned to walk through the hallway of glass arches projected with fusillades of colored Redon starbursts. It was small wonder that the congregants were primed for awe and amazement by the time they reached the Main Temple. As he forced open the great bronze doors depicting the Fall and Redemption of Man (with a *zaftig* Christ Renzo always felt looked suspiciously like Pastor Roscoe himself), he could see the Pastor at the main altar, between Hedberg's twin marbles of Tantalus and Sisyphus, directing traffic. Farshore smiled and motioned Renzo back into his private chambers.

— *I almost fell into a dead faint when I got your message*, Farshore said. *Spiritual crisis?*

— *Nothing so selfish*, Renzo said. *I wanted to tip you off, as our first line of moral defense, to a tentacle of temptation threatening the Christian psyche.*

— *Ah*, the Pastor acknowledged with a thin smile of recognition, *I see. The sentinel sending the alarm…*

— *…To ev'ry Middlesex village and farm.* It was a symbiotic relationship. Renzo fed the Pastor hints about devilish culture, and Farshore lent Renzo's clients the *frisson* of danger that made them irresistible to the underground. Renzo couldn't use this tactic more than a couple times a year, but it was surefire. A warning on Pastor Farshore's *Clarion Call* was good for 90,000 units and a dozen Q points. In exchange, Gestalt, through its Staff of Life subsidiary, helped keep the Pastor in cognac and Italian shoes. *It's encouraging that a man like you can do well by doing good.*

Farshore rose slowly and walked over to his humidor, clipping the end from a Cohiba with a cutter shaped like Jonah's whale. *Lovely, isn't it?* he said, gesturing toward a painting Renzo didn't recognize, a *sacra conversazione* in earthy greens and reds. *Since the earthquakes, Italian export restrictions are a thing of the past. Funny how things work out.* He delicately rubbed his ribcage at the site of one of St. Sebastian's arrows. *You know, I never accepted your theories of human nature, but I'm not fool enough to quarrel with success.*

— *Always leave the public wanting more. But then, the soft sell has never worked very well in your line.*

Renzo knew he was giving the cue for one of Farshore's well-rehearsed rants about the basic corruptibility of Man, the allure of the fleshly pleasures, and the need for constant and vociferous vigilance. But his laundry list beckoned, and by the time Farshore had gotten to Weimar Germany, Renzo's hands were clamped on the arms of his chair, waiting to catapult him out of the houses of the holy.

— *Serpents and savagery,* Renzo said, placing a microdisc case on the edge of Farshore's lucite credenza. *As pure an invocation of pagan passions as ever quickened the pulses of men. And women, we hope.*

Farshore blew a trio of smoke rings and coyly winked. *If it's as bad as all that, I warn you, I shan't hold back. I will attack with my full arsenal of rhetoric, regardless of cost.* He tapped an ash into a brass replica of Cellini's golden salt cellar.

— *Yes,* Renzo acknowledged. *We're counting on it.*

*****

Renzo had never before done so much groundwork for a campaign, and he had a warm feeling about its prospects for success. He had convinced Gunther Nadler at the Galerie Asmodeus on Broome to use Vyasha as the soundtrack for *Guts of a Virgin*, L'Infer's exhibition of viscera sculptures and corpseblood screenprints, an exhibition that would, thanks to Dax Frazee in the Mayor's Office of Even Public Temperament, be closed before a single patron had fainted, a single note played. He had even written tomorrow's *Post* headline: LOONEY TUNES AND MORBID MALADIES. But when careers were on the line, Renzo knew, you didn't take chances. Although most of the commerce flowed through computer networks, there were still a handful of stores that served as staging areas, meeting places for fans, collection hubs for retail data. A good launch event and prime product placement in the large population centers could still put even the stealthiest whisper campaign over the top. Some pre-planned shoplifter busts, news flashes showing discs stashed behind locked counters with FreshHell™ and the vivisection and sex games... These could push Vyasha over the top. It was time to visit Erasmus J. down at Distractions, Inc.

Renzo found him in his custom powerchair, working a couple in the Recreational Pathologies department. They could not synthesize MS, but for a moderate sum, they could give you a 48-hour case of EAE, the mouse equivalent. *It's quite exquisite. Every muscle crying out in a tangled whiplash ecstasy. The sweat pouring into your eyes like salty, mad hornets.*

You'll awake drenched and drained like a man who's fought a dozen Gettysburgs. But of course, it's not for everyone. Can I guide you to something milder? He could tell by the way the boy's eyes searched his partner's that the hook was in.

— *I'll try anything twice*, he said, grabbing two vials from the display rack.

Back in the office, Renzo reclined. *Used to be comic books and Die Hard discs. Custom diseases? Home brain mapping and retinal modification?*

— *In the words of Prof. Aziz-Durand, those kicks just keep getting harder to find.*

Renzo explained the circumstances of his new discovery, sliding a disc in Ras' player and surrounding them in a thick mist-blanket of thrumming heartbeats and cicada songs, from which emerged a piercing viola melody and Vyasha's wordless, keening animal cry. He could see that Erasmus, whose ear was legendary in music circles, instantly joined with the sounds. He had x-ray eyes and the twitching in his right hand had stopped altogether.

— *That is some transfigurational shit*. After a time, he had fallen back to earth. *What do you have in mind?*

Renzo sketched out a scheme: cultists trashing a carefully-chosen section of shelves, police presence, a public bashing of Vyasha's tunes, a small but angry demonstration, maybe later, a legal challenge. Erasmus laughed a little; in some strange way, he lived for this stuff, from the sable polish on his boots to the end of the golden braid he whipped from side to side along with the beat of the talking drums.

— The Pastor is already on board, Samson. The sacred and the profane.

Erasmus smiled again. *How come I always gotta be the profane, man? I can be pretty fucking sacred, if you catch me at the right time.*

Renzo counted out some currency slips and slid them under Ras' Wynton Beazley bobble-head. *God doesn't do bitter. Golden calves aside, I mean. Try a little gratitude.*

— I regularly petition the Big Man for a 26-hour day so I can properly catalogue all my motherfucking blessings. He punctuated his speech with a pair of blasts from his chair-horn.

— Our friend would have something to say about that, Renzo said, puffing out his cheeks. *Keeping the lights on all over the world could run into money. But I'll work on it.*

Ras traced the image of Giordana St. Ives on a ragged tour poster dotted with beer-bottle rings. *You know what they say. What doesn't kill us, entertains us.*

Renzo checked his watch, a pre-war Cartier tank. *Maybe everything kills us a little bit,* he thought. And entertainment was a part of the process. A consensual nano-cannibalism of the soul. CNCS. He'd have to remember that.

— Got to race, Renzo said. *I have a non-opening I have to attend.*

*****

The Altura digital frieze in his living room gave off eight pulses of topaz light, which told Renzo it was nearly time for his appointment. It had been a maddish, up-and-down week, and he felt relieved that he would soon have the benefit of Chisa's subtle attentions. It was hard to find a good psypros (*emotional trainer*, he chided himself, almost instantly) and even harder to keep her on long-term, since contracts were *verboten*. He and Chisa had been together for three years now, and he no longer knew what he would do if he could not have her to knead out his emotional knots with her blend of Socratic questioning, pregnant silences and simple radiance of soul. Many times he had maneuvered his commitments around her schedule, for he was well aware how many heartsick executives were waiting to soak up her time.

He answered the door and sighed to look at her, smallish, slender but full of kinetic energy like an acrobat, her long black hair positively pulsing with shades of henna and burgundy. Her face, which seemed to change each time Renzo looked at it, was shaded by the hood of a cape of crimson silk. He stepped aside and stared at the surefooted way her sandals navigated his teakwood floor. Without a sound, she made her way to the hall closet and took out her *yogen* screen, which she unfolded across the living room. Behind its glass, contoured and translucent to give a quivery ghost image, he could see her small expert motions as she lit the *ganriki* candles, technically illegal in the residential zone, but so vital to the ceremony. As Renzo sat, cross-legged, on his side of the screen, he could see her cloak fall to the floor, like a shower of scales.

Renzo watched her skin, the color of ancient bones, and he imagined the candle sheen pooling on her delicate shoulders like little gemstones of light. She began moving in a calm snake dance and quietly mouthing the word *open open open* in a breathy singsong prayer. How desperately he wanted to break the glass and touch her, but he knew the rules. And an incident would go hard on him with the bosses, not to mention constituting a Class D misdemeanor. So he watched and waited for thoughts to come, his fingers softsearching her ghost image in the cool glass. As he always did at the start of their sessions, he remembered something she always said: *we are always the most perfect we ever were*, and let the words guide him back, into the past, where he lay with Luma and their newborn daughter Emmaline, before it had all fallen away. Without expecting to, he heard himself speak:

    — *Kachi, can one ever get too good at losing things, at surrendering things?*

She stilled and placed her hands on the screen, a teasing gesture Renzo mirrored. His breaths were cacophonous, like the collapse of a building. He waited and imagined her eyes, always her eyes, looking into her private place, belonging to no one.

    — *Invite the pain,* she said. *Sometime, invite the pain.*

This seemed to disentangle him, and for much of the hour, he spoke and she heard, of the old days before success, of the quiet nights and the pleasures so picturebook it almost drove him crazy with redfaced longing: the kites in the park, washing

Emmaline's babyhair, dawn whispers in Luma's ear, redolent of raspberry shampoo. All this he had tossed away. He imagined his waterwords falling down the eternal curve of Chisa's resting spine, her gentle motions guiding them into a pool of pellucid regret. By the time the candles burned down, and they thanked the surrounding darkness in words she had painstakingly taught him, he felt bleached inside, the quiet lust an engine driving out sadness the way hard exercise purged the body's poisons. For the only time in his week, he felt clean. Through a slot in the screen, her elegant fingers handed him a card on which were written, in elaborate calligraphy, the Japanese words for focus, renew and invent. It signaled session's end.

— *Where are all the girls like you?,* Renzo whispered, his lips to the slot. *The ones with the sight?*

— *Hidden,* she answered. *Where we will remain.*

However much he admired Chisa's strength and grace, he always pitied her a little, too. Although her caste were the way to love, they were denied love. They were the ones who held open the door for everyone else. He and his friends helped keep them in that place, and the thought of it pained him just a little.

*****

Things had gone well. Gestalt, on one of its house labels, Sleeper Cell, had slipped three tracks into the datastream, and the buzz had built slowly, beneath the surface, an infection. A half dozen websites had reviewed the songs in terms ranging from curious to rapturous. Their NerveNet™ monitor Carlos had detected significant interest on the index of social nets, and ambient mics from Charleston to Coos Bay had logged indications of attention in the randoms. Add an appearance on the crawl of the *Sentinel*™ holocast (with a twinge of grimace from talking head Atlas Brees that cost Gestalt a weekend at a Phuket sex resort) and you had some real intrigue, an irritant under the collective skin, something they could build on.

For weeks, the murmurs grew, fed by events both planned and spontaneous. The Second Church of Christ Scourge of Sinners in the New Secession burned discs and memorabilia, the frenzy building until the flames engulfed three Salvadoran housekeepers dressed to resemble the hazy wire photo that was the sole picture of Vyasha Gestalt had leaked. *Waste not want not*, Renzo thought. The Happy Family Council, a Pennsylvania-based subsidiary of Gestalt's corporate parent, did a Congressional show-and-tell of scans showing the brain on Vyasha, the regions governing sexual violence and appetite tinted an angry chartreuse. The company-sponsored tribute act, Lawrence, Massachusetts' Snow Leopards, surprisingly, begat three more started by honest fans. But nothing, they knew, ruined an act's popularity like popularity, the way a violent explosion cancelled out a raging oil-well fire. So Renzo was careful to avoid mass exposure, gossip columns, awards and celebrity boyfriends. Vyasha was delicately brought to a slow boil, name-checked by only the cleverest commentators, always with a suggestion of corruption, of aboriginal sorcery. By the fall, *The Unseeing Eye* reported a groundswell of e-blasts demanding live shows, and Vyasha was smuggled, *via* unmarked motorcade, to the City, to work with dancer Soren Lundvall and the installation artist Denizen on a semi-secret concert tour.

The 12th floor of the Hotel Vollard, where Vyasha and entourage were ensconced behind a subtle but ruthless security force, had become a pilgrimage point for Gestalt insiders and *cognoscenti* like online semiotics guru Roy Hauptman (who seemed to toss away monocles the way hair-metal guitarists once discarded plectra), holodeck sex star Marduk and her troupe of muscular functionaries in their matching pleather codpieces, and the Latvian film director Lajos Rivka, who spent a week of all-nighters watching his cinematographer Mortice film the back of Vyasha's neck with a 1980s camcorder, for what creative end no one could guess. Renzo and Arky divided their time between the old Turpitz Brothers sewing shop, where Vyasha's band rehearsed; the Vollard, where they looked over set drawings and costume sketches while a newly-fashionable Magdalena (looking like Delphine Seyrig in *Daughters of Darkness*) hovered in mother-lion mode over her new obsession; and New York's loose circuit of evanescent and secretive after-hours joints, whisking Vyasha in and out after no more than 30 minutes in each. She barely had time to test her jumbled but emerging English. She did, however, leave a series of *paparazzo* vapor trails, the fruits of which Gestalt judiciously parceled out to media favor-seekers.

— *Must we do this now?* Magdalena asked in an uncharacteristically testy manner, tapping an expensive-looking wristwatch. *It is after two.* She squeezed Vyasha's shoulder, and the vulpine beauty, perched self-consciously on the edge of her chair, threw Mags a look of gratitude that Renzo felt hung awkwardly on her face. Vyasha began to slam closed an album of drawings of chinchilla snow suits for a planned polar production number, then caught herself, lowering the cover without a sound. *Must we?* Renzo thought, dismayed by Mags' newfound gentility.

— *I suppose there's time enough*, he said; then, to Magdalena, *can we offer you a lift?* She brushed him off dismissively, without a word, without a glance.

— *Whatever became of the little girl swayed by b.o., bad manners and Irish accents?* Arky joked as they crossed the lobby. *Our Mags has become a loy-dee.* Renzo seethed a little at Arky's cheek, at the prospect of losing Mags, at his own inattention. He noticed how the scattering of people in the Vollard's modernist lounges had metastasized from wide-eyed fan types to jackal-eyed journalists and process servers to paste-white amateur ghouls, sallow-cheeked in secondhand medieval finery and costume-shop cloaks. They seemed to be trying to talk themselves into something sinister and unwise that Renzo had no wish to stick around for.

— *Gravedancers*, Arky said. *But these are the crazies who'll stick with us.*

– Careful what you wish for, Renzo said, grunting under the weight of the great bronze doors that led onto the 63rd St. pedicab stand.

*****

There is no success like failure. – B. Dylan
There is no failure like success. – Lord Sweetwater, M.B.E.

Two quotes were carved over the door at Gestalt's home office, and they perfectly bracketed the career track they had planned for Vyasha. Her fame would start as a nervous whisper, build to a mumble then a grumble, and finally ascend through outrage, scandal, *cause célèbre*, contrarian embrace, critical reassessment, and, finally, tragic legend, each phase expertly micro-managed from Gestalt's complex of monitors and data libraries. By early October, the murmurs were gathering, perhaps faster than Renzo would have liked. He had embargoed all interviews and released bonus tracks laden with backwards-masking through only the most incestuous members-only networks. *Signet* magazine had run a piece with a handful of exclusive and very artistic photos, blurred through rain-soaked stained-glass windows. The standard rumors had been planted that she was the voice of a washed-up session singer, a computer program, some unholy amalgamation of whale songs, hummingbird wings and the grinding of machine-age gears. The plan was to let select cadres of fans see her in live performances spread across widely-dispersed population centers in dark media markets: Kampala, Sarajevo, Quito, Winnipeg, Brisbane, Dar Es Salaam, Montevideo, along with a smattering of real/mythical private shows for world leaders and opinioneers. Then, there would be a week of shows at New York's New Agora, a tantalizing, multicasted glimpse for a curious world, just to make the cultish fanatics feel betrayed and embattled, to make them clutch her more desperately to their breasts. Everyone who had bought a Velvet Underground album, they said, started a band. Everyone who grabbed a piece of Vyasha would start a sect.

When the time zones permitted it, Renzo would jack into the live feed and watch their investment turn the lonely halls into something sacred and haunted, her voice sidewinding around Adam Hart's viola or skating on the glacial echoes of Pal Karlsson's glass vibraphone. Most new artists were rehearsed within an inch of their lives, slaves to structure, but Vyasha would move in and out, expanding and contracting rhythms like lovers' breath, and taking the band with her on a net of telepathic cues. Renzo wondered if the band was even aware of where she was leading them. In Karachi, the Mayan sacrifice encore culminated in a low, throaty whisper like a panther growl, the last notes met, not with cheers, but a stoned, reverential silence neither Renzo nor Arky had ever heard before. Renzo tried to get the real post-mortem from Magdalena, but could only elicit tour expenses, box office receipts and quotes from bewildered but respectful reviews in Beirut broadsheets before the

TransVoice contact faded. Even the arrests in Haifa and the bottle-throwing in Cairns came to him as generic newscrawl bytes. He marveled that, in such an entangled world, he could feel like his artist was a freshly-released helium balloon, beautiful and shining and lost, forever lost. And the more lost she got, the more the people around her seemed to find her, and to find things in themselves. It was exactly how the process was designed to work.

But in the midst of it all, even as Vyasha's star rose, Renzo could feel himself fading.

After New York, they would stash their charge away under a haze of conflicting rumors, Dylan after the crash. Maybe at Wildwind, maybe at Arky's place in Constanta. Give a taste and take it away. Basic pusher/pimp logic. People would think her a fever dream, find it hard to believe she had ever existed, until Gestalt reappeared her and swooped in for the real fuck-you money.

The metrics – the quants and quals – had been trending strongly for weeks. JeremiAds™ had given Vyasha a golden pyre for her stream of condemnations in church bulletins, Secession lunch counters, Indian casino bingo parlors and swap meets. The Trenchcoat Index of Disenfranchised Youth put Vyasha among Che, Divine, Rimbaud, Klaus Kinski, Reich, Hopper, Mishima, Brady and Hindley, the Honeymoon Killers. Her first tracks were gaining commercial traction day by day, but the right way: *Riptide* made one the nation's fifth most stolen tune. It meant people were too afraid to *buy*, a situation they could remedy while preserving the air of anti-corporate sabotage. Once things went aboveground, in a year or 18 months, Vyasha would have rebel cred that would insure decades of sky-high licensing – more if she was lucky enough to die the right way.

Renzo was humming along aimlessly to a live feed, watching his computer screen as a blanket of Hebrew and Arabic characters enveloped Vyasha, wide-eyed, mining some animal music from a foreign stage, when Arky sidled in, wearing a look of concern, a sheaf of printouts under his arm.

– *Wanna see something crazy?* he asked.

– *Drummer for the Dimestore Phonies asked me that in Tempe once. Never again answered in the affirmative.*

– *This might interest you.*

Renzo recognized it right away. It was a standard research kit, the kind the free NYU interns threw together. On top, Arky had laid the sort of red and black Nesbitt graph he had seen 500 times before.

– *Ever seen one like that?*

The Nesbitt pulled and analyzed data from all the receptors and all the libraries. It was a shelflife predictor used to estimate revstreams from long-term clients. For the universe of consumers of an artist's output, it pictured shape-of-demand. The x-axis represented intensity of exposure; the y, urgency of need. In virtually every instance, the universe of fans could be plotted along a gently descending curve that represented the impacts of media overkill; the slope of the curve reflected the public's degree of tolerance, and often determined whether a net or label would put that extra promotional dollar into a performer's flagging career.

But Vyasha's graph was different. At 30% saturation, the graph split in two, and a steeply ascending line knifed through a long cluster of points that threatened to spill off the page.

– *The "forked tongue"?* Renzo asked, his voice rising, incredulous. Those in the industry who glanced at the academic literature recognized the pattern, a phenomenon that had existed for years in theory, like some unseen subatomic particle, but that no one had ever seen materialize for an actual artist. *Is that even possible?*

– *Apparently so.*

The y-curve, or, as it was known in industry slang, the *forked-tongue*, was to antipub what giant ants and mantises had been to the atomic energy industry of the 1950s. It was Bigfoot and the Jersey Devil. It was Roswell, before the Snake River excavation. It meant there were fans whose Attachment and Consumption Energies would continue escalating past 80, 90, 100% saturation. It meant they were building a monster.

– *Lord S. will never go for scuttling the City gigs. Not now*, Arky said. They shared a long, stupefied silence. *So do we wake up Megalon and go hunting for Godzilla?*

Renzo fidgeted with a little wind-up car that he set down, to spin in doughnut after doughnut, until its spring-driven energy petered out at the very edge of his desk. *I only hope,* he said, *that we do have to hunt him down.*

*****

– *So crabby*, Sadie said, in her flirty Moneypenny voice. *You should be on top of the world.* And, truly, the AmbiGauge and related indicators agreed. As the tour rumbled across the globe, Vyasha's shows grew bigger, tickets more hotly coveted. At irregular intervals, shows were called off, generating angry news items and making ticketholders edgier and more expectant. The most discussion, by far, concerned an explicit recreation of the death of Isadora Duncan at a private birthday show for a Chechen militia general, a show most notable for the fact that it never happened. It was a thing of beauty. Yet alongside the breathless reviews and mystified speculation were persistent sidebar items about unruly crowds, backstage invasions, and odd bouts of politically-motivated violence. In Monterrey, a drug cartel splinter group, all in the guise of Santa Muerte, broke windows and burned devotional effigies outside the provincial theater Vyasha was playing. Any unrest was good unrest, Renzo knew, but the build-up of weirdness unnerved him, made Vyasha's ascent hard to enjoy. In Clearwater, Florida, a Farshore radio broadcast condemning Vyasha's "Love in The Place of Skulls" spurred a progress of autistic and Down's Syndrome children ending with a mass mock crucifixion on a local high-school football field.

And there were the crazygrams, one a day for the last ten, pasted in letters cut from paper magazines, soup labels and children's cereal boxes. Renzo had to admire their artistry, drop capitals elegantly cut from multi-colored packages of

MegaBran and Mold-Resistant Rice Clumps. A labor of mad love, he thought. But the messages grew more and more threatening:

SORRENDER GIRL SINGER TO US O TRGIK RESULT

WE TAKE VYASH FOR SAFEKEPING

U XPLOYT, U PAY

In three days, the entourage was due back in the states, but the FBI field office, called in at last by an insistent Security Director, treated these warnings as troublesome pranks by teenage MurderNet subscribers trying to emulate the notorious exploits of their pet killers. Special Agent Creech had been in the office barely twenty minutes before rudely stuffing the notes into individual sandwich bags and tossing Arky a business card with only the field office's public complaint number on it.

— *They're treating us like fidgety assholes*, Arky muttered as the elevator door closed on Creech's backside.

The mood among the band and crew was best described as guarded relief when they limped back into town. Even the entertainments Lord Sweetwater staged at the Sangre de Christo (where Gestalt housed the Artist and her core entourage) seemed to distract the invited luminaries only slightly. The gleaming ivory and mahogany sexual acrobats from the Circus Horribilis show moored on the West Side piers were exemplars of grace and flexibility, their twinings making fantastic human sculpture through the glaze of cinnamon incense, and Naropa Aswari's expressive saxophone jazz gave everything a lazy, debauched ambience, but Vyasha, unmoved, did not stray from the sofa in her sunken living room, where she nibbled on root vegetables and fielded questions from a rapt nucleus of admirers. Chamblee Sanders, the smooth-pated chairman of Columbia's demonology department, and holocast host Livia Wasch peppered her with questions on the shamanic powers of music and natural healing, and she, not fazed in the least, sometimes answered in soft imperfect English, and sometimes whispered answers to her interpreter Magdalena, who stayed glued to her side, clutching her hand with very public tenderness. Renzo did not want to scatter this air of tranquility when he finally cornered Mags, and omitted his story of the latest note, which warned of the illicit power of Vyasha's message, and arrived in a box of what seemed like the singed ashes of birds' wings.

— *She won't go on Wednesday*, Mags announced. *Gervais wants her to sit one out. We'll do the proxy show by tape loop and hologram.*

And, in fact, Tuesday's show went off without incident, the set greeted by cheers from an upscale crowd polite enough to be almost alarming. Wednesday was a frigid night, the air moist with the threat of snow. It was the bracing feel of the wind that made Renzo decide to swing by the theater to see that evening's set. From his vantage point at the back of the room, he gazed at the impressive stage set, expensive mint-green curtains over a reconstruction of the Trailblazer space platform, Hirsh Graves' guitars standing in line at attention behind an elaborate cubicle of keyboards and servers holding arias, news broadcasts, and nature sounds from all the continents. His eye was drawn by an ashen wisp swaddled in a dull blue-gray felt cloak, guided to an aisle seat by a pair of Indian ladies-in-waiting. From her wave-motions and the glint of amber, he knew immediately who the silent, unrecognized figure really was. Renzo wondered what she would think after finally seeing herself perform. But the Wednesday crowd was young, rowdy and conspiratorial, and the morose figures in their almost-uniform black paratroop sweaters and bondage trousers made Renzo feel old and out-of-place, so, when the lights went down and a hungry howl filled the room, he buckled his waistcoat and retired to the lounge at Esme's across the street, where he could watch proceedings on his networked micro-tablet.

Snow had begun to fall when the waiter returned with Renzo's Jack and ginger, which he used to wash down the Omnivox tablets that gave events a sense of slow, easy clarity. If he didn't know better, he would say that the spectral image onstage, chanting and gesturing, pulling magic from the corners of the cavernous hall, was Vyasha herself. The rolling solace of the pills began to rock him, and he thought he saw looks of foreboding drift over the shaded faces of Vyasha's band, accompanied by echoes of gentle tumult, like those surrounding a drunken fight, from the orchestra pit. Lazily, he tapped through the various camera views, finally settling on a feed of the audience in the expensive premiere seats. A chill he interpreted as a draft from the doorway held him as he watched, in video time-lapse, three black-clad figures duchamp to their feet, igniting makeshift torches with cheap cigarette lighters. From outside the frame, other scuffles were erupting, soundtracked by muffled sounds of half-formed ladyfear. Cloth wicks flared. Makeshift firebombs illuminated the crowd's pinched, anxious faces, the incendiary cocktails flying toward the stage and erupting into violent streaks of St. Elmo's Fire.

It was beyond description, the way the hail of flares fell, and the shrieks and low male commands rose and jumbled into some kind of panicloud over the elegant old venue, fire spreading across the walls like something out of old newsreel footage of decapalm burning off the foliage around Timorese guerillas. Renzo's pills, which disassociated painful neural connections, turned it all into a play of radiant colors that mesmerized him so that he was unable to rise or call out, even as the first burning patrons exploded onto the street and the sidewalks broke out in mad carnival displays of terror and rescue. *Fever fervor flame*. Renzo did not turn to scan the victims, for he knew that Vyasha was already gone, and with her, whatever pith was left inside him.

*****

After it all, the reality left to him was one endless, tumbling day/night that he traversed along a bread-trail of pills – Mentira to remember the steps

103

that led him there, Lethemax to draw the spirit-briars from his skin. Still, he had managed to distill one thought that pulled him along like a scream in the nightmare forest. *My great gift has been for losing things, tossing them away without guilt or bitterness, and now the world has repaid me in kind, left me interred in my glass-and-hardwood prison-tower, mail pressing under the door, unheard messages stacked on the data console.* All that left an impression on him now was the vision of Chisa behind her screen, that flowing grace-dance he loved so much and that, he knew, would very soon also slip away. *There's a dream-kingdom that's mine,* he thought, *and it's always and only mine, and it lives beyond Chisa and her gently rolling landscape skin and all her luckless wisdom, and there, I have a chance to be clean and valid again, to atone.* He had no voice, but he felt himself asking her to explain how things had come to be the way they were, and he waited.

Smoke, she said, touching the surface of his vintage cedar globe of the world with those lovely, spidery fingers. *All a sacred smoke.*

WHO'S AFRAID
OF TOBIAS WOLFF?

   — *'Atta boy, Shooter! A tray and change!*

It was nice to finally get a kind word from Nathan Chang. Ever since he had come over from *Dellinger's*, he had been putting the fear of GOD!® into the whole *P's and Q's* staff, trimming back on perqs, calling for live meetings, bringing in Billy Dean as Ombudsman to conduct random nanoaudits…My blast on the Japanese bras that dispensed flavored breast milk stayed up on the PNQ.lit site for 3:13, earning me some serious Pay-Points, maybe enough for the hyperbaric chamber Rikki kept droning on about.

   — *Don't want to get too worked up over second place,* I said. I needed to sound like a striver to keep Chang in my corner. His favorites always got the best placement, and that made a difference. One wrong move and you could wind up in the back pages near fitness or education.

   — *Perish the thought, Superstar,* he went on. *Nuñez is out. Deano found too many good facts in it. You're the champ.* "Man Castrates Pooch Over Leg-Humping Incident" had been the talk of the office, hanging around for all of 7:08. An instant classic. But the *Stranger Than Fiction* stuff couldn't be too factual; that was cheating and could get you sued. So the week belonged to Tek Symmyns! As Dr. Chaudry might say during one of his big Religion of Me encampments, "It was a toehold on the mountain of Personal Power."

The traffic was heavy on Constitution Ave. due to the Congressional winter session, but I didn't mind. I loved the sight of the Capitol all floodlit, the brilliant rainbow hues – crimson over the House, the Money Green dome, the Passion Purple Senate. It made me a little nostalgic for the Freespirits, no matter how hard their Empathy Laws made life for a journo. It was almost impossible to prosecute newswriters now under the Originalists, and that made things a whole lot easier, but I was going to miss this colorful landmark once the Leadership could scrape together the Reagans for a monument's worth of Purewhite. Stuck at a crosswalk waiting for a pride of Solorides to pass, I tuned my audio to Dylan Rewired. Ever since the Germans had isolated the algorithm, you didn't hear man-written originals anymore, but people didn't seem to care that much. It never bothered me that "Bullrush Child" was SimulSound, because those gospel harmonies could lift me like a fistful of Vitalon. And with a big night ahead of me, I would need all the pep I could muster.

I was really getting into it when – just my luck! – my audiochip message bell started ringing.

*– You have a message from…RIKKI SYMMYNS. It will begin after this helpful word from Pro-Stet. Pro-Stet: Nature…Only Better…*Much as I hated these commercials, especially the artificial organ jingles *(No aches and pains/Or bulging veins…)*, I knew the dangers of declining a call from the wife. So I cranked up SymBob and waited for Rikki's voice.

— Hey, Bear, where you at? she cooed. She sounded agitated.

— Almost to the Potomac flyover, I said. *With a little luck, I'll be nuzzling that downy neck before you're through watching Fat and Frisky.* I could hear her chuckle and inhale deeply. I imagined her leaning back in the Iso-Chair, all the stress flowing out of that beautiful, rippling red-clay back, those graceful, serpentine porphyry arms.

— Oh, you! Don't make fun. Don't forget we have tickets for the Senate tonight!

No chance of scrubbing that. For weeks, I had been hearing the ancient refrain: *we never go out anymore,* until I could barely stand it. So I called in a few favors from the guys at the Center For Voodoo, and scored some giga seats for the Midnight Rumpus at the Capitol. It was budget season, and there were some fireworks over the last of the public wheat stockpiles, so tempers were high, the old men were working at the top of their games and tickets were scarce as polar ice. I was feeling pretty proud of myself and with Templar away on a school trip, I was frankly looking forward to a little full-tilt sensopressure. It had been days and days, and, besides, I had earned it. No mediation required this time, cousin!

— I am so dialed in, Kitten. After the show, we are going OFF-off-line and getting all kindsa tactile. And that's covenant…

******

3 FEBRUARY, 11:18 P.M.

Micronesian cuisine was never my favorite. After a dinner at Colonia, I couldn't care if I never saw another banana leaf. But the snapper was fine, and the palm wine had got me glowing, so I was in a good mindframe when I handed the Agogo's drivecard to the valet parker at the Capitol gate. And Rikki was turning heads as we strode down Monsanto Corridor. No question about it; my wife was a stunner. That subtle mix of bloods – the Malaysian, the Iroquois, her mom's Egyptian roots – blended to form a woman of lithe and compelling exoticism. I had never liked the "egghead" look, and I was damn glad her black tresses had grown back to shoulder length, but the electrolyzed brows were growing on me in a big way. She definitely moved like nobility, and the roll of her shoulders made the citrine microcrystals on her wrap positively dance. The lines of her bone corset really made the most of her trim, tight belly.

– *I love the new outfit, but bone? I'm not made of money, Chipmunk…*

– *Never fear, my love*, she beamed. *It's only laminate. From Khoikhoi.*

– *Mmmmmm! You sure know how to wear it, Babe.*

It was another sellout, and *les voodouns* had done me proud with third-row on the aisle. The sound system was spinning old 20th century Dixieland jazz and, as I scanned the gallery, I could pick out a celebrity or two. Marella and Dezzie from PlanetTeen's *Watch Me Binge!* were parked in the

Commonsense Party section, squired by some Navy men in dress whites. The lights dimmed, and a very familiar face mounted the podium.

— And a fine good evening to all of you ladies and gents! You know me! From Holovision 3-D's Useless People, I'm Your Bro, Ken Dreams, and boy, are you in for a rollicking good time tonight! So zoom in those peepers and tune your audiochips and buckle up! First up, it's Equal Rights for Dogs with Sen. Bailey Biddle and his Canine Caravan! Raheema Dutt and Kandy Kane Carbo are going to musically debate the Sex Traffick Tariff, and we've got everyone's numero uno political Pagliacci, Fuzznutz the Clown, in another fine mess. And music from the Andrew Keister Septet, with DJ CastorOyl! Seminal! Then, to cap it all off...oh, you lucky people... it's a tribute to Uncle Remus from America's Grandpa, Arch-Senator Rollo Greenjeans and Our First Daughter, the luminous, jim-dandy Wholesome Hackett! So let's get jovial, Americans!

Next was my favorite part: the March of Senators, led by the Rex Radnor Dancers in their translucent dermex catsuits. It was quite a scene.

— There's Abdullah Crumb! I love his hair!

— See that desk where Calyx Arthur is sitting? That used to belong to John C. Calhoun!

The downside of a hyperethnic wife was that I always had to poke her in the ribs to remind her to stand during the Anthem. But by the time the recording got around to the bit about *The cauldron of achievement/God!'s® trophy on the globe*, I was tingling with excitement, ready to see our mighty system of laws at its glittery best.

The guy next to me, an older fellow with a Maori face tattoo, leaned over to stage-whisper: *Nobody can accuse these guys of slacking…I've been back three times and I haven't felt cheated yet!* Mr. Man sure said a mouthful. It was high spectacle all night from a real cast of professionals. Geech Durwood, the stalwart centrist from Missouri declaimed, in a wonderful, pure tenor, on the benefits of renewing the Tax-Free Territories, while twirling his statuesque chief of staff Isolde in a sensual minuet. Rikki, who never showed the slightest interest in tax policy, gave my arm a gentle, loving squeeze. And then, before you knew it, it was time for the main event.

Rollo Greenjeans (O-Alabammy), at 116, was the longest-serving member of the Senate. He was a simple processor at the CorMaCo megafarm at Clementine Falls in the '20s, when the Originalist drive to change Alabama's name pushed him to center stage. His tall tales, earthy laugh and virtuoso banjo-picking made him a natural public figure. Since attaining the rank of Arch-Senator in 2058, he didn't come to the chamber much anymore, but his flamboyant witticisms kept his recorded performances on the multivision and cemented his status as the country's biggest politainer. I had to admit he still looked pretty spry as a couple of tuxedoed members of his backing chorus wheeled him in. For tonight's revue, he had shed his trademark eelskin suit for demin overalls, workboots and a wide straw hat. The chorus fanned out, and with some vintage softshoe steps, cued the band, who struck up the sort of rural ditty that might have watered Stephen Foster's eye.

Back inna days 'fore the patents was filed
The Man done saved the day!
Da wheat fo' da bread was growed buck wild
The Man done saved the Day!
Da wheat done died in da frost an' flood
The Man done saved the Day!
While da farmers woiked in da knee-deep mud
The Man done saved the Day!

Dem sto'-bought genes
Dem sto'-bought genes
Da Man make sho' you get yo bread and greens!
Dem sto'-bought genes
Dem sto'-bought genes
Make da high-priced taters and the bestest beans

I couldn't keep the toe of my snakehead boots from tapping. A great gold banner, emblazoned with the names of all the top agra concerns, unfurled and a spotlight picked out a pigtailed calico figure across the room. I knew every inch of that figure, and seeing it again sent an icy down my CNS.

Helena Hackett was a research librarian at the Museum of Weather when we first met. I was researching a story on coastal erosion, and we flirted over digiclips of churning seas and embattled wildlife. I was single then, and I hadn't forgotten all the moves yet. Smiles and jokes turned to kisses under the sheltering arm of the Angel of Free

Enterprise in Financier's Park. Even then I could tell she was destined for greater things. She sparkled. I can't explain how, but the light shim-shimmied off her, her eyes, her lips, her hair. And when the time came to unwrap the Holy of Holies at the pinnacle of lust – hell, even that seemed to throw off its own light. Every cell a star. I was smiling contentedly, but the inside of my head was fizzing like a water cooler full of Sweetabs. She spun out of the corner and twirled into Old Man Greenjeans' lap, leaning back to thrust out a milk-white leg that could have been carved by Canova. And when she sang, she brushed away all the info cobwebs:

From the field at harvest time
The songs are bright and gay
No worm or weevil, rust or rot
Can still the rondelet
Nature's bounty, green and good
Our tables will attend
Through corporate science, wise and kind
Our treasure to defend!

This was the one that got away – too ambitious, too willing to shill for politainers for a grim truthartist like I used to be. It was Rikki who was the right woman at the right time, the smile at the end of the gauntlet, after all the rage and spite had been squeezed out of me. But the hole Helena left had a very singular shape, and no lady, however sublime, could snugly fill it. There were always gaps where the nerves were a little raw.

The older lady at the end of the row, by the looks of it old enough to remember the Great Hails, dabbed a pair of glistening eyes. It would not be long before Wholesome and Greenie were playing this number before the Twelve Earnest Persons for enactment. The Twelve had been stacked against BetterFood for the last couple of years, but recent hit holovision films, and the big robot-infidelity scandal coverage had elevated hardliner persons-plus Gripp Pretty and Griselle L'Ange onto the tribunal, so patent extensions on designer seeds and soils were likely to sail through. The Originalists were rising again.

So much politics, personal and otherwise. Made it like work. I concentrated on dissolving a headache and tried to focus on fun and frolic.

– *Look at those Little People tumble!* I said. *Just like the Kiev Circus.*

– *Oh, Honey,* Rikki sighed. *Tonight has been the best. And it's not over yet...*

******

4 FEBRUARY 8:14 A.M.

The multivision timer was set to Introverted Life and it threw into the center of the room a gorgeous hardbody in one of the new Valkyrie designer swimsuits. It was a bit of an inside gag, setting the Rise-N-Shine to *What Is Your Problem?* We got a charge out of waking up with one of the regular trio of celebrity holochix cooing their little encouragements.

— Oh, hell yes! I cheered. *If it's Thursday, this must be Syzzle O'Banion!* The night had been rewarding as hell, and we were both feeling lazy and silly and indomitable, like rich kids on a dizmax bender. Each of the hostesses had her own vibration, but Syz was my favorite. She had a real 1980s vamp; everything was more, more, more. The thighs and ass of a cyclist or swimmer, peerlessly squeezable breasts, a French-curled thunderhead of platinum hair. She hovered over us, smiling a mischievous smile that could convince a Freespirit to club the last koala.

— You have so much to give. It hurts me to hear you talk that way. I really mean it. Let me show you, Muffin… Her hand reached out beckoningly and I could not resist throwing off the covers and letting her intangible i-fingers flutter near my full-grown manstick. I liked the way the light played over my texture implants: yakuza pearl. Best thing Rikki ever talked me into.

— Geez, Rikki snorted. *You are such a clod. You are beyond beyond.*

— Sorry, Babers, but you know me. Syzzle is sex.

I had a lead on a good story for later. Gibraltar E-feeds was hyping the live date of *Who Knew They Were Men?* and I had a sit-down with the author, a big local forensic kinesiologist who was sure to say some printable things about Marilyn Monroe and Patsy Cline. Chang had promised me masthead placement and if the Machete Mobs down in the Provisional States kept relatively quiet, my blast might just hang around awhile. I could never explain the public's lingering obsession with Carrie

Underwood, but I was determined to make it work for me. For us. T-Bird, my little Muskrat and me. Our mob.

— Know what? I think I'm gonna make some breakfast. What do you fancy?

— Besides this? I asked, putting a gentle bite on a tender little medallion of salty hip flesh. My mouth was watering. Rikki hardly ever cooked anymore, what with all her charity work and the school Vigilance Committee, but before we got married, she had been quite a little chef. She still had a Get Out of Jail Free card from her days cooking at the Directorate of Parking. It came in handy; you never knew when you were going to find yourself in the middle of a sympathy suicide or a roadway collapse.

— Damson and plantain extract gridcakes? Mmmmm, I'm making myself hungry! She seemed as happy as an oiled-up gameshow contestant in the MoneyPit as she stirred batter and skimmed the morning scuttlebutt on the digital slate. *Oh look. Ouida Peeple has a new contest to rebrand the Alpine police action against the Gruppe Weltlich. I'm thinking the 'Swiss Watch.' Get it? Because we're 'watching' them...*

— I must be the luckiest man on earth, or thereabouts, I chimed.

The double-tone in my audiochip meant a call was coming in to our vidscreen as well. I threw on my robe and walked into the living area to switch it on. The sender was Mrs. Kinsella, the vice-principal at Temp's fasttrack prep. I was a little surprised to be hearing from them; at this moment, Temp should have been touring the Deadwood Crater with his Astro-Security class. She didn't even wait for my salutation.

— *Mr. Symmyns, good day. I suppose you're wondering why I called.*

— *Temp OK? Not an accident I hope…*

— *No, no, nothing like that.* She was fumbling for words. *Can you and your wife swing by my office this AM?*

— *What's this all about? Did Temp do something?*

Silence.

— *I think we should talk in my office. There are… complexities…*

******

4 FEBRUARY 11:06 A.M.

The GoodLife Superior School was the capital's most exclusive, an incubator for judges, administrators, state security, the real movers. There were six or seven applicants for every slot. When Templar was born, I was working at the last of the purist newsmagazines, *Symbion*. I covered the energy beat. That's when I started keeping my private file. Hard news was dying, and it was getting tougher and tougher to sell the editors on the indigestible: bribes, little genocides, free energy scams. I let the players know that I didn't miss anything, but I was in the game. I would keep the lid on for the odd favor. When a name we all knew was paying off some of the President's people and a couple of the Earnest to keep a big geothermal field in cowboy

116

country from becoming a national park, I got wind. It was worth a first-grade slot at GoodLife. Ten years earlier, it might have bought me one of the man-made islets off Old California, but everyone knew that scandal was a buyer's market, so I grabbed what I could still get: a meaningful life for my boy, a chance to rub elbows with the infoscenti at soccer games and car washes. I hated going to that place, a hideous egg-shaped Ahtisaari monstrosity at the end of a West End cul-de-sac. I always felt a little dirty, and I wanted us to be clean.

— So, didn't she say anything? Rikki was worried, and it really spoiled her look. It gave her those concentric forehead-lines that made her look like she was wilting.

— Best not to fret, Sillygirl. Let's not go lunging at phantoms.

Esther Kinsella always made me laugh. In her floor-length kurotoroko kimono and her hair in a tightly-lacquered bun, she looked like the 1980s vision of The Future, contrived and overweening. Her speech was amateur intrigue, breathy and unnecessary. This little drama could have been about drug dealing, but then again, it could have been a dress code violation or a hacked electronic permission. You just never knew.

— Ah, Mr. and Mrs. Symmyns. Please, sit down. I found her formality unsettling. *Can I get you something? Water? Sani-bowl? Comfort mask?*

— No, no, thank you, Rikki sputtered. *I'm anxious to know what's going on. I'm a nervous wreck.* We had not even begun and she was already massaging that aerodynamic neck with a kava towel.

Esther eyelocked us for a gratuitous instant and reached into her desk drawer for a black plasticene bag, which she threw on her desk with careless bombast, like trash.

--*As a member of the Vigilance Committee, Ms. Symmyns, you helped adopt the Inspection and Seizure Guidelines. And you know that we often use class trips to conduct our looksees.*

Again, needless pathos.

– *Okay, I interjected, so you found something in his things. How bad could it be? Is he dealing drugs? Passing around Blood Moths?* They were endangered, but kids got a little high from chewing the wings and used the dyes to give themselves homemade tattoos.

– *Not exactly.*

I'm thinking to myself *Can we please get on with this?* They find a couple of Ultrexas or a vibraglove in the kid's locker and it's snakepit time. I mean, kids will be kids, right? And nowadays they were literally dying of stimulation. They were putting themselves in the hospital just to get a little conscious sedation. GOD!® knows I had spent many a class-hour backbenching, hunched over my TabulaRasa, fascinated by those free-circulating blasts of Calysto Gadd – *Can't Stop The Mucus* and *The Orifice*. Seems like babyshit today, but it was worth a nod back then. Hell, and I turned out alright. Better than alright. We were up-and-comers.

– *It's not the magic again?* Rikki asked. *For that I blame your Mr. Argenbright. Don't you watch what goes on in your classrooms?*

Esther visibly tightened, mumbling some spit about getting defensive.

— *Maybe I should just show you.* She tipped over the bag and a bunch of square, multicolored paper bundles tumbled out.

— *Books*, I blurted, without meaning to. Of course, I knew what they were, making my living with words. But I hadn't seen such a collection in quite a while, not since my post-grad days. To be honest, I was more fascinated than angry. They were paperbacks, old, well-read, but in surprisingly good condition. It explained where all that holiday cash had been going. As I leafed through the trove, I recognized a few of the titles, but others seemed strange. *Last Exit to Brooklyn. Sexus. This Boy's Life. The Ice Shirt. The Lathe of Heaven.* Still stuck at the bottom of the bag was a fat copy of *Ulysses*, something my old professors had talked endlessly about, but that I had never read. Or seen, for that matter.

— *We see your point*, I said.

Mrs. Kinsella seemed dubious, preoccupied, watching a pair of Japanese gardeners trim a topiary hedge in the shape of a Viking.

— *Do you?* she asked. *I'm not at all sure. I've asked Dr. Sutorious to join us. He's the company's consulting psychologist.* At the threshold stood a stout, aggressively unfashionable man in a houndstooth jacket and baggy pleather trousers. He was already breathing heavily by the time he reached the taupe divan and settled himself.

— Of course, he said, *no laws have been broken, so let's not get too excited. But this is sort of...tightrope behavior.*

— Curiosity about the forbidden, Rikki offered. *The old story.*

— Forbidden? Not forbidden, but discouraged. You see, all the studies have generally found that certain fictions tend to have negative effects on young people and their situational fluency. That is, they tend to depress, frustrate or confuse. And to inhibit the kind of N.O.W.-based conditioning that grows achievement.

— Healthy. Eager. Real. Earnest, Esther recited. *Narrow Our World.*

We had gotten an earful of this pseudo-science when we had enrolled Temp in First Year. *Keeps the kids focused on the is. Mastery, not mystery.* It was all designed to keep the youngsters competitive with an entire planet scrapping for jobs, resources, wealth, allegiance. We were too enlightened to censor, but we turned all our guile toward persuading the young away from inventing stories, especially ones that looked at tough questions, at people forced into terrible choices.

— We'll certainly talk to him about his spending habits, I said, *but we're still just talking about a couple of books, right? Not to minimize things...*

We all looked at each other, and Esther's assistant cracked the door and beckoned us into an anteroom.

******

The room was windowless but comfortable. At its center was a 3D holodeck for, I imagined, performance reviews, press availabilities, quarterly trustee conferences. Esther looked twitchy and out of sorts, like a P.I. with hoverdrone footage of a cheating spouse.

— *Let me set up what you're about to see*, she said. *For insurance purposes, we have been forced to record all extra-curricular activities...including your son's Citizen Service Project.*

I had encouraged Temp to get involved with the school's CAC chapter: canned food drives to feed the incarcerated, transporting legally-competent seniors to the polls, shit like that. It was great resumé fodder and a chance to meet the next gen of some big-name families. And it wouldn't kill the kid to develop some feeling for the disadvantaged. I watched as the room filled with images of students filing in, joking, gossiping, being regular bubbly boys and girls.

— *Is that Lambda Carteret?* Rikki whispered. *Hasn't she grown...Holy crow...*

— *Great resolution on those images.* She was a foxy little bambi all right. That bullet bra was practically putting my eye out. And her mom was chairman of the Digital Journalists' Forum. I told T he should cozy up to her, but he was a little thick in the romance department. He got that from the Egyptians. Too wrapped up in playing Infernal King with all his little Australasian friends, I figured. As I watched, uncomprehendingly, Templar slipped on a black robe and five girls folded white refectory napkins into some sort of odd nurses' caps.

— *All right*, Rikki fumed, *what is this then? What the HELL™?*

— *We don't have the audio, but our History Department believes it's Arthur Miller's The Crucible. From the American 1950s. A reenactment of the Salem Witch trials. Not a big moneymaker.*

Lambda fell silently to the floor writhing and shivering and reaching for the sky, alongside four other girls, including the local prelate's daughter, a dark, leggy little beauty with red, belt-length extensions who rolled and sobbed with an almost old-style sexual gusto. I grabbed an Annual Report from a side table and put it in my lap, so Rikki wouldn't see that I was getting a little firm down in the engine room.

— *So*, I asked, *some little sex game? Kids will be kids, am I right?* I could see on their faces I was getting no validation from anyone. *Better that than drugs, anyway.*

— *I wish it was that simple. I think we're seeing an outbreak of...drama. We're seeing it in other clubs, as well. The International Skeptics were caught in auditions for Some Like It Hot. Fitness Boosters were distributing contraband folios of My White Devil and earwitnesses heard our Engineering Studies Council humming what we believe to be the libretto of Flower Drum Song.*

— *We're sorry*, the doctor went on, *but our intel places your son at the center of this. We believe he's the instigator. Student Zero, if you will.*

So that was it then. I reached out and clutched Rikki's wonderful hand, letting my finger caress that terrific art deco tanzanite ring I had bought her on our last anniversary. I had been part of the GoodLife family long enough to know dismissal language when I heard it. These guys were true believers. They didn't buy into halfway measures. I expected T to get the boot and the Dragon Lady did not disappoint.

— *Now, now, this isn't a death sentence,* she droned. *There are many options for a bright, talented boy like Templar. And we have wonderful relationships with the three d-cons in your district. All wonderful schools!*

The words we dreaded. The *desconsuelos* movement had begun in the Provisional States, as a way of redirecting the children of families with deteriorating prospects into a reviving service economy. Soon these institutions of lower learning began to spring up in all sectors of the nation. It was true the District's d-cons were better than most – one even had Algebra, those years when students wanted it – but there was still no way around it: it was a come-down, and a very public one.

— *We feel it would be best to make the switch before Templar gets back. It would save him the embarrassment of packing up in front of his friends.*

— *We find it's very important to let young men save face,* the doctor said. He couldn't even look me in the eye. *To deconfront.*

Rikki seemed to have checked out completely. So what could I do? Fight over a day or two? Make the boy stick around where he wasn't wanted? Force him into scenes that would be the talk of all the dads at the Plugg Inn and the Harriers Lodge? I signed the Transfer and Release and the Personal Goods Receipt and got Rikki the HELL™ out of there. She looked like she had just walked away from a three-way wreck and, in a way, I guess she had.

— *He gets it from you*, I grimaced as I slid into the driver's seat. *Teta Bakhoum and her snake dancing or whatever*. I didn't even care I would be stroking my own pearls for a while. They had all let me down.

******

5 FEBRUARY 8:12 PM

Templar had positively bounded up the ingress ramp, breezed through the entryway and spiderholed himself in his livingspace without so much as a *Hola!* to Rikki or me. Not all that unusual, but behavior that took on a sinister undertone now that I knew about his clandestine fixations. I had always given the Little Shooter a lot of slack in the old leash, but now my cerebellum was overflowing with the most evil imaginings: a school copy of Bremer's *Entrepreneurial Responses To Natural Disasters* hollowed out to hold a semi-legal photocopy of *The Basketball Diaries*, my heir and scion matching soliloquies from *Death of a Salesman* with that shady al-Quarami kid on the 3D webcam his Aunt Starla gave him for his First Prostration.

— *Post-pubes*, I sighed, mostly to give my brain some sounds to process, to stop the cavalcade of imagined indignities. Rikki just squinted into her vanity, squeezing cellulose microjections into her incipient crow's feet. I padded over to Temp's door, gently rolling my knuckles across and inching it open just a nose wide.

— *Hey there, Ranger, how was our crater looking?* His eyes were locked on the holodeck, where several European heads of state in multicolored sumo *mawashis* ran a dash towing what appeared to be plumbing fixtures, while the crowd, mostly mustachioed men, fired roman candles and whirled New Year's noisemakers. *Macedonia was almost out of it last night. Coming back?*

No acknowledgement at all. It was so hard to take when juvenile petulance began to turn into growed-up passive aggression.

— *Your hole is still hole-y.*

— *Still holy*, I muttered, forcing a smile.

— *Wholly idiotic.*

It had not been so long since my Occupation Forces tour in eastern Canada that I had forgotten the persuasive power of the thumb to the eye socket, or the unerring efficacy with which the heel of the hand could be applied to a youthful Adam's apple. But in my peripheral vision, I could see Rikki hanging back nervously, ready to dive in and calm hostilities. I had ignored the threat of her intervention once before, and my collarbone could still predict a rain squall better than high-end radar.

— *Okay, there, Big Bear, your mater and I have something we'd like to chat about.*

Again, stone silence.

— We were thinking it might be a tonic for us to yank you away from the books and take a little vacation. Whaddaya say?

With nary a change in expression, he picked up his handheld and jacked up the volume to drown us out. My digits were a-tingle and I could hear the blood *whoosh-whooshing* inside my head. I went over to the console and hit "disengage," plunging the room into a sepulchral silence.

— They found out about your novels and your little thespian exploits. Yeah, that's right. You're expunged, kiddo.

For a sec, he just looked sadly relieved, then, mussing the tuft of his Mohican, he clicked the holo back on. Only this time, it was in full omnicast mode, the room full of spectral Vegas nightclub tables filled with 1950s swells, and the chatter of mobsters and the idle rich, the popping of champagne corks. With a cold precision, he bounced to his feet and froze us in a glare of defiance.

— Whether I'm right or whether I'm wrong/Whether I find a place in this world or never belong/I've gotta be me... I had to confess being somewhat impressed by his tremolo, his stage presence. For an instant, I was transported, but Rikki's elbow to the ribs catapulted me back to my senses. I pounded the "off" switch again, in the process, sending an old Sgt. Freewill action figure on a headfirst swandive into the imitation Navajo throw rug.

— That'll be enough of that, Mr. Bojangles. We had a little chat with your prefect. All about those little afterschool productions of yours.

– Do you have any idea what this means? Rikki shrieked. *And me treasurer of the Monitors. You were on fastrack!*

Unmoved, his face a mask of unbowed rectitude, Templar clicked us into the courtyard of a Tudor palace, the air filled with the smells of horse and honeysuckle, Thames River mud, roast meat and human sweat.

– I do none harm/I say none harm/I think none harm, he said, hands folded serenely and piously before him, his face wreathed in a forced modesty.

– Oh no, you don't! I interrupted. *Don't you go getting all ecclesiastical on us, not after all the pheasant and foie gras we had to skip to get you into a good school, on a decent social path. You did this to yourself.* I poked the console, this time twitching with rage, dissolving the English castle back into the mists of time. I had hoped to hear some contrition from the lips of my only child, but he just pouted for a moment, then clicked his way into a dirty 1970s municipal courtroom, stalking the floor like an anxious, caged simian.

– I'm out of order? You're out of order! You're out of order! This whole trial is out of order!

By now, Rikki had heard enough, her eyes filling with a slow-boiling menace. *Trial? That's a laugh. Where do you think you are? You've already been bounced. You're done. For you, it's the d-con, or the Better Youth Brigade.*

I was a little shocked at the way my little wren had brought the hammer down. Temp seemed to gather himself – to circle the wagons, emotionally speaking – then grabbed his Kevlar flak jacket and shoved his way past us, toward the door.

– *You can't silence me by shutting me up in a d-con! Imagine! Don't make me laugh! I'll be running auditions for Short Eyes within the week. Órale!* He slammed the door with authority.

– *What the hell is that supposed to mean?* Rikki asked.

– *Odelay…*I chewed this over for a second. *Can't be sure, but I think he might be threatening to turn old-style Republican.*

******

12 FEBRUARY 1:48 P.M.

So now it's all about damage control. Henny Muller and Hoover Shelby and the rest went straight into the neighbors' insta-rator. Once Templar got over the initial sulk and settled into his Information Retrieval studies, we started him with a good psych and got him on subcutaneous Rectamine® twice a day. The spitting and nighthowling were a bother, but, I mean, like Dr. Chaudry reminds us, children are the We of the new Nows. The other Tenth-Years at GoodLife figured out what was up when Temp never came back and their club meetings started being regularly moderated by ed-marshalls. The staff went into mute mode, squelching any chatter about the afterschool Broadway bacchanals. (Could you imagine? Senators' and army generals' kids dancing something called *West Side Story*?) Without her school activities, Rikki lost touch with the other poshmoms and started spending whole days pacing in front of the holo, developing an unsettling attachment to *Oddities!* and the pirate skincasts. All the Orotaine was putting weight on her, making her arms go jiggly. Down at the newsite, the whispers were flying. I could tell. Chang blanked my expense account and kicked me upstairs to the vegetable bin, letting me compile the monthly *Same Old Song & Dance* politainment supplement. My signature key said *Editor*, but everyone knew it was really a scheme to decelerate me, to keep me out of the real headline Points. The last guy who held my job keeled over reading news releases at 103 and drew his pay for a year after that. And Chato Nuñez, whose son Manco taught Bio-Containment at Loveless d-con, was riding high with a scandalcast in development on StraightToHell®, eight straight weeks at the top of the newsroom duration derby, and Sycorax Lutz, a wild new fitness-host wife with abs you could grate onions on. Assuming, of course, you could find natural onions in the Developed Zones.

In fact, my audiochip is telling me that's Nuñez now. I wonder what he needs from me?

RODGER PIDGEON IS DEAD
(May 14, 2017 – October 22, 2063)

Contemporary music's "last word" silenced after sudden illness

By Dore Feldsher*

Providence, R.I., November 6, 2063: Cold drizzle from the autumn sky hung all around the restive swarm of mourners outside the Mortech Necroplex Parkside East. It collected in the folds of plasticene mourning cloaks, glued medieval tunics to the bodies of tattooed tribalists huddled in office doorways, slicked down the long, straight hair of pretty pre-Raphaelite princesses and gently smeared the letters on homemade signs and banners painted with sadly suggestive slogans and song titles.

ASK THE LIGHTNING

PITY POOR YORICK

RETURN TO US THE SUN

Everywhere hung the sweet smell of the violets piled in the pre-designated Public Memorial Zones.

Since the dataclouds had two days earlier reported the news that Rodger Pidgeon — troubadour, songwriter, political irritant, style icon, and cultural reference point for a restless and dissatisfied generation — had succumbed to a drug-resistant viral infection on tour in Southeast Asia, a general air of repressed anguish had descended on this New England enclave of low-rise business blocks and ethnic restaurants. This epicenter of post-mortem angst sits just minutes from the leafy residential street where Pidgeon was born nearly half a century earlier, the introverted only child of a theatre group *dramaturge* and an energy firm research librarian. If you sat quietly, you could still almost hear the nursery bells of the ice cream trucks, the laughter from games of soccer and tag.

"History conveys a special imprimatur onto firsts, but Rodger Pidgeon's was a career rife with *lasts*," lamented post-rock musical archivist and writer Lyman Casey. And, indeed, Pidgeon, at times, seemed destined to close the book on one after another vestige of popular music tradition. His was the last million-selling "album," the last musical release pressed on CD chrome, the last successful stand against claims of artistic plagiarism. Pidgeon and his band The New Cathars played at the last major European outdoor festival, the riot-scarred and financially-disastrous Bergen Rockarneval of 2058. It seemed that everywhere Pidgeon went, he was barely a step ahead of the imploding pop *zeitgeist,* and this endowed his music with both a melancholic poignancy and the simmering danger of vital energies seeking new outlets, new channels.

"He was the first superstar," Casey summarizes, "without a signature medium. He was like a man without a country."

Early in life, Rodger Earl Masters Pidgeon was a frail, quiet child. He enjoyed a tight connection to his mother Sofia, a Smith College graduate who filled their spacious John St. home with the sounds of music, both from her baby grand piano (to which Rodger took eagerly in his early teens) and a large collection of recorded world musics. Her curatorial nature was a trait she inherited from her father, Wendell Glidden, a well-travelled Third World economic development consultant. It was these early influences Sofia assembled that may have been responsible for both the exotic instrumentation and the activist worldview that informed much of Pidgeon's mature musical work.

This background, coupled with an aversion to conventional academic studies, made Pidgeon a natural candidate for enrollment at the recently-opened Charlesville Progressive Vocational High School in the fall of 2032, where he joined the Electronic Music program as a trainee technician. There, according to headmaster Janice Romweber, he demonstrated "superior enthusiasm and aptitude," learning to repair and restore traditional keyboard and electronic instruments, including one of the east coast's oldest, museum-grade theremins. "There was scarcely an hour of the school day," she recalled in a 2050 *Calliope* magazine interview, "when music wasn't pouring from his cubicle in the reconditioning shop. It was clear he was more artist than tradesman."

During the winter of 2036, Pidgeon, along with school friends Dennis Kitsos and Aubrey

Morgenthaler, decided to capitalize on the fashion for ambient electronica by forming Dark Matter, a trio whose lifespan was largely spent rehearsing on Charlesville's stock of secondhand keyboards. Little remains of the band's output, besides a brief tape of a 14-minute, one-song school talent show performance. In a holocast interview for local news broadcast in 2041, Morgenthaler recalled Pidgeon's burgeoning desire for a paying gig, and shortly following Dark Matter's one and only live set, Pidgeon used the school's weatherbeaten 1984 burnt-orange Farfisa organ to audition for a slot with another contest entrant, the successful Tex-Mex-flavored dance band Los Maquiladoras. The impressionable Pidgeon fell briefly under the influence of leader Ramses Ramirez, a confident, charismatic young man who introduced him to (in no particular order of importance) women, stagecraft, geopolitics, and the melancholy ballads of Doug Sahm and Freddy Fender, whose songs would provide the slow-dance interludes in the group's otherwise boisterous live shows.

The band maintained an active – perhaps too active – gig schedule, and after a houseparty in the spring of 2037, Pidgeon was seriously injured – suffering three cracked ribs, a fractured humerus, and a femur broken in three places – when a car driven by bassist Orel Menses swerved off a New Haven road and struck a telephone pole. He was forced to convalesce at home for seven months, and it was this period, during which he was confined with his family's estimable library of music, books and videos, that was to have the most profound effect on the development of his writing style. In that way, his career echoed that of an idol from the previous century, Bob Dylan.

"I thought my life had ceased," Pidgeon writes in an unpublished memoir held in the collection of Brown University's John Hay Library. "I mentally played and replayed my funeral. But once I tired of this charade, I began the work of reconstructing my mind and, more importantly, my soul."

Day after day, Rodger retreated into the family library, travelling the wine-dark seas with Odysseus, touring the netherworlds with Dante, conquering the known world with Alexander the Great, surveying the carnage of Antietam and Omaha Beach, traversing Holden Caulfield's inner minefields, parading through Nighttown with Leopold Bloom, and reliving the tortures of Scott's Antarctic trek. He marched with Van Slyke against the Aarab Ozgorluk Ordusu and treasure-dove to the undersea caverns of Infierno Azul with Pintor and his Atlantis Raiders. The entire canvas of world history and literature was unfurled to him. He became, as he put it, an "accompanist to the grand human march toward salvation and oblivion." Working on his mother's antique Quaglia mandocello or the old Wurlitzer electric piano she set up at his bedside, he began to explore in earnest the mechanics of writing songs he crooned into her ancient TEAC reel-to-reel.

"I call it my cocoon phase," he told *Record Herald* editor Henrik Obermaier in April 2057. "And when the cast came off, I was transformed. An artist."

Of the 75 songs he wrote during his convalescence, his parents had one, "Cavalcade of Wonders," a nostalgic tour through P.T. Barnum's American Museum, pressed onto the A-side of a vinyl record to celebrate his recovery. It caught the ear of a local amusement park owner who was organizing a tour of animal acts, weightlifters and sword swallowers to promote his attraction, and soon became the tour's theme song. When the local amusement company was sold to the Zurich-based Diversifizierte Attraktionen GmbH the next winter, Pidgeon's song went along, becoming the signature for DA's international advertising campaign. Soon, Rodger was being recognized for his broadcast commercials and listeners were clamoring for new songs and personal appearances. On the strength of his homemade demo, the 21-year old Moog repairman was launched as a rising recording star.

So great, in fact, was the clamor for new material that DA launched its own record label, Miasma Records, to release and promote Pidgeon's first LP/CD *Pity Poor Yorick*, a sampling of his better home recordings that included the title track, the romantic "Eleanor Lamb" and "Age of Mirrors," a glittering dulcimer-tinged reflection on the fleeting nature of beauty. *PPY* caught the fancy of audiophile vinyl collectors and, with 1.3 million units sold, the 200-gram 2039 pressing of *Yorick* became the last-ever vinyl LP to go RIAA-certified platinum.

Like many talents of the time, Pidgeon rode a bumpy but energetic wave of technological innovation to his global celebrity. He worked against the backdrop of the Chamelia program, the groundbreaking software whose "creative algorithm" could imitate the style of any writer, past or present, and whose biannual upgrades perpetually threatened to undermine the work of thousands of authors, journalists, poets and composers. Additionally, the 2041 passage of elaborate federal tax incentives (including the highly-punitive Download Tariffs) designed to rescue the embattled music industry ushered in a decade of unparalleled invention during which artists also struggled to keep pace with evolving modes of recording and playback. Somehow, the range of Pidgeon's thematic and instrumental influences always enabled his music to successfully translate to ever more complex and esoteric media. First, there was the holodisc, patented by Holmstrom in 2042, its 3-D imagery seemingly tailor-made for Pidgeon's chiseled good looks; MBC's 2044 Vibranet sent the cavernous echoes of his mournful dirges directly through sonochips embedded in users' temporal bones; lastly, the 2050 Bosch DreamSense® system coded the surreal images of Pidgeon's romantic song cycles into electrical dream stimuli. In each case, one of Rodger Pidgeon's capstone works slammed a door on one medium and eased open a portal into another. Somehow, he endured and prospered.

2042 saw Pidgeon, then a yeoman with a solid, but unspectacular, cult following, release the holodisc that would be the first tentpole of his success, *Not By Sight*. On this disc, he was joined by the first of his regular backing ensembles, The Entrail

Prophets. In addition to providing him with a fuller, richer sound, the group included violist and dancer Hanelore Walz, his lover and muse for the remainder of her life, and songwriter/multi-instrumentalist Zal Darabont, who would remain an artistic combatant/collaborator through all of Rodger's most significant work. In *Not By Sight*, Pidgeon adopted the *persona* of a ragged, penniless seer, cursed with visions of mankind's historical failures, struggling to find hope in a fragile and uncertain future. Songs like the nightmarish "Trabzon (What Endless Road?)" and "Wheat Field With Crows" showcased his newfound depth of field, while the title track is sung in the voice of a visionary portending an actual, physical paradise:

> *The uses of fear*
>
> *The alchemy of need*
>
> *Bring us to safety with surpassing speed*
>
> *My walls dissolve*
>
> *I greet the night*
>
> *An all-embracing fortress for the brave contrite*
>
> *Looking down on troubles from a wond'rous height*
>
> *Achieved by faith and fervor*
>
> *Not by sight*

But it was not simply America's technological seascape that was wracked with turbulence during the early years of the 2040s. The Wall Street Kamikaze Suicide Clusters of 2041 and 2042, along with America's questionable role in the Sub-Saharan Grain Wars, had driven the nation to something of a spiritual *nadir*, and *Not By Sight* was adopted as the informal soundtrack to a generation's search for moral atonement. It was partly happenstance and partly *kismet*, then, that Pidgeon's 2043 tour crossed paths with Father Emer Crabtree's St. John, Missouri-based Tabernacle of All Things, Sanctified. Crabtree's doctrine of Pure Intention appealed to Pidgeon and millions like him who, liberated from issues of unintended consequence, took The Vow and became junior deacons. Crabtree gave Pidgeon and his collaborators license to speak out against injustice during a volatile era, and Pidgeon gave Crabtree credibility among the youth he attempted to evangelize. The relationship peaked during the recording of 2045's percussive *Soft Cat Feet* (the first internationally distributed vibradisc) when Crabtree performed the wedding of Pidgeon and Walz at the foot of Bolivar State, Venezuela's Angel Falls, what Crabtree described as "God's perfect shower." The ceremony was holocast live to 16 countries and, for the rest of that year, fans at outdoor Entrail Prophets shows were baptized by a fleet of Crabtree's gaily-painted crop-dusting biplanes.

Unsurprisingly, the freedoms endorsed by the Tabernacle occasionally gave way to license. It was particularly common for members to experiment with the plethora of new drugs being legally and semi-legally marketed by the freshly-deregulated pharmaceutical industry. Pidgeon proved partial to Praesix™, a psychoactive compound that fractured users' "personalities" and assembled one or more new configurations from shards of memory and experience. During one Praesix trip in early 2046, Pidgeon was "reconfigured" as Adelet, a Turkish rifleman from the 1915 Armenian genocide, an identity assembled, he later surmised, from high school history lessons, television documentaries, and Jordanian and Syrian military diaries in his family's collection. Pidgeon spent ten weeks in a Taunton, Massachusetts psychiatric facility, and his publisher Hanta Music was forced to sue for control of 35 songs recorded in Adelet's voice. (Bootlegs of dubious provenance have fetched $300-$450 on internet auction sites and several cover versions have been recorded, but no formal release of the tracks was ever authorized.)

Although the synergy of Rodger's music with what Crabtree called "the holy yes" made Pidgeon a figure of international notoriety and influence, the union proved as short-lived as Pidgeon and Walz's 18-month marriage. After allegations of misused donations, Pidgeon parted ways with the Tabernacle in the fall of 2047, enlisting manager Riis McKenna and veteran record producer Tugg Djirksen as his new inner circle. Djirksen was behind the boards for 2049-50's *Pathways To Perdition* sessions in Nashville and, once again, Pidgeon shifted thematic gears. The new record was a concept disc loosely linking modern

139

political concerns with themes from classical mythology, and yielded his biggest hit, "Ganymede," which grafted the tale of a low-level anti-capitalist street fighter onto the myth of the legendary cup-bearer of the Hellenic gods:

The boxers and the bouncers said you had no sand

Just an actuary's son with a faggot's hand

You moved all around the grid

Hit and run and hid

Not a pin to show for what you did

Push-button Billy the Kid

Your own phony legend might have calmed you down

On the trip from class crusader to clown

You didn't see it all was just preparing to drown

Hang on to pills and pretty girls and all your favorite bands

When it's time to throw down, nothing ever stands

Not born to lead, never freed

Fetch another round

Our pretty Ganymede

Sales were modest until 2051, when Calumny Records issued the DreamSense® edition of *PTP*. As fate would have it, Pidgeon's lyric landscape of ancient, windswept mountains, trash-covered urban streets dotted with the figures of lost salarymen, and starcrossed lovers wandering moon-strafed cul-de-sacs tickled the electric junctions of pop's collective unconscious. Goldenfleece.com reviewer Dee Comingore's REM-sleep review of the disc declared it "a font of haunting and indelible nocturnal imagery that validates the psychic power of the medium." Millions of listeners took Comingore's advice, establishing DreamSense® as music's dominant new format, dooming the vibradisc, and giving Pidgeon his greatest commercial success. So great was Pidgeon's career peak that even the infringement suit filed by a Tucson restaurant, claiming his track "Staircase Girl" ("A temple is no place for a staircase girl like you/So climb down from my pediment/My church of awkward sentiment...") stole its tune from a series of interactive billboards, failed to wound his growing prestige. Rodger was ultimately vindicated, but not before the three-year legal battle cost him over $600,000 in lawyers' fees. Two years after the verdict, federal legislation raised a plaintiff's threshold of proof and made such actions, effectively, things of the past.

The 2050s were a largely fallow decade for Pidgeon, who disbanded his short-lived early-music project The Sanctum Sanctorum to focus on litigation, his domestic reunion with ex-wife Walz (rechristened "Ardeia Walz" after watching a flock of herons being sucked into a jet engine) and his political opposition to the federally-sponsored "decommissionist" movement. The creation of these life-cessation camps attracted vociferous opposition from artists and intellectuals, and Pidgeon's bitterly ironic "The Lovely Void" (recorded with filmstar/activist CherryRipe TigerCub Kyndal) became the resistance's rallying cry. It was Pidgeon's ragged solo set during the massive 2057 pro-existence rally at Oregon's Kalapuya Raceway that stemmed the growth of the camps and limited them to processing invalids, military deserters and the mentally ill. But the political infighting left him bitter and distant, as evidenced by his last major interview, given to *Reliquary* magazine in the spring of 2058:

> Q: What is art?
>
> RP: Art is just publicly-exhibited revenge.
>
> Q: For what?
>
> RP: Virtually everything. Not paper airplanes. Or honey.

After the highly-publicized Bergen fiasco and the controversy over his refusal to assume the premiership of the newly-independent socialist Republic of San Severiano later that year, Pidgeon might have stayed permanently retired from public life. But a small, independent label in Presque Isle, Maine issued a collection of his unreleased tracks,

Supine in the Beauty Arcade, to benefit the family of Darabont, who succumbed to esophageal cancer in summer 2059, and this release revived interest in an artist the mainstream had begun to neglect. Although the songs were mostly somber and decidedly lo-fi, some stood, Pidgeon scholars today assert, among his very best. Take, for example, the velvety folk reverie "Last of the Unbroken Stallions," the hypnotic, harmonium-tinged "Constable Clouds" (later, a hit for synthelle spokesmodel Kerilee™) and the percolating guitar rave-up "Life in Retrograde":

I was a soldier until somebody led me

I was a poet until somebody read me

A lover till somebody wanted to bed me

I was a dead man till you kissed me deadly

Circumstances conspired to push Pidgeon back into the limelight. His lavish chain of Innerfresh plasma infusion bars entered bankruptcy in 2061 during a lull in his catalogue sales, undercutting his once-considerable net worth and impelling him to undertake a final tour of small-capacity halls in Asia, Australia and New Zealand commencing in August of the following year. But this was not the daring, energetic performer of years past. Walz's 2060 self-immolation suicide in response to the proposed Tripartite Partition of the Continental Economic Zones had taken a permanent toll on Pidgeon's psyche, and the pressures of life on the road soon made his scars manifest. Although The New Cathars' Dixieland arrangements of his greatest hits were received with polite appreciation by tour audiences, Pidgeon became increasingly distracted and morose onstage, forgetting lyrics, haranguing audiences for seemingly minor lapses in etiquette, and frequently lacing sets with long, single-chord solos. A visibly-drained Pidgeon was taken ill after a show in Vientiane, Laos and pronounced dead several days later on October 22 at a western-style hospice in Phnom Penh, Cambodia. His body was returned, with little fanfare, to Providence for mandatory quarantine, autopsy and cremation in early November.

Perhaps the last critical analysis of Pidgeon's career should be Obermaier's, from the *Record Herald* fansite:

> Ultimately, the tragedy of Rodger Pidgeon was his overwhelming ambition: to unite a past he had missed, a tech-obsessed present that undervalued transcendence and beauty, and a future too uncertain to support a durable artistic vision. He would have been more appreciated in another time. Any other time.

But the real last words, fittingly, are Pidgeon's. Chiseled in marble at the Mortech crematorium's memorial wall are words from his anthemic "Corridors of Used-Up Men," words he famously described as "not boast, but warning":

NEVER LOVED
NEVER ASKED FOR LOVE

His legacy will certainly be how wildly he underestimated both his own passion and his public's lingering affections.

Farewell, Poor Yorick...

Rodger Pidgeon Selected Discography:

"Cavalcade of Wonders" b/w "Lightning Head" (Godot Records, 2037) (limited edition of 100)

Pity Poor Yorick (Miasma Records, 2039)

Not By Sight (Miasma Records, 2042)

Soft Cat Feet (Hanta Music, 2045)

"Peaceable Kingdom"/ "Fingers Holding Sand"/ "I Heard The Voice" / "(All I Got Was This) Lousy Tee Shirt" (vibradisc offered to audiences at Emer Crabtree's "Born Innocent" Revival, summer 2045)

Syrian Jezebels (Underground Discs, 2047) (bootleg edition of songs recorded in Taunton State Hospital; two-vibradisc set released under numerous names and covers)

Unbelievers Fright/Wrong Turn at Golgotha (Hanta Music, 2048)

Pathways To Perdition (Calumny Records, 2050)

"A Drawing-Down of Blinds" / "Against Desire" (DreamSense® demonstration disc distributed to attendees at Napa Valley TechFair, Calistoga, California, February 2051)

"The Lovely Void" (free microsheet given away with August 2055 edition of *Protest!* magazine, edition of 3,000)

No Backward Step (with CherryRipe Kyndal) (Life and How To Live It, 2056)

Shitting Where I Eat: The Very Best of Rodger Pidgeon (Mainway Nightsounds, 2057)

Supine in the Beauty Arcade: Songs For Zal (Arcadia Music, 2060)

Various Artists, *Ever-Rising Road: The Songs of Rodger Pidgeon* (Hanta Music, 2061)

Consolamentum Live on the South Island (Maritime Music, 2062)

Never Asked For Love: The Political Mind of Rodger Pidgeon (Hanta Music, 2062)

What Do Ya Want For Nothin'? B-Sides, Rarities and Retreads (Recordhound, 2062)

"Deaths of Ice" (sound collage installed at Mortech Necroplex Parkside East, Providence, Rhode Island, November 2063)

THE GOOD WORLDS
ARE ALL TAKEN

Maj. Gen. Erwin F. Casson, Ret. thought, as he waited to lose consciousness: *Today is the first day of the end of my life*.

It was alarming how quickly American lives could change direction in the post-Barysau era. 2045 had seemed full of promise. The Green victories in the elections of 2040 had crumbled after the humbling defeat of Democratic Europe forces in Belarus to the combined Russia-Kazakh bloc. President Santa Cruz had snuck in for a second term, with a little help from hackers in Missouri and Ohio, but polls were showing major anti-Green backlash brewing and the quiet men behind munitions and fossil fuels had begun to plan for a full-out blitz in the '46 mid-terms, in advance of an Originalist presidential push by Uriel Gadisson, two-term senator from West Texas. Americans could always be relied upon to act out of fear, and everywhere along the east coast, people were watching the skies. The electorate was ready to turn and that meant good times for the right-wing generals. The country would fall into their laps again.

Then came Moldova.

Operation Foxfire was intended to extract a team of U.N. agriculture consultants, including an ex-Olympic women's gymnast and the daughter of Gram Illesley (who gave cancer kids their last wishes on virofeed commercials) being held by pro-Russia insurrectionists. Casson's man in the field was Col. Ed Laudrup, a public relations guy with little field experience that the White House had set up as Hero. Laudrup did what no good combat veteran would do – underestimate the enemy – and he walked his assault team straight into a nationally-televised ambush. The viral grenades and bombardment by placements of Russian-made rail guns took U.S. forces completely by surprise, and the Americans did the one thing worse than die – they ran. Live. On every net. The Originalist momentum evaporated overnight, every tavern and roadhouse in the states was sponsoring memorial services for Starlight Kidd and Dina Illesley, and the Green committee chairs in Congress were clamoring for heads they could nail to the city gates. Casson, who had been tabbed for Joint Chiefs, was "advised" to consider a silent back-door departure.

It still made him sick to think about the televised court martial of the so-called "Ghost Platoon." Of course, it was all theater: the way Creg Veder strutted in front of the tribunal in his gold dress uni; the humiliating, pinpoint interrogation of the wet-eyed kids and the seething lifers; the lurid descriptions of trenches abandoned with MREs freshly-opened and half-eaten, letters from home unread, when the barrages began. Veder was about to be promoted to major and handed some bullshit advisory job in the Santa Cruz administration, and everyone involved with Foxfire – all hard-liners, *go figure* – were set up as doddering, disloyal and deadly. Nobody had been executed for cowardice since Eddie Slovik, but damned if they didn't haul all 24 survivors in shackles out to Moab Proving Ground, douse their bare feet in oily conductant and march them across the execution grid specially constructed for the occasion. The whole thing was deeply classified, but, of course, some adjutant slipped pictures to a Congressman's aide, and in 12 hours, the images – tangled bodies smeared with excrement -- were everywhere. It was a thousand times worse than Abu Ghraib, a whole platoon of dead deserters and the Pentagon forced to be the guest of honor at a catered shit-banquet. By the end of the month, the President was cashing his blank check, cleaning house, pushing out everybody who could help the Originalists seize the Oval Office. Not a shot was fired. And, in an ultimate *fuck you*, Aden Van Meagher, that downy-skinned Ivy League poltroon, made Casson write the condolence letters. The worst kind. *We regret to inform you that your husband/son/partner died like an unclaimed mutt...* It was the sourest parting note a military man could have.

"Don't sweat it, Winn," Dick Graybill from Armed Services had joked, "nobody commits suicide jumping out of a basement window. The lightning strikes the mountaintop." But Casson was pissed, bitter at being served up like a suckling pig. There were ways of finessing debacles, creating evidence of more heroic stands or, where this was not feasible, disposing of bodies with more palatable cover stories. He had seen it done, and even pulled it off himself once or twice. The country could not have known how glad it was for the small defeats he had spared them. But this time, it was all too comfortable for the White House to air the "truth." Within three months he was out, shooting skeet in BigSky, and, as it so often tends to, his health soon crumbled under the weight of anger, regret and excessive leisure. The Starrett's was diagnosed two days after Christmas 2047 and, by spring of 2048, he was on full bedrest, eating through a nasogastric tube under the tyrannical oversight of a Bosnian HappyHome nurse named Gretel.

Enter PermaSom™. By the mid-2030s, there were too many damaged kids coming back from Syria, Libya, Gaza, Ukraine and other open wounds for America's smoke-and-mirrors economy to handle. There were no jobs, and the VA was so far overwhelmed they were farming PTSD cases out for meditation and biofeedback. In desperate straits, DoD called in DARPA to cook up an outside-the-box solution, and, ever the innovators, they developed the dormancy wreath and the algorithm to run it. The concept was "dormancy" or "de-commissioning," a sort of happy coma or permanent dreamstate, custom-fitted to give the subject a pleasant inner life while his husk was filed away in a sort of cryogenic warehouse. The costs involved were just a tiny fraction of what job training, medical care and counseling would be, and the savings let the services sweeten the deal with fairly gaudy benefits for the families: cash, annuities, tuition credits, housing allowances, accelerated pensions. In 2042, a syndicate of old Pentagon guys based in Schaumburg, IL –

PermaSom – bought the technology and signed a services contract to run the dormancy program for the government. Within a few years, the corporate mascot, Sopor the Sleepy Bear (voiced by the Wily Wizard from Saturday morning cartoons, Duncan Poundstone) was everywhere: virofeed ads, NFL halftime shows, and holiday parades, singing the omnipresent company jingle *peace and calm/with PermaSom*, and civilian families with infirm relatives had made the company #38 in the *Largesse* Fifty. Casson hated the thought of being filed away, but his care would cost a fortune. Ariel, who was battling Parkinson's, would have her own expenses soon, and Nathan, with his two kids and his paltry salary as an Adjunct Professor of Printmaking, was hardly in a position to accommodate sick parents. The bonus money would be a godsend. Reluctantly, he signed on. Sometimes, he thought how funny it was: Santa Cruz was a town bandits robbed in western movies, and here he was, on the poorhouse steps because he had refused to steal under Norm Santa Cruz: not from the oil-rich coffers of Qatar, not from the fleeing warlords in Libya and the Sudan. As much as he hated his lack of options, Casson hated far more that he would be helping to make Gordon Samm, a crummy flier and a dishonest 12 handicap, rich with his business. *Rotten short game*, he scratched in a note to Ariel with a withered left hand, *worse C-E-O...*

By late 2048, Casson had little with which to occupy himself besides returning the odd video message from a nostalgic former colleague, and, as the days grew short, he found himself spending more and more time with his "Preparing 4 Forever" packet, adding details to his Dormancy Plan, refining and revising until he seemed to have imagined every square foot of his mindspace, every minute of his retirement.

His psylocale was based on his childhood home of Fort Temperance, Kansas, but with many, many key improvements. He would not be a skinny, shy kid picked on by The West End Jackals. There were no Jackals, and he would be 6', 190 lbs., and a varsity sprinter on the Kennedy Cavaliers. His house would be an unpretentious, aluminum-sided 1950s ranch, his car a restored vintage GTO. Meghan Treehorn, his girlfriend, would be slimmer and blonde, from a home not shattered by divorce. The Armour plant would not put his and Meghan's fathers out of work, but would churn out a steady supply of meat byproducts for a hundred years or more, while he rested in PermaSom's Coronado, AZ storage facility, supercooled to a chilly -118°C. The Cavs gridiron 11 would roll to a thrilling state title year after year, always besting the hated Etheria Elks in new and suspenseful title games. Winters and summers would be mild, springs blazes of flowering color, autumns stained with gold and rust and faint melancholy. Dad would finally be elected Rotary president; mother would escape the nervous whispers of local churchwomen scandalized by an annulled marriage; Rosie's breasts would be a manageable size, stilling rumors of licentious behavior spread by the local spinsters. Brendon Foss and Elroy Sievers would never crash in Mr. Foss' Ford Fiesta on Prom Night after sneaking some of their illicit bourbon whiskey. Lori Chatsworth's brother Ray would not die during Navy basic training. Roscoe's Dairy Vault would never be razed to provide parking for Lumbertown. Everyone's favorite teacher Joe Pemberton would not be forced to retire by Hodgkin's Disease. Founders Day would not be suspended after Herm Legler's gay rights boycott. The flags at City Hall would never fly at half-mast, there would always be a free swing at the Mason Way Playground, and every third baseball from the pitching machine at Chaz's would be a grooved change-up, ready to sail off Winn's favorite Louisville Slugger. Lightning would never strike Miles Ranford's barn, engulfing in flames his pair of jet-black colts and a senior year's worth of party plans. Ft. Temperance would have no angry minorities; the only blacks would be Delton Davis and Jim Maxwell, and they would be ROTC, leading the Cavs' victory parade to Llaemle Auditorium. The Natives from the Kickapoo reservation would cheerfully sell their crafts at the Saturday Swaps Jensen's would hold in its rear lot. By Christmas, Casson's plan had swelled to 98 single-spaced pages crammed with dense, almost obsessive, detail.

The process was long, involved and painstaking. Once Ariel submitted Casson's plan and it had been reviewed for safety, sanity and soundness by the Processing Board, Casson was brought in for lucid-dream coaching sessions, after which his REM-state brainwave activity would be recorded in a half-dozen sleep studies, followed by exhaustive (and exhausting) exit interviews. Science had the ability, the salesman had explained, to translate wave information into words and pictures. Dormancasting was simply a mode of reverse-engineering, learning enough about the subject's neurological wiring to turn his ideas into electrical micropulses that could be fed back into the parietal lobe, prefrontal cortex and amygdalae to trigger the comadream vision. PermaSom's computers were then sophisticated and fast enough, he was assured, to sustain wave patterns indefinitely. Their rep made it seem so reliable, and their literature was full of testimonials from satisfied clients whose loved ones were sailing on endless ocean cruises, enacting perpetual Roman orgies.

When the time came for Casson to be wheeled into the DreamSalon, he felt ready. The nurse slipped on his headphones and he closed his eyes, clutching a Derrick Thomas football card with as much strength as his palsied fingers could muster, gently synching to the sounds of the Gin Blossoms' "'Till I Hear It From You." In a matter of moments, he was home again, reflexively reaching into the pockets of his cargo shorts, searching for the coins that would buy a maple walnut bomb from the Dairy Vault truck, whose chime recording of "She'll Be Coming 'Round The Mountain" roused the children of Belton Park from their games of pickle and hopscotch. At the corner of Lanyard and Mountjoy, he watched Meghan and her sister Lee, still in their field hockey skirts, look up to see him and smile, schoolbooks clutched modestly to their chests. A red-headed woodpecker chipped rhythmically at the trunk of the Boudreaus' ancient sugar maple. Past the fire station, Mrs. Arsenault, town librarian, tested the microphone at a dais set up in front of brownstone Glick Library for Veteran's Day speeches. He was of a mind to saunter over and revisit the old display case of Gutzon Borglum's small clay busts of famous Kansans, an exhibit he had always loved. He would look into those pioneer faces and think of how Borglum would grow to carve Mt. Rushmore in the Black Hills, an achievement not unlike the peaks Casson would ascend in his own military career.

"Winn," old Charlie Weathers called. "Grass needs trimming. You look like a kid who could use ten bucks to take his girl out." Casson was a little embarrassed to be busted for penury in front of Meghan, but Charlie was a great guy, and anything he could do to help a grunt who had assaulted Omaha Beach on D-Day would be time well spent. He was full of contentment, and, when he turned onto Liberty Street, where Dax Grace and Gar Classen gunned their old Chevrolets in a make-believe drag race, he felt his pulse quicken with youthful envy and knew that he was mentally and emotionally locked-in on the right milieu for his de-commissioning. He could smell the smoke from The Barbeque Pit and his insides roiled with acid. He could practically taste the tang of brisket.

"Any bad memories associated with that place and time?" the oneirology aide had asked him, later, in the debrief.

"Yes," he had said, forming the words with some effort. "Stomach ache. Too much butterscotch pudding." All else was sunlit and full of promise.

The early months of 2049 were hard. Casson required a ten-day hospital stay for pneumonia in early February, and spent three days after he returned home with a former lieutenant organizing his private papers and crafting an Interim Asset Disposal Plan. With the remaining mobility in his hand, he signaled instructions in American Sign Language, relying for the rest on Gretel, who had learned to translate his deteriorated vocabulary of grunts and wheezes into English commands. Only his military training, his refusal to succumb to even the most severe hardships, kept him going. But by late March, a faulty catheter led to a troublesome UTI that four different courses of antibiotics could not vanquish, and he had begun to lose vision in his right eye. When the night sweats kicked in, Dr. Cunningham suggested that it might be time to check in to the local PermaSom intake depot and launch the dreamlife.

Dr. Jake Cisneros, gloved, masked and gowned, recently snatched from a Neurology residency at Regents Hospital, ushered Ariel, Gretel and Casson, freshly washed, dressed in full army regalia (for, he presumed, the very final time) and arranged on the nickel-plated wheelchair that had been his Christmas gift from the Leesburg VFW, into Consultation Room B, the showplace they reserved for FDA inspectors, major shareholders and VIPs.

"Billings Kuperman was through here last month," he said, assembling briefing books for the three. "Professional rodeo can be so cruel. One ticked-off bronco can ruin your whole day." Only Gretel, hardened by her legacy of strife, chanced a furtive smile.

Casson sat, stoic, while Cisneros waved a seemingly endless stream of waivers and acknowledgements in front of his face for him to "read." *Do they think me an idiot?* he wondered. *Do they think I don't know why I'm here?* It offended him that almost every piece of paper to which he shakily affixed his mark was designed to exculpate the company from some sort of liability, but he knew these were essential prerequisites to his near-death homecoming. Acknowledgement of Experimental Technology. Inventory of Personal Property. Appendix B: Fillings, Prostheses, Implanted Medical Devices. After 45 minutes, it was finally time to execute the Dormancy Bailment Agreement. Casson skimmed its impenetrable provisions, until a paragraph on page six made him shift uncomfortably and exhale heavily to get the doctor's attention:

R. **Conditions of Dormancy:** Subject hereby agrees to indemnify and hold harmless PermaSom™ from any and all damages resulting from the terms and conditions established for Subject's dormancy, including, but not limited to, those set forth in the rider attached as Appendix A hereto. Under no conditions shall PermaSom™ incur any liability for any injury, physical or psychological, incurred during Subject's dormancy, other than injury caused directly and proximately by the physical misconduct of its staff during the execution of its duties as expressly provided herein, and adjudicated during AAA arbitration as provided for in Section G.(2)(a.) of this Agreement. It is stipulated by the parties hereto that dormancy conditions not expressly set forth in Appendix A are not reasonably foreseeable by the parties hereto and are not covered by the terms of this Agreement. PermaSom™ disclaims any covenants or warranties, express or implied, with respect to Subject's dormancy conditions; Subject understands there is a risk of developing adverse conditions not directly stipulated, and expressly assumes any and all such risk as a condition of entering the custody of PermaSom™.

Cisneros seemed to have expected Casson's reaction.

"Some of the guys call it the George Spigott clause," he said. "Inside joke, I guess. Nothing to worry about, I think. Even now, the electrochemical processes that occur in the brain are a little bit mysterious. The mind, it seems, has a tendency toward equilibrium. What do I mean by that? Well, in the testing phase, some of the subjects who had designed optimal worlds saw unforeseen features or events – what we used to jokingly call 'gremlins' – creep in. Maybe the dreamgirl has a deep man's voice, or the jukebox at the jazz joint plays polka music. Little hitches to keep things from getting too perfect. That's why we're now so careful. Our post-dream exit interviews were introduced to reduce the incidence of these imperfections."

"I've overseen 38 of these," Cisneros japed, "and I haven't had a single sleeper complain." Gretel laughed quietly into her palm, unconcerned, it seemed to Casson, about being overheard. He felt he was doomed to spend his last years as a punchline for a conga line of overachieving Hispanics.

Casson felt the gooseflesh rise along his naked arm and thigh as the door to the Preparation Room closed. "Just relax and we'll have you back home before you know it." The preptech, a youngish Asian woman – Mongolian, he guessed, from her narrow eyes and broad face – cradled Casson's head and fed him a 5 mg Valium in a paper cup. Another tech, an Indian man with wiry, muscled forearms, gently slid a PICC line into his arm, calmly whistling a raga Casson failed to recognize. The steel wreath was icy against his temples and he winced drowsily, saying ugly mental goodbyes to duplicitous politicians, scandalmongering journalists, opportunistic doctors and even the lone mother who kept an angry vigil outside his home with a hand-lettered sign that read "Turncoat." At last, he could leave them all behind.

Those first moments seemed to last for days, as Casson's custom world spread itself before him. He did not know, at first, where his mind was. For a while, his consciousness was a slideshow of freezeframe images – a schoolyard brawl, a family breakfast, his father and Uncle Ron shooting grouse in the meadow outside of town -- always on the verge of disintegrating in loud hues of amber, scarlet and blue. Then, like a film finally coming into focus, his perception cleared, giving him a muddy but familiar view of streets and buildings from his youth. Slowly, his other senses caught up until he could at last feel locks of long blonde hair tossed by a stiff April breeze, feet pressed solidly against the gravel (flecked with glimmering nuggets of ground green glass) in the back parking lot of The Prairie Schooner bar. He was loving the feel, wiggling his Converse sneakers side to side and enjoying the crush of stone when he was shocked alive by a blast from the horn of Ernie Van Tusten's cherry Silverado.

"Samson! Sometime today, huh? I got a delivery coming."

Leaning against the brick wall, Casson surveyed the street, his eyes picked out Meghan, fake-pouting, wrapped in her kelly green Kennedy varsity jacket, looking perfect enough to punish a man, to drive a best friend's dad to the knife-edge of scandal. He used to have nightmares in which she went down on his friends, laughed at his chainstore clothes, his untutored tastes in music and liquor. But now, she would be his and his only. She would never even glance at Zack Himmelman, the all-Jackson County point guard with an offer from K-State; Bill Carmody, the steel guitar player from Rustlers' house band; Ethan Dignan, whose family owned half the town. She would be his, and he would have a century or more to invent, with his grown man's mind, new ways to explore and test her devotion. He slid his arm snugly around her waist and together they turned up the main drag.

"Looking good, Shit-Hot. Drop around later and I'll sneak you a shot of Beam."

Not likely, Casson thought. *I'll be well occupied.*

The world around him was everything that had been promised: temperate breezes; a busy, but uncluttered flow of traffic appropriate to a thriving Midwestern town with a brilliant future; fragrant bowers of roses and daffodils in well-trimmed front yards; healthy, cordial townsfolk attending to the day's business; just enough conspiratorial teens, freshly loosed from a spring schoolday, to make a grown-up feel alive and alert and vigilant. *And yet.* The girls seemed too erect, apprehensive, like actresses about to be called to read for an audition. The clouds of fresh-bread smell that should have issued from Perriman's weren't there. The marquee above the lobby of the Hillendale Theater was adorned with a jumble of red plastic letters, still waiting to be arranged into coherent words. The Andrews' Lhasa Cosmo, who had always chased Casson along the sidewalks after class, just stood stock-still, yelping angrily at the mannequins in the front window of Marie's Le Parisien Fashions. There was a general air of unrest up and down Liberty Street. The Palace Tea Room at the end of the Whaley Road cul-de-sac was already boarded up and abandoned, its front window marred with a golf ball-sized hole. And then, suddenly, the answer was there. Casson could now feel the feathery touch of foreboding, an unrest of which he had been only dimly aware, along the back of his neck. Something like an unclean haze had begun to invade the edges of his peripheral vision and, in an instant of intuition, the nature of things came into focus.

"Winn, are you okay?" Meghan asked, sweetly squeezing his arm. "You seem about a thousand miles away and it makes me a little bit – I don't know – nervous, I guess."

All along the sidewalk, he felt it. He saw it in the wobbly outlines of things. Lines of vapor, like heat rising from a desert floor, had begun to ascend and arch along the street. Against the brownstone façade of Gabe Hebner's flower shop, he swore the heat swirled into shadowy ocular orbits, almond-shaped, like those of wiry Joey Kreutzman, the first private who had walked across the execution grid, and below those orbits, a plume of smoke seemed to trace the shape of an unaccusing smile. This recognition was the key. Now, Casson saw the forms of others, all the Ghost Platoon's members, rising into something like a wraith-canopy all along the busy street, then growing wider and larger and higher into a thin new atmosphere that spread across the heavens. In the teeming air, he caught the hulking outline of Gardiere the quiet corporal from New Mexico and, for an instant, his rueful, translucent glare floated over the familiar face of Mrs. Graves sweeping the day's candy wrappers from her strip of sidewalk. And beyond Gardiere, Casson saw and sensed new tongues of air – not just his own soldiers, but exhalations more ancient, from all the secret and public wars, intimations of the thousands, maybe millions, who had fought and died in years, decades, ages, previous. And they rose and spread, thinner and thinner but always there, into that lapis spring sky he had so carefully planned, hemming in sun

163

and clouds with a quiet presence he felt like a stagnant sort of moral weather. Meghan's face bore a look of helpless concern, like that of children he remembered staring at bruise-purple skies pregnant with winds, the sort of winds that might, in a few minutes, take away all you had or imagined. He wanted to touch Meghan with steady hands and whisper *don't, don't be afraid*, but there was no sense in faking it. He was scared, too, for he knew that these mists would be forever with them, sometimes as puffs of breath or wind, sometimes thickening into an encroaching fog or a looming black thunderhead ready to pour tepid rain, always natural-fact, reminder, indictment, insult; there to censor the air they breathed, the music from the horns of the marching band's trombones, the golden sun, the cold and universal prairie moonlight. He and Meghan would be forever swimming through it, drowning. Every breath would add a little more of the sweet spirit-poison.

Casson knew would not be happy here. He would not be still.

JOHNNY BROKEN, JULIE GONE

A Play in One Act

Setting: Simon's modest but neatly-kept studio apartment, complete with peeling paint, fancy moldings and high ceilings – the sort appropriate for a young teacher or graduate student – in a small Northeastern college town. The front door at stage left opens into a combination living room/bedroom. The downstage space is sparsely furnished, just a work table and computer, at the appropriate height for Simon's powerchair. The table is cluttered with pill bottles, tissues, bottled water, soda and energy drinks, and a pair of small plastic hospital urinals, all arranged to be within easy reach. Against the back wall are a pair of guitar stands on which sit a Fender Jazzmaster, beaten up from many out-of-town gigs, and a newer Guild 12-string acoustic. Alongside them is a stereo cabinet whose shelves hold a vintage turntable, cassette deck and Pioneer amplifier. At the cabinet's foot sits a 1984 Tascam PortaStudio, a nest of cables and effects pedals, a pair of Sennheiser microphones, and a small Marshall guitar amplifier. A Japanese screen divides the room; at upstage right is an unmade futon on a wooden stand. At far right, a window opens onto the river. Next to the window sits a small, portable television on a low stand. Scattered around are a lifetime of music magazines and trade paperbacks, a handful of oversized hardcover art books on Schiele, Bellini, Bonnard and others. The overall effect is that of a well-lived life bursting the seams of a home too small to hold it. The walls are adorned with a number of items: a family photo from a long ago summer picnic; a signed poster from a mid-80s Dream Syndicate show, framed under glass; college and law school diplomas; an ornate yard sale mirror in a carved wooden frame; a large framed poster of Jacopo Bassano's unfinished Baptism of Christ. Above the futon is a framed Eugene Atget photo of Paris shrouded in mist, the picture wreathed in a decorative Persian shawl. During Simon's moments of solitary reflection, the pictures on the wall become windows on Simon's psyche, screens through which a host of voices speak.

Time: The present, a mid-week in late summer, just after dinnertime.

Cast of Characters:

Simon: A disabled attorney and part-time musician in his mid-50s.

Jessie: A friend of Simon's from his school and rock band days.

Beatrice: Former partner of Simon's in an unsuccessful love affair.

Eddie: Ex-bandmate of Simon's, long dead from a drug overdose.

J.C.: Simon's imagined version of a Christian savior.

Philpott: Simon's literary and intellectual icon, also long-deceased.

Lawrence: Simon's estranged father, dead since Simon's teens.

Laurent: Simon's paid caregiver.

Delivery Man

The Thrushes: Familiar phantoms, advisors, tormentors, objects of fear and fantasy, chorus for Simon's ongoing internal struggles.

> *Eurydice*
>
> *Electra*
>
> *Dora*
>
> *Bryce*
>
> *Rhoda*
>
> *Cleo*

****

It's early Tuesday evening. Simon works intently at his desk. He is a bit unkempt and moody. An oversized Cleveland Indians baseball jersey hides a small belly born of chronic inactivity. His hair is long and a little greasy, pulled back from his face, and he has an untended goatee to cover a newish double chin. His eyes reflect a low fire slowly running out of fuel. Laurent, angular and impatient, emerges from downstage left, holding a spray bottle and a roll of paper towels. From offstage right, we hear the distant sounds of traffic and people on the riverbank below.

Simon: Hmmm. Laurent. *Lau-rent. Loh-rahn.*

Laurent: Yes?

Simon: Just thinking aloud. Interesting name. You have any French blood?

Laurent: Well, for one thing, you're saying it wrong. It's not Loh-rah. Just "Laurent." American. Like *low rent.* Kids used to break my balls in school. Mr. Low Rent.

Simon: Still.

Laurent: Still what?

Simon: Don't like it. It's ethnically inappropriate. It's like naming a black man Yuri. Or Nanook. Or Seamus.

Laurent: You never heard of Black Irish?

Simon: Black Irish aren't technically black.

Laurent: Besides, lots of brothers have French names. Africa was colonized by Europeans. Belgium. France. Continent is full of French names. *Patrice* Lumumba. *Laurent* Kabila. Hell, the West Indies were all French names, and that's where you crackers got most of your slaves from.

Simon: *Us* crackers? My people were still in Europe until the 1920s, *mon ami.*

Laurent: Just making a point. The language is lousy with Creole French. French for black is *negre.* 'Nuff said. Ever heard of Jean-Michel Basquiat?

Simon: Okay. You win.

Laurent: You worry about more silly shit than anyone I ever worked for. I oughta walk out of here just on GP.

Simon: I need to distract myself somehow.

Laurent: From what?

Simon: From life.

Laurent: Life. When you start getting all maudlin, I know it's time to go.

Simon: True dat.

Laurent: Now, *that's* some ethnically inappropriate shit. Need anything before I go?

Simon: Can you open up the window? Polluted breezes help me sleep. They chase me right out of this world.

Laurent: All right. Well, I'll see you. Try not to make yourself crazy with nonsense, Mr. L.

Simon: You're no fun at all. Let's not say *au revoir*. Let's just say *à demain*.

Laurent: Well, motherfuck...

Laurent exits. Simon fidgets with items on his desk, more to prevent himself from accomplishing anything than for any other reason. He clicks at his computer, takes a pill with a swallow of bottled water, squeezes a stress ball, clicks the television on, listens to a few seconds of pointless opinion being traded on a news program, then clicks the television off again. Simon's movements are halting and awkward. It's apparent that he has difficulty maneuvering his bulky chair through the narrow spaces his apartment affords him. The silence surrounding him is oppressive. After a time, he wheels over to the window, where the dusk light is just beginning to fade. Simon absent-mindedly serenades himself.

Simon: I'm try'na disappear before the end of the
      night

      I'm close but I can't seem to get it all-the-way
      right

      Just a fevery moan

      Between the skin and the bone

      A whisper in the din

      To fill your mind with pictures of the places
      we been…

Simon reclines, flexes his fingers, debates inwardly for a moment, then takes another pill and closes his eyes, waiting for the drugs to relax him. There is a knock at the door.

Simon: Come in.

Jessie peeks in. She is five or six years younger than Simon, still tall, lean and tomboyishly athletic. Her face, severe in a way that's almost Native American, is taut and handsome. She is happy, but has not seen Simon in years and circles him cautiously, as one would circle something rare and unusual, freshly excavated. They embrace gingerly, awkwardly, as tightly as the chair allows.

Jessie: Well, well. Long time no see, Simon. You put on a couple. I ought to be mad at you. How come you never come around? Ellis thought you were dead.

Simon: He's half right.

Jessie: No. I mean legitimately deceased. I almost fell out when I got your weird-ass phone call. Can you imagine? Voicemails from the abyss.

Simon: Nice to see you, too, ladyfish. Hey, thanks for coming. I wasn't sure you would. You never seem to age. I look at you and it's that last Rounders show all over again. You look like you bathe in virgin's blood.

Jessie: Don't bullshit me, kid. I was always just a phone call away. Shame on you for not calling. For letting yourself calcify in this little rock & roll coffin.

Simon: *Calcify.* Sorry, that sounds so *clinical.* Sounds like you were eavesdropping on my last session with Señor Marcos, my old physical therapist. He was supposed to be getting me active. Bringing me back to the world. I told him this fluid in my legs is making me feel like the Tin Man. I provided him an almost theatrical cue for him to tell me I was being "discharged." Sounds so much better than "abandoned."

Jessie: That doesn't sound good.

Simon: Either I was hopeless or my insurance was running out. They sound the same. Sorry to see him go. His compliments of my *pretty eyes* were the closest thing to action I've gotten in years. Well, at least his departure gave me time to work on my memoir. I'm nearly up to The Greta Years.

Jessie: Greta. How is Lady Skidmark anyway?

Simon: *Skidmore*. She went to Skidmore.

Jessie: Whatever.

Simon: She's long gone. She went off to lawyerin' school three years ago. At Vermont. She wants to lobby against GMOs.

Jessie: What? Muscle cars?

Simon: No, genetically modified foods, dummy. Frankenfoods. I wasn't enough of a charitable project for her.

Jessie: Well, then. So you lost out to an ear of corn?

Simon: You never liked Little Pigeon, did you?

Jessie: About as much as any pigeon. An aerodynamic rat. Shitting on everything.

Simon: But thanks for that corn image; that's a keeper. How's Ellis doing?

Jessie: Fine. He's getting his real estate license. Can you imagine? Some family buying a dream home from him? Clifford got him into it.

Simon: Good a scam as any, I reckon.

Jessie: You reckon? *(Laughs)*

Simon: I reckons. *(Longish pause)* There's them that takes and them that gets took. Nice to see you guys are on the winning side. But what kind of host am I? Pull up some futon. There's some Paulaner in the fridge. Some Old Grand Dad? I just recently decided to take up my old hobby again. But I never drink before the sun is over the armrest. I figure as long as I'm never walking again, staying steady on my feet becomes a non-issue. No medication like self-medication.

Jessie: Sobriety didn't take for you, either? No, no thanks. I'm just enjoying seeing your old fright mask again. Jesus, but you disappeared, you idiot.

Simon: It's surprisingly doable. It's shocking how little trace we really leave, and how few people really try to pick up our trails. After a while, they stop trying altogether.

Jessie: Is that a dig?

Simon: No, not at all. I know it's mostly my doing. It's so much work to keep up, and when you do see people, they have to see you like this. And you have to see them seeing you like this. It wears you down. *(Pause)* So, did you get it?

Jessie: We get right to the point. Fuck you, too.

Simon: I thought you might have people to go, places to see.

Jessie: No. Nothing. Just my crusty old pal.

Simon: Sorry, I'm just a little on edge these days. You'd be amazed how much energy I spend on menial shit. Just getting the groceries in, and the bills and banking done and shit like that. And with that wild winter we had, not knowing if my guys were going to show up. Man, do not take those good legs of yours for granted. *(Takes a beat to relax)* You really do look great. Great. Ellis is a lucky guy. I mean it. *(Another beat)* I guess maybe I act so businesslike out of fear, fear of nostalgia. Look at this little monastic cell. Sometimes I feel like all that beautiful past would just suck me right in like a whirlpool if I let it, and make me one of those bawling, insufferable old bores that repels peers and frightens small children. You even still wear that old Raincoats button, the one the doorman at the Locker gave you. Here, why don't you throw your coat over there...

Jessie: Always the knack for gracious living.

Simon: I should have a set of crash test dummy coatracks like Eddie used to have. Remember the converted firehouse over on Ferris Street? *(Pause)* Remember that? Jeez. I haven't thought about that joint for a little while. Not since 'NBS did the birthday thing last October. Eddie...

Jessie: Do you remember Eddie's birthday, the day we all went out with a keg to Blair's Falls, and drank and swam and played guitars, you and me and Eddie and Trudy and Clifford and those two girls from the jewelry store on Howarth Street?

Simon: The ones we called Chip and Dale? And that fragrant squatter guy who followed Wendy home from junior year in Rotterdam?

Jessie: Mats was his name. Dutch Mats. That was a good day. And Clifford and I split a quart of George Dickel and you played me "Circus Fire Dream" for the first time. Or what there was of it.

Simon: Uh huh.

Jessie: *(A nervous pause)* And what happened then? Do you remember that?

Simon: Surely.

They sit for a moment with the memory.

Jessie: I really liked you then. Asshole. You had a way of cocking your head and looking around corners like you were expecting to find something to fight. *(Pause)* Always something to fight. I would have done just about anything for you then. Anything. Even crazy shit. Which reminds me. *(Nervously extracts an object wrapped in cloth from her knapsack; unwrapped, we see it is a pistol, a .38 revolver)* Well, here it is. It took some getting.

Simon: *(Seemingly shocked by the sight of it)* Well. Wow. It should be so ordinary. I guess seeing a fantasy object so many times in movies, it becomes invested with some kind of mystical significance. The very ordinariness of the real item becomes… extraordinary.

Simon holds the gun gently and examines it with perverse fascination; it is filled with wonder and power and danger, like a mystic amulet.

Jessie: The only thing extraordinary was the price. $350.

Simon: That's OK. I got it. No worries.

Jessie: I still am having a hard time getting my head around this. You with a gun.

Simon: Protection. My door is open a lot. I've got guys coming and going all day. Sometimes they show up with friends. I mean, who knows who these guys are the agency sends? A two-bit job like this… It's not like these are bonded guys. Some guy walks in and sees musical equipment. Lady upstairs got some expensive jewelry taken last month.

Jessie: If you say so. Why not just buy the thing at a store? I feel like I'm setting up a second-story job or some underhanded shit.

Simon: Well, your old pal has some dusty old skeletons. There was that coke bust. And all the police involvement after Eddie died. Like anyone gave two shits. We know it was nothing, but who knows what kind of questions…?

Jessie: All right. Sure. Well, be careful. The guy said it could jam.

Simon: The guy?

Jessie: Do you really want to know?

Simon: No. Good. Done. Done deal.

Jessie: You been writing again? I see you're hanging on to the old four-track. Old Lucille.

Simon: Oh, hell. That's a whole other thing.

Jessie: Yeah?

Simon: Yeah, I started dicking around with it after I watched that old Martin Sheen movie on TCM. The one with Sissy Spacek.

Jessie: *Badlands.*

Simon: About the runaway lovers on a killing spree.

Jessie: Yeah. *Badlands.* Terence Malick before he got boring and metaphysical and whatnot.

Simon: Yeah. That story, the doomed couple on the run, got me writing a bit. Calling myself Brother Sun, I think.

Jessie: Ha. A concept album.

Simon: I like to say "song cycle." It got to me somehow. All that space, and nothing they needed anywhere. Nothing but doom at the end. I guess I'm becoming more and more drawn to lost causes. Really lost causes.

Jessie: Just so you know, it's kinda been done.

Simon: I'm afraid to think of what hasn't. But a man keeps himself amused.

Jessie: Well, thank God for that.

Simon: Don't underestimate the power of amusement and distraction. *(Pause)* I don't know how monks do it. All that nothing. Some people dream of it. Just peace and quiet, like those two things go together or something. But Nothing has a life of its own. Nothing is a cancer. The less and less I have in my life, the less peace there is. Nothing is like a weed. It grows and crowds out the real peace.

Jessie: You're still working.

Simon: Yeah, there is that, but that's not much. Pat doesn't really need what I do. He mostly just keeps me on as an old friend of the band. He knows I need the benefits. I'm not complaining. But a student could do what I do for lots less. One day he's going to realize that. That's why I tried to start writing again. To push the Nothing back. Nothing repellent.

Jessie walks over to Simon's acoustic guitar and picks it up.

Jessie: So play me.

Simon: It's hard some nights. It's like using someone else's hands. You gonna bust my stones?

Jessie: No promises.

Simon: Seriously.

Jessie: You know you're waiting for me to.

Simon: If I nod off in the middle, it's my pills. They do that.

Simon picks up his guitar and strums, tentatively at first. It has been some time since he has played for an audience, and, as he tunes, he watches Jessie's face for confirmation that he is doing things correctly, that the guitar has not lost the power to make him more than he really is.

Simon: Let me be the kind of man

      A girl might keep around

      Just sharp and fair

      Not full of air

      Dishonestly profound

      A man with sunlight in his eyes

      A man who's straight and plain

      No schemes or implications

      No bargains to explain

      Just a pure green light

      Who's gone tonight

      For friendlier terrain

We'll be famous anywhere

Doing everything we dare

You'll see

Answer all my interrupted prayers

Girl, your eyes are deep and clear

Your voice is heaven-sent

Need a nod and sigh

An alibi

No need to reinvent

Without the contemplation

Or the urges to repent

Gonna sew up my design

Holy blood and holy wine

Babe won't it be fine

To live outside the line

Forever free

We'll be famous anywhere

Doing everything we dare

You'll see

Answer all my interrupted prayers

Transfigure my confusion

Into reckless zeal

Don't need nobody's virtue

Just be right and real

Come take a trip with me

Out to the silent sea

We can hate the jails and jailers

Like they hate the fearless free

We'll be famous anywhere

Doing everything we dare

You'll see

Answer all my interrupted prayers

I won't ask again

No time to reach "amen"

Don't have that kind of sheen or *savoir faire*

Just answer this man's interrupted prayers

Just answer this man's interrupted prayers

Jessie: *Badlands* to *Worselands*.

Simon: *(Softly)* Johnny Broken and Julie Gone...

Jessie: What?

Simon: Did I say that out loud?

Jessie: Uh huh.

Simon: A fragment is all. Still working on it.

Jessie: Okay.

Simon: *(Offhandedly)* Johnny Broken and Julie Gone/Made a wish on the final dawn/To live forever/To live no more/To finally learn what all the shit was for...

Simon goes quiet.

Simon: I suppose that's my opening.

Jessie: For...?

Simon: Wow. Now that you're here, I don't know how to ask this.

Jessie: Uh oh. That sounds kind of ominous. *(Pause)* Tell me I'm wrong.

Simon takes several long breaths trying to translate his thoughts into palatable words.

Simon: No. No. Jess, I've always thought we had something in common. Something deep.

Jessie: Oh, shit. Don't try to snow me. I've got this hot feeling in the pit of my stomach. Is it money? You know if we could...

Simon: No, not even close. You've got to let me tell it.

Jessie: All right.

Simon: You and I, we come from kind of the same place. All the stories about your mom and how that went down, and the way your sibs were with *you*. The money stuff. The insurance. And your dad leaving.

Jessie: What..?

Simon: No. Let me finish. You were the one who saw how things could turn out when you got a raw deal. And when real hard-luck shit had to be dealt with. Eddie. Do you remember how good you did with him after that first problem?

Jessie: Mmmmm.

Simon: What would we have done...?

Jessie: Such a lot of good we did in the end.

Simon: And Petra, when she lost it that first time.

Jessie: That was a long time ago, for you to be bringing all that shit up again. Best left buried.

Simon: See? You could see the hard truths and deal with them.

Jessie: This is going to a real ugly place.

Simon: I don't have to lay it out for you. I mean, shit, look around, man. *This is it*. Where does life go from here? No place. This is as far as I go. This chair. Do you see any way out of here, because I don't...

Jessie: You gotta be kidding. That piece isn't for protection.

Simon: It is. From bankruptcy. And old age. And insanity and self-parody.

Jessie: Oh, ho! And you want me to, *what...?* Witness...?

Simon: Not exactly.

Jessie is silent for a moment.

Jessie: Oh fuck. Oh, you crazy fuck. *Fuck me. (Pause)* I'm sorry, it's just that I thought maybe you knew the first hundredth millimeter of a *fuck* about me. What gives you the slightest inkling I could do that? You morbid, sad fuck.

Simon: It's the greatest chore and the greatest favor a man can ask, and also the greatest compliment a man can give. I want you to escort me out of this life.

There is a pause – impractically long, totally silent.

Jessie: I should slap holy shit out of you. *(Shakes head)* You total asshole. Asshole. No, I... To what do I owe this... great... *honor* anyway?

Simon: Do you remember what you gave me for my 20th birthday?

Jessie: Yes. I think, a book.

Simon: Any book?

Jessie: I don't remember. What has that got to do...?

Simon: It was *The Letters of Vincent Van Gogh.*

Jessie: Yeah, sure.

Simon: Nobody ever cared enough to give me something like that. To match me with something that pure.

Jessie: It was just a book.

Simon: No, no, it wasn't. *The Rolling Stone Record Guide* is just a book. *Watership Down* is just a book. This was a message. A connection. Mostly, it was a warning. A sign: Danger Ahead. I should have listened, Jess, but I didn't. Only you...

Jessie: You're reading too much into it. Way, way too much.

Simon: Some lady on the bus saw me with that when I took it out of the gift bag. Strange lady. Never saw her before. Know what she says? "You are so lucky to have such a friend. Hang onto her." And she was right.

Jessie: So why didn't you?

Simon has no answer.

Simon: Hmmm. I didn't know.

Jessie: You didn't know much.

Simon: Thoughtless gifts are for family to give. They are the ones who drown you in things you don't need or use. The real measure of a connection is the rightness of gifts. You are the one. You need to do it. Or the ceremony has no meaning.

Jessie: What would Beatrice say about that?

Simon: Don't drag her into it.

Jessie: Our Lady of Hard Truths.

Simon: She's gone. She's well out of it and we should leave her out. I only thought of you. Only you were tough enough.

Jessie: Tough. Gee, thanks. Y'know, you always said the most unintentionally hurtful things. You really did. But I never minded, because you were skinny and quick with quotes and had sculptor's fingers. And good hair. Montgomery Clift hair. But you didn't know how to be nice, not without hurting people. Always took short cuts. You couldn't just let people work out their own stuff. You always pushed them away. You never let anybody love you or hurt with you. Sometimes, a person needs the dignity of her own pain. Get it?

Simon: Pain…

Jessie: No. This is where *you* keep quiet. I mean, killing yourself? Really, Simon? Saying you're not going to miss the friends who love you? What kind of shit…?

Simon: I never said it.

Jessie: Yes. Your actions said. Your actions and your intentions. How kind. How very kind. Nice leave-taking.

Simon: I miss you already. I miss you now. I miss everybody now. That's the pain I'm saying goodbye to.

Jessie: And what about us? What about me? Aren't you saying goodbye to the people along with the pain? Can't you even let us share it with you just a little? Did it never occur to you that we can take a little bit of the pain away? *(Slowly, sadly, kisses his forehead)* Think outside your skin. Jackass. Miserable old jackass.

Jessie notices on the desk an envelope Simon's hand seems to be protecting. She grabs it from him and starts to read.

Jessie: Oh, sweet Jesus. What the fuck?

"Let your search end here. I did this thing. Me and me alone. Hunt no one for this crime, which is not really a crime at all, but, rather, a pardon. In a related file, you will find directions regarding the final disposition of what remains of me and my assets. This is not the act of a madman, but one sadly and ordinarily sane. I act out of diminution of good: love, pleasure, connection, hope. I have squinted hard at the future and found no encouragement, just the stalling of research scientists deeply concerned over the welfare of lab mice, more than willing to consign discoveries to a pharmaceutical company vault for an honorarium and a pat on the ass. Human life has, through the awful disciplines of war and economics, become cheap and inconvenient, a rigged casino game. Life is a manual of cons I never got around to reading and mastering. I am not prepared to live forty more years in a room, like a bookcase or a flowerpot, entertained by only the withering of body and mind, and the coarsening of the world, a revenue source for corporate mercenaries. I was meant for better; I will not submit to that. To those who helped, I wish a life spent wresting pleasures and satisfactions from the hoarders. That, and not too much pain. For the rest, I have nothing at all. I ask only that people occasionally dig out our music and smile, for the sake of Eddie Jay Lane, Jim Dragicz and LeRoy Masterson, if not for my own. They deserve that. Beyond that, I ask nothing and am entitled to nothing. I don't leave in hate, only in haste. Simon Losman."

Wow. You have got to be kidding. You great horse's ass. Did you leave enough money for the statue? Every martyr has to have a statue. You in a toga with a couple of cherubs. Cast out of something that rusts and corrodes.

Simon: Don't do that. Don't make it cheap. It ain't cheap.

Jessie: Thanks for not ratting me out, anyhow. Thanks for that. Lame piece of shit.

Simon: You're mad.

Jessie: First of all, I'm not gonna do that for you. No one is. *Freak*. Do you think any of your friends could live with that? Jesus. How could you leave people to pick over such a mystery, like a wound reopening, for years? Decades?

Simon: You're looking at it all wrong. A man can't live for others.

Jessie: Some of us have *only* lived for others. Besides, anyone can see this is just some pussy impulse, some whim. Not thought-out at all. From a purely logical perspective, it would never work. People would hear the noise.

Simon: Use a silencer. You can make a silencer with a soda bottle.

Jessie: Why would someone use a silencer to commit suicide? And if I threw it away, the police would find it and know that someone else was here.

Simon: Someone.

Jessie: Like me. I told people I was coming to see you. At least three people. My prints would be around here. And I'd show up on some closed circuit camera.

Simon: If they bothered to look. You give the cops an awful lot of credit.

Jessie: And someone would find me and test my alibi. They would test me for GSR.

Simon: GSR?

Jessie: Gunshot residue.

Simon: I have gloves. The guys use them so they don't have to touch me when they wipe my ass.

Jessie: No. And your fingers wouldn't lock around the gun like they're supposed to.

Simon: You could put it in my hand and point it, like so.

Jessie: Are you kidding me? You could do all that and still need someone else just to pull the trigger? Are you that weak? *(Pause)* That tells me you're not ready. That this is just some stupid, attention-seeking funk. I'm not going to let you. I'll tell someone.

Simon: Who? Who's left to tell? You won't.

Jessie: Why?

Simon: Because of why I picked you for this mission. Because you were friends with Petra. You were with her at the end.

Jessie: She was far worse than you. She had Lou Gehrig's. She was much worse.

Simon: We are points on a line that ends in the same place. Do you remember what happened when she tried and failed?

Jessie: Of course, dumbshit.

Simon: The police and the hospital. The guardian and the drugs and the restraints? The coldness and all the freedom she lost? You would never do that to me. Could you have two of those soul-rapes on your conscience?

Jessie: I could start coming over.

Simon: I don't want you to come.

Jessie: You really mean that? I guess you do. *(Hurt)* I guess you do, at that.

Simon: "Everything I loved was taken away from me, and I did not die. There was nothing I could do."

Jessie: What's that?

Simon: Just something I heard. A movie. An old movie.

Jessie: Baby, I won't do it. It can't happen and I'll tell you why. You're lucid. You're not in pain.

Simon: Physical pain.

Jessie: You can still think and feel and create. You're still a fucking *participant*. You're still recognizable.

Simon: I'm alone. I'm unloved.

Jessie: *Loved*. Don't make me laugh. *Loved* is not a prerequisite for entry in the human race. Tell me you know that, at least. *Loved* is a bonus. *Loved* is money on the sidewalk. All you need be is *eligible* for love. That's all you're promised. And as long as that long shot is on the board, you are *eligible*. No matter what the odds. You want some hard truth? Stop feeling sorry for yourself, you selfish asshole. You terrific, selfish asshole. I love you. I do. But you're about eight different shades of fucked. *(She is almost crying now.)* You had better not let this happen, you *fuck*, because I'm not going to Hell to bail you out.

Jessie waits a moment for Simon to answer, her eyes full of something that says she would not – could not – see him again, then exits in exasperated silence. For a time, Simon hangs his head at Jessie's rebukes. One can almost see the gears turning as he tries to form a Plan B. The phone rings and Simon lets it – five, six times, before picking up.

Simon: Hey, Pat. What's going on? Yeah, yeah, yes. He just left. Uh huh, always. But... I don't know ...he's alright. He's good. Shows up on time. Does his thing. Not easy to get people to show. This one guy, this one guy, claimed the same road was closed four days in a row. Like he couldn't figure out... Him? I don't know. Canada maybe? Always talking about Americans like we're the Other. Yeah. Yeah. I will ask. So what's the latest? Good, good. How did your thing go over? Your thing. The CLE talk. Great. Well, they never do. Yeah, let's talk about timing. Obviously, your wish is my command, right?

The doorbell rings. Simon reaches for the wall buzzer to open the front door.

Simon: No, nothing. Just the door. Uh huh. I know. I am so sorry. It's just that my place is miniscule. Could you just throw it in a closet somewhere? Did he say that? Sure. Okay. I understand. Let me work it out with Ted. This week. Later this week.

There is a loud knock at the door.

Simon: Come in. *(Louder)* Come in!

Delivery man enters, with a box.

Delivery Man: Shall I just leave this for you?

Simon: Umm, yeah sure. Just drop it on the counter. I'm on the blower here.

Delivery man exits.

Simon: Oh nothing. Nothing. Just a box. You know, more bad news. More med stuff you don't want to hear about. So, I'll deal with that stuff, but – can I just run something by you? Something that makes me feel a little, um, I don't even know how to say it, Pat. Kind of silly. But you brought it up and now it's on my mind. Only take a second. Yeah, well… I just get a feeling… I know I don't come in anymore, but I still feel like I'm part of the, the overall oper… It's just I get this image of me getting moved into a closet. Sure, I understand space is at a premium. I totally get that. It's just for someone in my situation, being packed away carries this whole… Uh huh. Sure you're not. Sure. I appreciate. All right. I'm glad. I'd like that. Let's set that up, definitely…

Simon picks up scissors and slices open the box, removing plastic packages of catheters, which he holds up and examines with an expression of disgusted resignation.

Simon: Okay, and the Sorenson docs... I ran into a coupla hiccups, but... Oh, okay. Really? Why was that? 'Cause that might create... Oh, she is then? Yes, surely. I can send her what I've got. The note and the P&S... I'll do that now, if it has to move on that much of a fast... No. No prob. Sure. The other? Yeah, I can get you the memo. Fine. Fine. And I'll arrange to get that stuff out of Jeff's office. Right away. Cool. Cool. Later, Pat. Yeah. Be good.

Simon hangs up the phone. He grabs an open pill bottle, pouring one into his mouth and, after a second's hesitation, electing to wash it down with a swig from the open whiskey bottle. He sits for a moment, waiting for the drug and the drink to punish him. His eyes roll a little.

Simon: Huh? Hello? *(Softly)* What the f...? I thought I just heard...

The silence continues. Simon looks down at his hands, feeling the roll and tumble of the booze. He closes his eyes for a few beats, then, calmly, returns.

Simon: Shit. Out of sight, out of mind. I must be out of my mind to expect more than charity from a place like that. *(Places head on desk, defeated)* Where's my portable inspiration? *(Wheels into the bedroom and looks through books, selects a volume)* Time for a little sanity, a little reading break. Something noble and uplifting for a change. Something for the ages. Like...?

Something is happening inside the large mirror; the normal reflection vanishes and the image of the author

Philpott, a bearded British gentlemen of considerable refinement, late-60s, appears.

Simon: Why do I bother with it, the law? So much bullshit. *The law is an ass...*

Philpott: "Law was the Japanese screen he placed between himself and the indecent predations of life. He was endlessly fascinated by the perpetual, unequal wrestling of shadows, while invoking the magical intercessions of hoary old justices and slumming medieval monarchs. The membrane of jurisprudence stretched but, in his trembling, insect mind, never fully sundered."

Simon: *Notes From A Lost Expedition.*

Philpott: I should be flattered.

Simon: I need you, man. You remind me of the work that matters. The conjurer of social delusions.

Philpott: Ha. The *slayer*, perhaps. Another one of those nights?

Simon: They've been coming. More and more.

Philpott: And one invokes the divine insanity of literature to animate the quotidian clockworks of everyday life. To make the pointless relevant again.

> The icy peaks of NothingThere,
>
> They scrape the chill and silent air.
>
> They scale the heights, without a sound,

The men no kindness ever found.

They cannot love, they cannot learn,

And from their climb, they can't return.

Their songs, a plaintive *Miserere*

Around the peaks of NothingThere.

Simon: I had no idea you wrote verse.

Philpott: Landrum wouldn't touch it. It ended up in a tiny college literary journal, long defunct. No reason you'd know it.

Simon: Very, very nice. Mr. Philpott, you're the man I consult for insights. I'm, I don't know, running out of psychic petrol. What can one do when life becomes…a net energy *drain*, sucking more from you than it can ever offer?

Philpott: But it always has so much to offer! You hold my answer in your hand!

Simon: *(Reads cover of book he is holding)* Ian Philpott, *The Graveyard of Everyday Saints.*

Philpott: Page 84.

Simon: *(Reads)* "McGlone looked out distractedly at the awakening evening city. Chalky women from the aircraft plant ducked into doorways, looking for quiet spaces to prepare their masks and dances for the promenade of promises and narrow escapes. Streetlights, traffic lights, candled windows, splashy galaxies of multicoloured neon, glimmered like stars against the encroaching darkness. Small groups of young men scuttled along the mechanized pulse of Arcadia Street, transacting what he imagined were small, forgivable crimes. The pulse of music on the glass pane foretold, he thought, dozens of little collapses and pyrrhic victories, a nightly epic poem recited by hundreds of clubgoers and prostitutes and firemen and journalists and emergency workers, then, lost in the silty industrial breezes of Carnevon. It was all so transient, so instant. Nothing he saw or felt or imagined would survive him. Performance was the only real art; violence the only real law; appetite the only real philosophy. Because, like Helena said with gloriously carnal relish: *it was all the now*. Everything else was a construct, wishful thinking. Law, art, ethics, fashion, medicine... they were all methods – imperfect ones, to be sure – to bottle up, to divert, or to remedy the damage caused by, the lone driving principle of human life: wild, unconstrained Will. The Will to dominate, to impose, to satisfy every kind of want. McGlone was sure that, left to its own, unmediated devices, humankind would do precisely what the new war was now giving it license to do: tear itself to pieces in a splendid Dionysian Technicolor *melée*. He had accepted this and, under Helena's awful caresses, even begun to embrace the entropic pageant. It would be a marvelous thing and he felt privileged to be able to see it."

Philpott: Decay, erosion, destruction! In its way, as fascinating as any birth or creation.

Simon: But... even a man's own?

Philpott: "Those deaths are sweetest, most affecting, that strike nearest the heart." Pg. 114.

The dim twilight is massaged by the flicker of distant, rainbow neon through the window at stage right.

Simon: Ah, there it is. Regular as sunrise. The sign at the old Vincennes Candy factory. All over the country, they know this sign. What does that say, that the whole world knows your town for a sign from a factory that's been closed for 70 years? During the war, they converted it to making rations for the army. Nice, right? But Harry Truman goes after the owners for overcharging and shuts the place down. Three hundred sixty people out of work. Then, in 1988, this historic preservation group buys the sign – just the sign – and restores it and lights it up, and it's been lit ever since. The factory stays shut, dead as the dodo, but the sign stays on, like a taunt, a reminder of something good that could have existed in the world, could have done good for people.

Philpott: Is there anything more beautiful than a splendid ruin? One day, this will be as venerated as the Parthenon or the viaducts of Rome. Any decay is artmaking, whether it's a society's, an industry's... or a man's.

Simon: Surely. *(Reads)* "Dr. LaPlace had been able to sew McGlone's cuts, set his bones, turn back the advancing colonies of bacteria in his leg and abdomen. But his increasingly sedentary and somnolent life had given rise to an ague the doctor, with his sophisticated diagnostic protocols, could not begin to fathom. McGlone's inward intellectual flame had begun to cool. Once the complex of impulses labelled *soul* began to atrophy, he knew, it was only a matter of time before the empirically measurable faculties fell, like the walls of an imploded skyscraper."

Philpott: I give you a glimpse of the world behind the world, Simon, the wonders behind the wonders. Yours is a life free of leisure and style and diversion. Yours are not the mediated meditations of pay-per-view and infomercials and pre-recorded museum lectures. Your warders have abandoned you and left you to roam the prison corridors unattended. In the low rumbling of a bowel you hear the crashing waves of mystery oceans. The keening whine in your cochlea is the whirring music of the spheres. Yours is the postmodern disease, man surrendering to his overwhelmed, haywire defenses. Your corruption, your collapse, is a rehearsal for Ragnarok. The Singularity. Every ultimate disaster -- biological, technological, psychological. You have a gold circle seat. How many of history's avatars would have loved to trade places with you on your journey? Society is shedding its skin all around you. You should have your notebook open, my son. This is the one and only Last Chance.

Simon: I never...

Philpott: Limbs and faculties are used up and jettisoned, one by one, like the stages of a Saturn 5 rocket. Nothing more than process. Did the crew of Apollo 11 fret over the discarded hardware, or did they focus on the journey? The discovery? Where are you going? New reaches of inner space? A teeming new wilderness filled with perils and unimagined vistas? Orozco painted with one arm. Beethoven was deaf, Titian and Monet almost blind at the end. The body is just a container for the soul, and a shabby one at that.

Simon: I think of the body like a balloon, that takes the air and segregates and defines it, makes it a new thing with new value.

Philpott: It might be, if the air inside was the same as the air outside. But the breath that animates you is unique, different from the air inside any other balloon, like rare perfume. Does a bottle give the fragrance its value?

Simon: Still, one can't help but wonder *why*. Why me? Why was I chosen for all this good fortune?

Philpott: I do believe you have the answer. You just bought it.

Simon: *(Digs through book pile and finds a newly-purchased volume) The Future Assassin: Conversations and Contumely.*

Philpott: The inevitable collection of interviews and ephemera. I was always dead set against it, but

Landrum was adamant. One's estate only has so much incentive to safeguard literary legacy. See pg. 18, the *Guardian* interview. With a horrible stoop-shouldered fellow named Van Cleve, if I recall.

Simon: Ah. *(Reads)* "Man's nature is assault. In an environment of safety and leisure, he attacks the only feasible target – himself. Christian nations kill their God, artists deconstruct their own disciplines, and the body attacks its own neurologic infrastructure. I silently pray for foreign enemies, an endless battalion of enemies that can be overcome, because man will never overcome himself."

So true, Mr. Philpott.

Philpott: Ian.

Simon: Sir Ian?

Philpott: Oh, Simon, give an old man some credit.

Simon: Such observations are bought with a lifetime of experience, a lifetime of war and love and travel and technological change, a lifetime spent in up-close observation of social evolution and upheaval. How does a man adapt to a life of imprisonment, of house arrest, caged like a zoo animal? I'm sorry. I'm getting overwrought.

Philpott: *Outside* is an optical illusion, Simon. Scientists studying fractals have discovered that, by measuring the dimensions of a single tree, we can learn encoded information about an entire forest.

What if, within the byways of the human body -- the patterns of nerves and capillary veins, the rhythm of our hearts and respiration, and the electrical activity of our brains -- was information about the whole human race, the planet, the pattern of expansions and contractions of the universe over time? All the codes and equations were there inside your skin, just waiting for the right type of slow, conscious cognition to figure them out? You would be running hither and yon, to all corners of the world, not to discover, but to *avoid discovering*, to bury beneath an avalanche of motion and anxiety and sensation a library richer than the lost trove of Alexandria! What if that all-too-human sense of ingrained restlessness was placed there to protect those secrets like one of those Indiana Jones booby traps? What if yours is not a disease at all, but a step forward in evolution? The loss of a faculty no longer needed for man's progress, and the growth of a *new* faculty, a new kind of awareness? How can you say this is not so, and that you don't merely await the support of a species that has yet to catch up? You have been given a wondrous gift. You should be savoring the inward journey on an expressway devoid of onramps and interchanges and visual distractions. We are all travelling there, but you will be an early arrival with the best parking space and the shortest walk to the scene. Experience is a trap because it confines our thoughts to what we have seen and heard. Travel is an inconvenient relic of an age gone by, an interruption in the only journey of note, the great virtual caravan that carries one from the Siberian

Steppes to the villages of the Maasai to Balkan peaks to the floor of a Nevada livestock auction, faster than the speed of thought. That trip to the chemist or the dry cleaner a source of nostalgia? Banish it! The sizzling interchange of electronic networks, that moving sidewalk of requests and replies with their patterns richer and more complex than any Mashad carpet, is the new Grand Central, the new Kennedy International, and the termini of those nets are here in the eye, the unfathomably dense circuitry of the brain. You have opportunities for travel no explorer could have imagined in Livingston's day. From the headwaters of the Nile to the canals of Mars, and growing by the nanosecond.

Simon: I'm falling apart.

Philpott: There's poetry in it, Simon, if it's done gamely and gracefully. The world is nothing if not a sculpture garden of decaying masterworks, a ballet for the halt and dying. Await your cue. The show must go on.

Simon: But it's all fake. It's all delusion and make-believe.

Philpott: Then make yourself believe. Those are the muscles that need strengthening.

Philpott vanishes. Simon picks up the bundle with the gun inside to place it in a drawer, but for a moment is transfixed by the gun, as it catches a spotlight. The mirror goes hazy, and in it appears the somber face of Eurydice.

Eurydice: The world will continue without you
around

Scarcely a whimper, scarcely a sound

Simon: Ah, heavenly shades of night are falling… To what do I owe…?

Eurydice: New loves are courted; obsessions are
found

Scarcely a whimper, scarcely a sound

Simon: *(With mock grandiloquence)* My harlots! My harpies! My tormentors! Loves of my life! I might have known. What took you all so long? I missed you so! Maybe these pills don't get me tight as fast as they used to. Stay with me. Sing to me, my beauties! Bring me all your razor-edged luck and poison advice. Come back here, you crazy mythic Lolitas! Or is it *Lolitae*…?

Eurydice: The answer that humanity's been sold

The timely end, as valuable as gold

That saves us from the shame of growing
old

Simon: With voices soft and sane, and eyes so clear

An old man's great desire, and greater fear

Eurydice smiles coyly and is gone. Silently, the images in the gig poster shiver and coalesce into the pale, sunken face of Simon's old bandmate Eddie Jay Lane, long dead from an overdose, but still nervous, hungry, looking around like a spider whose web is being plucked by a constant barrage of potential prey. There is no peace in him.

Simon: Eddie, it's good to see you again. How long has it been?

Eddie: Don't you remember? October 1989. The Lawrenceville Hotel.

Simon: Sure I remember. The last Venus Hunters show at Porter Street.

Eddie: Good show, considering.

Simon: That sick girl with the video camera and the jean jacket trying to climb over the monitors.

Eddie: Yeah. Weird.

Simon: Whose party were you at again? When it all happened?

Eddie: Party. If three guys can be a party.

Simon: It was never the same after that.

Eddie: Nothing is ever the same, period. Even when things are the same, they aren't the same.

Simon is silent for a beat.

Simon: So, I guess you know. Things have been better.

Eddie: Yeah, I see.

Simon: Do you?

Eddie: Uh huh. At least your hands work a little, guy. At least you can still play now and then. Or whatever you call that noise you make.

Simon: Soundsplatter.

Eddie: Yeah, right. You've still got that. Some of it is okay.

Simon: Some. Thanks, I think...

Eddie: The great assassin of rock and rollers: *sensitivity*. What's going on with that acoustic shit? I do not approve. Would not have flown with the Hunters.

Simon: Hey, I'm not 27 anymore. I'm not entitled to grow up?

Eddie: Not that much. You're a rocker and your sword and shield is confusion. You're the all-American alien boy. You're coming from a place of raw love and desire. You don't know and you don't *want* to know. You're not part of the *game*. When you start understanding, you have to start explaining, and then it's not rock and roll anymore. It's something preachy and pretentious and *adult*. Did Joey Ramone ever explain why he wanted sedation? Did Mick let us in on why he couldn't get satisfaction? You've gotta be a little bit lost and bewildered because that's where the fucking asshole belligerence comes from. It keeps you outside, banging on the door.

Simon: What if it breaks down and you find yourself *inside?*

Eddie: Then you're Sting singing about Nabokov and Oppenheimer and international diplomacy and shit. Doing duets with Nevilles.

Simon: Which ones?

Eddie: Any of 'em. Tito. Tito Neville.

Simon: *(Laughs)* I wish you were still here. I still need you.

Eddie: Obviously. "Dusk turning Faulkner rust." Really? Oh, *man...*

Simon: Do you hear it all?

Eddie: Just about. The electric stuff could work. The sweet voice over the top of that din that sounds like walls coming down. That works. That's your poetry.

Simon: You're speaking for me now, huh?

Eddie: You can see a lot from here. You'll go round and round looking for answers until you see how stupid that is. Then you'll be right where you ought to be. Ours is a poetry of inarticulate rage. We build castles out of mud that stand forever.

Simon: Forever?

Eddie: Well, a while, anyway. A good while. Inarticulate rage for an inarticulate age. See, I'm writing your songs for you, even now.

Simon: We could make a hell of a comeback.

Eddie: I had to die. You can't be remembered if you don't die.

Simon: That's sounding pretty good right about now.

Eddie: There's a bunch of that feeling going around.

Simon: Always.

Eddie: But worse than usual. Worse all the time. You should hang around for a while yet, though. I wish I had done more. Finished the Auburn demos for that last album. You don't get the right monument if you die too soon. They don't even know what to build it with. You have to leave them the bricks and the blueprints when you're alive.

Simon: So, music is supposed to keep me alive, is that it? Die middle-aged. Leave a beautiful *corpus?*

Eddie: Music. It's kind of a sad memorial. But, shit, it's what we got, guys like us. People try to make it into some marble palace, but that's wishful thinking. Makes no sense. Music is not about beauty, or rebellion, or magic. Not for me. That's a lot of bullshit. For me, music was an ugly thing, about conquest. Conquest of boredom, conquest of despair, conquest of insignificance. Conquest of obscurity, of oblivion, of time. Beating that shit over the head. And music always loses. Always. And we do it anyway, because *we don't care*. That's the glory and stupidity of it all. Heroic futility. *Don Quixote* by the slice.

Simon: Nice.

Eddie: I read a little in school. I wasn't crashed out all the time. Rock and roll gave me something nothing else could. A chance to hit back. You could, too. Just open your ears.

Simon: What do you mean?

Eddie: Your little fugitive girl. The one you've been chasing. She could be nice. She has a lot to say. You never let your girl speak. *(Pause)* You don't listen. You never did.

Eddie vanishes. Simon reflects for a moment. He looks at his hands, flexes them, frowns, takes another long swig of whiskey. He lights a cigarette, which hangs from the corner of his mouth. We can see, as he grabs his Fender and plugs it in, that he is trying to recreate some kind of rock and roll vibe, and that he is almost getting there, almost surmounting the age and the inactivity and the isolation. He steps on a fuzz pedal and begins to channel some golden mud, somewhere between Darklands Jesus & Mary Chain and early Jacobites, harsh yet inviting:

Simon: There's a gun on every side

And all I want to do is ride

Watch the freedom promise hide inside your eyes

You're the garden and the spring

Source of everything

I'm king inside a Taj Mahal of lies

Your holy loving saves

But the graves are dug and they spread the powdered lime

So baby, baby, all we have is time

Too much to confess

Got an hour, maybe less

And no return address after the show

I'm scared by what I done

It's time to cut and run

The sun don't reach the place I gotta go

I'm wine and you're the grail

We're in their jail and they falsified the crime

Now baby, baby, all we have is time

Like suggestion to a spell

Like the desert is to Hell

Like a gesture to a full-on pantomime

The money's all been spent

The world is cold and bent

Just skin and breath and voices, yours and mine

Love's the sentence; faith the only crime

Baby, baby, all we have is time

I'll tell you good and plain

I only offer pain

Sheets of driving rain that block the sun

Strike those angel strings

I wanna be the one that sings

Of wings that carry losers on the run

That alone might be enough

Wanna sing our love but there ain't no pretty rhyme

'Cuz baby, baby, all we have is time

It's slipping, baby, all we have is time

Simon sits in silence, occasionally broken by the chiming of an undistorted string, sounds which turn into a somber improvised instrumental, like the soundtrack to a film about forfeited dreams. The screens go dark, and the serene faces of the Thrushes appear, one in each.

Electra: The long and aimless walks in foreign streets

The pulse of woman's breath from perfumed sheets

The coda that can't fade, but just repeats

Cleo: The feel of books before you crack the spine

The taste of veal washed in Italian wine

The light, to one who's slowly turning blind

Rhoda: The slow advance of palsy on the limb

The longing as the autumn sun grows dim

The wild hair in need of patient trim

Dora: Trembling hands that fight to turn a page

Fingers that no woman's hands engage

A body, once a blessing, now a cage

Bryce: The eulogies unwritten and unread

While friends keep bodies neatly dressed and fed

Who noticed him alive? Who mourns him dead?

Eurydice: No scholar can predict what God intends

These years for which no gold can make amends

So all is well that ends, *just simply ends*

Simon's song finishes. He sits, just thinking. He takes another long drink of whiskey, just holding it, imagining how he looks to his spectral audience, enjoying the flavor, before swallowing.

Simon: It's just not a special evening without my harem. I feel like I could write your life stories, every one of you. Was Eddie telling me the truth? Is that who you are? All the girls' voices we never heard? Come back to show us how much they really knew? To share all the stuff they understood in their time of youth and beauty, before they had to unlearn it all? So is this my second chance, or just revenge? Tell me. Tell me now, or else...forever hold...

The Thrushes start to dim.

Come on! Don't you fucking float away, you teases! You, you stand-by operators! This thing of yours, this *busy signal*, this lifeless, deathly cold -- *your* cold -- one day, is going to embalm the world.

I wonder how the other half lives? The half that's not one of us beautiful people, eh, ladies?

The Thrushes fade. The figures in Bassano's painting have begun to flow and melt like an animation. The image of the Christ begins to move, gain solidity. It speaks like an older, much wiser, but slightly worn-out friend:

J.C.: You are not beautiful. You may never be beautiful again. In fact, you don't look very good at all.

Simon: Wow. You really know how to hurt a guy.

J.C.: Who would know if not us? We built the prototype. I knew I'd be dragged into this eventually. We always get the call, when folks run out of drugs and food and women and other assorted vices.

Simon: I could use a hand. Things have gotten, I don't know, *weird*. Cold. I'm running *out*.

J.C.: Of what?

Simon: Strength. Resolve. Ideas. Faith.

J.C.: Ah. Faith is a tricky one. You know, you either have it or you don't. You can't really pull up to the pump and fill up.

Simon: "Act as if ye had faith…"

J.C.: "And faith will be given to you." Do you guys even *listen* to yourselves? Fake it 'till you make it. Walt Disney *via* AA *via* David Mamet. Not one of ours. We're not quite so easy.

Simon: Okay. I'm weak. I'm confused and weak and not big in the faith department. I'm not one of the saints or martyrs. I'm asking you. I need an answer. Tell me where the joy is hidden. Tell me how to live. *Why* to live.

J.C.: More than we already have?

Simon: I could really use a little clarity. Can't you give me something? Can't you?

J.C.: I hate this part.

Simon: Why?

J.C.: *(Pauses to collect His thoughts)* We usually try to stay at arm's length, not out of callousness or cruelty, mind you. People get that wrong. Out of... how can I put this? Mercy? Modesty? Tact? Fact is, the world would be cataclysmically disappointed. It expects something that isn't there. There is no big, cosmic secret, no alphanumeric code, no incantation that will roll back the planet's woes. That's what you all want, isn't it? Some magical formula that will trigger the grand Global Headslap? *Ah ha! So that's it! We knew it! Tony Perkins is really his own mother!* And everything would be good again, like it never was before. But the world of men has ears of tin, my friend. Your hearing is as selective as that of the world's most co-dependent spouses. Hundreds of people wrote about me. *Hundreds.* And writers were rare back then. But you chose four and threw all the rest away. All the nuance. And now you come to me for answers? *(Laughs sadly, privately)* It's funny. The truth is, the answers really aren't that complicated. Every human hears them a thousand times in life without even paying attention. If We showed up one day at the top of the Eiffel Tower and repeated them with a ton of echo and a few lightning bolts, what do you think would happen? There would be a worldwide gallery of blank expressions and a great collective *that's it?* moment, and, then, a planetary sense of deflation and emptiness and embarrassment, like a species-wide depantsing. Can you imagine how anticlimactic that would be? What a punch in the collective gut? Hell, you're not stupid. Be kind. Protect the weak. Stand up for what's right: justice and beauty and charity. Don't butcher each other. There's not much more. There's not *time* for much more before you're dead. Do you need to hear it in Latin or Aramaic before you believe it? You people can be remarkably dense. Cute but dense. How long can you try to explain ethics to a puppy before it gets tiresome? Two thousand years or thereabouts? Guess again. Much, much more quickly.

Simon: Please, please, don't talk in riddles. That doesn't work for me anymore. It's too late for that.

J.C.: Now, now. Shouting won't work. All that will do is attract the cops, and you know they don't have the answers. They don't even know the right questions.

Simon: Why do you have to make it all so hard?

J.C.: We're not in the easy-answer business. We're in the mystery business. Always have been.

Simon: If you want a man to live righteously, why put him in a chair, from which he can't reach anybody, love anybody? Where all he can do is rage and stew? What is it? A punishment? For what? To what end?

J.C.: Very cold, and getting colder. The affliction is no punishment; the cure is no reward.

Simon: What about miracles? Aren't those rewards for faith?

J.C.: Please, don't count on miracles. We have to keep those few and far between, or they would lose their value. And fewer and fewer people have that kind of faith.

Simon: And a man might go insane trying to pay off his debts.

J.C.: We wouldn't accept payback. It would be all about the Grace. We give you things you don't deserve and never will. Why? Because we're good like that. Sometimes.

Simon: That's what we get? A whim?

J.C.: "The condescension of Heavenly grace..."

Simon: Your words?

J.C.: I wish. Thomas à Kempis.

Simon: You read theology? Rather a waste of time.

J.C.: We have enough. Enough to read our fan mail.

Simon: So there's no retribution, no settling of accounts, no closed circles. Our lives are Moebius strips that just go on and on, never reaching or returning, to no purpose other than the prevention of pause and reflection, because that way lay madness...

J.C.: Mankind just loves to put audacious words into my mouth. I suppose We gave him too much credit. Worry less about the Last Judgment and more about your next judgment.

Simon: There's so much that you could do if you would just step down from there and give us five minutes of plain talk. Plain, blunt talk.

J.C.: You want me to jump out of this frame? But you love things in neat little frames. Yourself, in particular.

Simon: Five minutes.

J.C.: I already told you. Figuring out the answers is what life is about. If we spelled it all out, it would be the ultimate spoiler. Like spoil-the-sweetness-of-human-existence-for-5,000-years spoiler. Trust me. Not good.

The lights come up again. Simon leans back, pours another drink, runs his hand aimlessly through his hair. His eyes, we see, have gone a little bit glassy. He sets down his guitar on his bed and rolls back to his work table. For a moment, all seems normal again. The spell of music and verse lifts.

Simon leans back and elevates his feet like a senior partner enjoying a moment of triumph. One by one, he picks up a series of Lucite paperweights containing small facsimilies of the "tombstone" advertisements for transactions he worked on as a lawyer. He smiles over the glory and silliness of his past achievements. The spotlight hits the

218

glittering object in his hand, and the screens show a panoramic city view, as if from a corner skyscraper office, as he speaks extemporaneously.

Simon: Calista, take a memo:

MEMORANDUM

TO: Patrick Clohosey, Senior Partner, Clohosey & Kurfirst

FR: Simon Losman

RE: Relevant Precedent/Constructive Eviction

Date: August 28, 2014

In the instant case, our client, Ambassador Properties, LLC ("Ambassador"), seeks clarification of relevant legal precedent concerning the doctrine of constructive eviction. In particular, may a tenant withhold rental payments due to landlord's failure to evict a neighbor whose nightly bouts of weeping, lamentation and ranting against the world's ills as depicted on nightly news programs allegedly render lessee's residence "uninhabitable"?

While the definition of "habitable" traditionally implicates the landlord's provision of essential services, *see Ellsworth v. Drummond Properties, Inc.,* 353 Mass. 213, 230 N.E.2d 12 (S. Jud. Ct. slip opinion, entered Aug. 4, 1967) (steam heat); *Miner v. Bardasian,* 345 Mass. 4, 182 N.E.2nd 265 (Mass. Ct. App.) (1962) (water, trash collection), other recent cases from this state and neighboring jurisdictions

219

have expanded the definition to include compelling interests in less intuitively obvious features and services.

In the Vermont case of *Lessard v. Fremantle Housing Trust*, Lessard, lessor of a house in Athens, Vermont, stopped payment of rent on his bungalow after Fremantle constructed a multi-family dwelling on an adjacent parcel, which structure obscured the view of Mt. Stratton from lessor's bedroom window. Judge Piersall's opinion held that respondent's action violated the implied warranty of habitability in that it "deprived the tenant of those essential psychic nourishments supplied by access to the wonderments of nature and the yearnings toward transcendence supplied to generations by the majestic Green Mountains," 136 Vt. 32, 429 A.2d 43 (Vt. Ct. App., 1978). Subsequent cases in New England expanded markedly on the holding in *Lessard*, opining that tenants might suffer so-called "constructive eviction" for a variety of psychological and emotional deprivations, *see Bromley v. Edgerton*, 472 A.2d 209 (Me. 1984) (construction work driving away songbirds and depriving tenant of "consoling music"); *1618 Farrar Square Associates, Inc. v. Dahl*, 126 N.H. 23, 490 A.2d 56 (N.H. Sup. Ct., 1985) (exposure to summer outdoor screenings of "overrated and historically dubious" film *Casablanca*); *Eglitz v. Casamayor & Sons*, 132 N.H. 216, 560 A.2d 109 (N.H. Ct. App., 1989) (refusal to evict neighbor whose late-night recitals of Wordsworth's "Intimations of Immortality" triggered "sudden and deep-seated bouts of melancholy"); *Calabrese v. Sisto*, 227 Conn. 19, 629 A.2d 43 (Conn. Ct. App., 1993) (refusal to paint over mural of woman whose "sea-green eyes evoked [tenant's] unrequited high school love").

While none of this is controlling precedent, the author believes the developing trend in this area toward the recognition of legal rights to solace, fulfillment and spiritual bliss makes Ambassador's position, at best, difficult to argue, and believes the firm should advise client to accede to tenant's request for a Zen rock garden and koi pond, contingent upon payment of a corresponding rental surcharge."

Inside the frame of the family photo appears the round, red, bearded face of Lawrence, Simon's deceased father. He looks quarrelsome and judgmental and seems flustered, as if he has just been pulled from a critical staff meeting. His eyes water, and he can't stop nervously cleaning a pair of horn-rimmed glasses several decades out of date.

Lawrence: Really?

Simon: No, but why shouldn't he have his rock garden? Why shouldn't we all? Some days I don't want anyone to have anything. Other days, I give away the whole clip joint to anyone who asks.

Lawrence: I would have hoped to instill in you better work habits.

Simon: You always did sober, competent work. It's what you were good for.

Lawrence: You need to care for your reputation, boy. A man is known by his work. It's the calling card he shows the world.

Simon: You always knew everyone else's business better than your own.

Lawrence: All that's real are what you do and how people remember what you do. The rest is just illusion, fantasy and bullshit. It's all we have and all we leave.

Simon: I wish I could say I remembered you doing more.

Lawrence: I did what I could. Taught a few. Kept a home. Made you.

Simon: Made me. Made me a wreck.

Lawrence: So it's down to this? Where are the people you're supposed to care for? A man assembles a family. But here you are, alone, calling on the universe to save your bacon.

Simon: I don't remember calling you.

Lawrence: When a man sends out the alarm, he doesn't always have a say in who answers.

Simon: "Assemble."

Lawrence: What?

Simon: Is that what you did? "Assemble" us? Like a manager assembles a team? Just like a scientist. No wonder it gutted you that we didn't conform to specifications. No wonder we scared you so bad.

Lawrence: -Ly.

Simon: *Badly.* Of course.

Lawrence: My expectations weren't so high. Unrealistic expectation is a malady of youth, like chicken pox. Our job is to endow our children with realistic hopes for the world.

Simon: You always wielded your frustrated ambitions like a belt or a paddle.

Lawrence: A scientist lives to undress the world, to catalogue the failures of faith and fantasy. We can't afford to live in the never-never. Reality is our laboratory. You could never quite deal with that.

Simon: To this day, I don't know why you bothered. Marking baby steps of a doomed race toward its unmourned extinction.

Lawrence: I did some good. Some of those measurements and calculations saved time, helped people do more. Made life a little more convenient, a little more bearable. Did you ever do anything to make life more bearable, even to yourself?

Simon: Besides leaving home? I only wish I could have taken mom with me.

Lawrence: You and your mother were dreamers, and ended up with the legacy of dreamers.

Simon: What was that?

Lawrence: The fear and the disappointment. The fear that keeps you alone and alive. That defines you. The fear that you weren't all that you imagined. And neither was this world. Or, for that matter, that *next* world you hang onto.

Simon: Anything you say.

Lawrence: The worst thing we can imagine isn't fear or suspense or anxiety, which last just moments; not pain or shame or worldly disgrace or humiliation, which are, at any rate, finite and, for some of us, may even contain some self-lacerating form of satisfaction. Not loneliness, isolation, or neglect, which can offer the fertile imagination time and space to flower into palliative strategies. The most unbearable, bottomless, gaping horror we can imagine is the one most easily confirmed by objective observation: that the thing we have chosen to designate "life" is simply explained as a single, improbable, utterly fortuitous reaction triggered by the chance collision of a handful of randomly-arranged molecules in one vast beaker of many beakers called "universe," and that all the many crystallizations, mutations, couplings, uncouplings, heatings and coolings resulting in bacteria, plants, lichens, insects, fish, dogs, cats, blood, skin, eyes, fingers, farms, smelters, huts, homes, libraries, castles, cathedrals, palaces, oxcarts, armadas, planes, trains, automobiles, novels, sagas, madrigals, symphonies, plays, operas, torch songs, cinema, mansions, cities, skyscrapers, religion, philosophy, science, painting, sculpture, technology, fantasy, comedy, tragedy, marriage, murder, treason, wars, empires, mousetraps, muskets, tanks, atomic bombs, computers, supercolliders, and the whole kaleidoscope of human feeling -- tears, rage, envy, ecstasy, piety, love, loyalty, self-love, self-sacrifice, self-loathing, self *itself* -- were nothing more than the foaming residue on the rim of that beaker; frozen, blasted by debris, worn away in a sliver of time, in a process utterly unnoticed, insignificant, never to be replicated in The Grand And Never-Ending, All-Encompassing Absence Beyond All Beyond. That *nothing* we concoct in the flickering chemical hiccup of consciousness adds up to anything that registers upon, or is acknowledged by, creature or diety. That neither we nor anything we do or say, write, believe, create or conceive is, in fact, anything at all. Our lives, loves, triumphs, sacrifices, sufferings have no value because there is no thing "*Value*." None at all. We fizzle, dissolve and evaporate, unseen and unknown, in the wild, frozen Lack Without Limit.

Simon: You sound nuts. Even nuttier than I remember.

Lawrence: *Inconceivable*, you say? We conceive it every day, a thousand times a second. It's the white noise in our ears that the entire din of human existence was concocted to drown out. This single fear makes and remakes us every minute. You think you're striking a blow against injustice with your little gun, that your end will be remembered as a tragedy, as a promise broken. But there is no justice. There is no promise. Only what the strong can steal and hide away. And you were never strong.

Simon: In your own way, I'm sure you blame me for this fix I'm in -- for eating badly, not getting enough sun, enough wholesome exercise. Beating off excessively.

Lawrence: You had more blameworthy habits than those, boy. Maybe you still do. You were always weak. There's something in your voice that tells me you love your chair, your disease, because it's an excuse to retire from life. The worst has already happened, and now you can relax and feel safe.

Simon: I can hardly speak to you.

Lawrence: I keep waiting for you to prove me wrong. You're like a wire-walker, wobbling, suspended between two icy, empty pits.

Simon: The more I remember it, the more our house seemed like a trauma factory, some twisted behavioral laboratory designed to turn out emotionless people. People impervious to everything.

Lawrence: Every interesting man suffers trauma. Maybe you didn't get enough. You certainly didn't learn from yours.

Simon: Learn what?

Lawrence: To expect nothing. To depend on no one. That life is a slow crawl forward without triumph or tragedy. To hack out a comfortable space for your own. To make progress, without surrender or complaint.

Simon: Or love or transcendence or empathy or inspiration. Fuck your acceptance. Fuck your world. Your world of inches was never worth living in. With all your knowledge, you never found a *reason*.

Lawrence: I never expected to. Knowledge is just a bunch of answers on a spelling test. Want the answers to the exam? Okay. Something is better than nothing. Love is the greatest something. Love of self is the greatest love. There. Right out of the Teacher's Edition. Did I plug that hole in your heart?

Simon: You're so empty. I can't even look at you.

Lawrence: A man has to be hard to keep from being worn away. And yet I hear more of me in you than in your brother. You're the apple who fell closest.

Simon: I'm sorry I disappointed you.

Lawrence: You were never a disappointment. Only a confirmation. Data from a failed experiment. We all were.

Simon: You want me to *do* something? What? Climb out of this chair? Dance a jig? Argue before the Supreme Court? Cure cancer? Break the bank at Monte Carlo?

Lawrence: Something, anything real. For you, it was only toys and games and play-acting. Play-acting at the things that matter. You found ways I never imagined to keep the world at bay: decibels, booze, pills, storybooks. It makes perfect sense that your body is eating itself. You were one big defense mechanism, always running.

Simon: You were the father of despair.

Lawrence: And you are my true child. Afraid to live, afraid to die, paralyzed and unhappy in between. My frigid universe made flesh. Did you ever really live, son? Did your games make you happy, really happy? You were so wrapped up in yourself. After your little friend died…

Simon: Leave him out of it.

Lawrence: …you couldn't even be bothered to call.

Simon: Ah, yes. Our little fireside chats.

Lawrence: Watch yourself.

Simon: I never told you how awful, how soul-draining those were. Those tightly-scripted three-minute miracles of dramatic economy. Greeting. Weather. Diet. News and sports. Closing. Sign off. As warm and personal as re-entry instructions from NASA.

Lawrence: Not stylish enough? Not Billy Wilder enough to challenge your formidable wits?

Simon: Not anything enough. Not anything.

Lawrence: You severed every tie.

Simon: There was nothing on the end of that phone. No substance at all. You could have been anybody. I could have been anybody.

Lawrence: But you were *you*, boy. That's the shame of it.

Simon: Do you know what it felt like, week after week, year after year, to get nothing? Just nothing on top of nothing? To feel no contact at all? To feel that you have no connection and that the voice on the other end will never, ever, make the effort to establish that connection?

Lawrence: We just needed to hear your voice.

Simon: *(Pauses)* Listen now. Listen to what you're saying. *We just needed to hear your voice.* Just needed to hear my voice. As what? Proof of life? Or was I like that little voice the phone company sponsors that you listen to once a day to set your watch by? Is that what you were doing?

Lawrence: Even such a small comfort was too much to ask.

Simon: Comfort. I wanted so much more than comfort. I wanted lives, enmeshed like gears, turning each other, involved with each other. But I got headlines and sports.

Lawrence: Selfish ass.

Simon: I got people who just wanted a voice, people who knew nothing, asked nothing.

Lawrence: Boy.

Simon: Cared nothing.

The lights go down again. Simon halfheartedly lobs one of his deal toys toward the screen Lawrence has just vacated, but his withered arm can only launch a fluttering effort that misses wildly. Simon is, for a moment, painfully conscious of his solitude. A storm of static on the screens signals the Thrushes' return.

Rhoda: A life, like fists, all clutched into a ball

        The stallion kicking out against his stall

        Because there is no one for you to call

Bryce: A boy that gloomy reveries enthrall

        A neck that feels the chill of coming fall

        Because there is no one for you to call

Electra: Hell is just a room, a chair, a wall

        The human instant, moving at a crawl

        Because there is no one for you to call

Dora: The world is all a joyous *carnevale*

        But you are not invited to the ball

        Because there is no one for you to call

Cleo: Across the whole of life there sits a pall

And that could be the saddest end of all

Because there is no one for you to call

Eurydice: God's fingers cushion every sparrowfall

And you are left for happenstance to maul

Because there is no one for you to call

Simon: Oh, fuck off, will you? Just clear out and take that poisonous old villain with you! I've decided. Yes, I have. You are not here to help me. You are from the other place, the hot place, come to sing me to my perdition. Old Lawrence probably gave you a lift. Demons! In Jesus' name I cast you out!

J.C. reappears in the sky over Atget's Paris, first as a cloud, then as an all-encompassing image. His demeanor is patient, but disappointed.

J.C.: You know you're doing that all wrong? You're not even dressed for it.

Simon: What if you could live as a series of memories in the minds of your loved ones and travel as stories and recollections? What if you could do away with all the physical shit? What if *that* was the afterlife?

J.C.: What if the afterlife was just a metaphor, you mean, maybe for the aftermath, the earthbound legacy of doing the right things in this life? How would that change things?

Simon: I could live with that. But that's not what people think.

J.C.: Yeah. When I said my Father's house had many mansions, I'm sure people started measuring for window treatments. Well, don't think you're getting the answer to that one. You take your chances like everybody else. That's what human life is all about.

Simon: Gambling?

J.C.: In a sense. An expression of belief. In the value of good works. In what they earn you.

Simon: What's behind door #3.

J.C.: Life is a trip. People hang onto it, even when it's bad. Even when it's dismal. People talk a lot about belief, but what percentage do you think really *believe*? I mean *to a certainty?* 1%? 1% of 1%? Why do you think we have to work so hard to sell eternal bliss? Because anything is better than nothing. If you are betting on death, you need to be a True Believer, because the less life you have, the larger those tiny worldly pleasures -- even the *possibility* of them -- grow to be. By the time the hammer on that pistol falls, the memory of biting into a firm, juicy Macintosh becomes the equal of a lifetime of beauty-queen kisses on the deck of a summer yacht. You should *feel* it, for just that instant of awareness. You'll feel all those imminently forbidden things -- snail trails of sweat on the cheek during a great run, the tender current caving your knees at the met glance of a pretty girl -- all cranked up, like a feather stroke on psychic poison ivy. And then, you go mad with life-desire -- I'll bet the Germans have a word for that -- then...w*hat?* Wouldn't you like to know? Life-love becomes infinitely pleasing and then, it's all yanked away, and for a span of time so small it can never have a name, you hurt with all the pain that ever was. Are you ready for that? Mankind's ultimate all-in bet. I like you. You talk a lot of shit. But are you all in? Hell, you haven't even lost a limb or an organ yet, you big baby. You're a lawyer, a bet-hedger, a risk manager, not a believer or a gambler. And let's not even get into the loved ones. Sure, they're not around for this part. They almost never are. But you and I know you have people somewhere that you're still fond of, and they'll hurt, a lot or a little. You never know. That girl with the big glasses in back of fourth-period trig who you kissed behind the bus garage at the Carsonville game and then rarely spoke to again? Well, she could see something online or in the hometown paper about your demise and fly apart like she swallowed a grenade. People are like that, Simon. You could be holding the detonator to a hundred emotional A-bombs, and that's another fact that gets Stonehenge-big as the hammer falls. To endure all that crushing shit, you had better be running *toward* something. And even so, if the Church is right, you may still have to sit in the penalty box for a thousand years. A thousand times a thousand. With no magazines. *(Pause)* So what about it? Are you all in? Are you a believer? Or are you just in it for the incense and frescoes?

Simon: Maybe there's heaven/And maybe there's not/Space is too frigid/And hell is too hot. I'd accuse you and Lawrence of working together, if I wasn't so sure that you'd never met.

J.C.: I don't share the bill with atheists.

Simon: No great loss. Their sets are always too long. And they steal your equipment.

J.C.: What about your sick friends? What sort of message would you be sending them? Ever think of that?

Simon: Sometimes, as a symbol, a man can be worth more dead than alive.

J.C.: *(Smiles)* Ah. A symbol. A symbol of what? Now I think you're seriously punching above your weight.

Simon: "Greater love hath no man…" Whatever happened to that?

J.C.: Is that what you have? Greater love? For what? Big gestures? Public sympathy? The sound of your own voice? For what? For whom?

Here it is: God gives you everything and, in the end, he reserves the right to take it all back. Done and done.

Life is a ballgame. You pay your money and you takes your chance. Sometimes it's a great game; sometimes it's a stinker. Luck of the draw. Even so, you think you've paid your money and you've got a right to be there. But the small print on the ticket says otherwise. It says it's all just a privilege and that management can bounce you anytime, for anything. For wearing the wrong hat. You walk through the turnstiles for the privilege of seeing whatever game you luck into for as long as management decides to let you hang around. But people are always going to go to the games. Kids are going to scream and shout. Junior purchasing managers are going to fake sore throats and play hooky from the office. Fathers are going to bequeath season tickets to sons. Because it's the Game. And being there is better than being anywhere else for as long as it lasts. Life is that game.

Simon: You sound like the ass-end of an old Billy Crystal movie. After he's come home to Anne Archer.

J.C.: I like Anne Archer. You could do worse.

Simon: Roll credits.

J.C.: You're not a credit watcher. You should be. You learn a lot from credits.

Simon: About what?

J.C.: About putting in work. About finishing. About leaving good things behind you, and making sure others don't get hurt.

Simon: No girlfriends were hurt in the making of this life.

J.C.: Something like that. You should open your eyes; you could learn from that chair, too, maybe. Things like suffering as road to purification. Service. Humility as highway to mental health. Doing a lot with a little.

Simon: What am I supposed to be? Some saint or something?

J.C.: It's not for everyone. But you can think of them as teaching tools.

Simon: Teaching us what? How to be poor and sick and miserable?

J.C.: Actually, most of them were ecstatically happy, almost to a fault. Don't even get me started.

Simon: I doubt I'll clear that hurdle.

J.C.: Like I said, not for everybody. Your lawyer friends might be put off if you started dressing like Francis of Assisi.

Simon: Just what I need. More abandonment.

J.C.: You might be underestimating the value of solitude. Nothing like forty days in the desert to clear one's head.

Simon: Don't tempt me. I might take the devil's deal. The whole "all the kingdoms of the world" thing is looking pretty good after three years in a room.

J.C.: *(Laughs)* That was a one-time offer. Not too sure what a good deal that would be today, anyhow.

Simon: So, poverty, sacrifice, chastity, humility. And that's all there is. Get a lot of takers? You getting me back for the missed Sundays and names-in-vain? Or is Heaven all tapped out of love and this is some kind of holy rain check?

J.C.: We get enough takers to keep the lights on, even now. And love was never the issue. Consider us as parents who gave you all we have. We mortgaged the house and now whatever choices, whatever answers, there are will have to be yours. You're a smart guy. Always were. We are not here for you. We are neither defined nor limited. We are to be loved, to be emulated, to be disappointed and supplicated, embraced and abandoned. We are here to scourge, to forgive, to renew.

Simon: I am asking my Savior *(pause)* to save.

J.C.: It has happened; it will again. And again. Be brave. Be worthy. Have value. *(Pause)* Good luck. Choose well. It will be all right.

He departs. Simon is confused, and touches the bottle to his lips, wetting them indecisively. His television snaps on, with moody shots from old noir movies, which are also projected, in blurry focus, on the apartment walls. The Thrushes have been waiting in the wings, and return.

The images are daylight scenes from a rundown American city.

Bryce: A child bothers sunlight with his cry

      The hive of city living comes alive

Dora: A trucker curses heaven at a light

      Two jousting lovers argue and connive

Electra: Skaters darn the thick'ning sidewalk throng

      A scuffed-up beggar makes his silent plea

Cleo: For moments, vapors compromise the sun

      Which reasserts its luminosity

Rhoda: An inbred urging drives the homeward swarm

      A play in which you'll nevermore perform.

Eurydice: The middle-class dilemma: Bloom!
      Conform!

      A play in which you'll nevermore perform

The images are now moody late-night scenes, perhaps from a story of shattered love and betrayal, or of a desperate caper that promised an escape but went tragically wrong.

Electra: A spastic move to flick away a moth

      A shiv'ring hand to pull a collar tight

Bryce: A breeze sweeps half-heard music through the air

      Mist makes shine the surface of the night

Rhoda: Doorways frame a soon-forgotten kiss

Autos rush to destinies unknown

Cleo: A street born under paintbrush of the moon

A nervous chill nests softly in the bone

Dora: The evening shadow's molten, changes form

A play in which you'll nevermore perform

Eurydice: A woman's waiting body, taut and warm

A play in which you'll nevermore perform

The images slow, fade, recede. Everything is peaceful for a moment. A thought emerges, as if from nowhere. In fact, it is from somewhere very deep.

Simon: I miss birds. Snakes and turtles, too. When I was a kid, it seemed they were everywhere. We had a little patch of woods in our backyard and, I swear, you could throw bread or seed on the ground and within half an hour, you'd find all kinds of birds fighting over it. Robins. Well, sure, robins. I mean, it was Connecticut. But also cardinals, blue jays, goldfinches, red-winged blackbirds. If you were good and quiet, there were even flickers and pheasants about. Right in the yard. Then, little by little, they just stopped coming around. Bet you notice it too, now that I mention it. But nobody mentions it. I mean, you'll never see an editorial about the shrinking New England flicker population. They just die, quietly, out of sight. This beautiful, happy thing. And maybe someone like me notices and maybe he doesn't. And then one day, they're just gone, as a price of more used-car lots or insurance offices.

And, for the most part, nobody ever knows or sees. And maybe every day for 500 years there's a change like that somewhere. How different does the world get then? And, what's really scary: *How different do we get?* They say there's a rise in middle-aged suicides in America. I'm not crazy, but what if these are related? Every day, 50 or 100 more guys wake up and don't recognize the world anymore. That's nuts. And it's not. Because a man is only supposed to care about the big things. So he wonders *what the hell is eating me? Why don't I feel right?* And it goes on for years like that, just getting worse, until...

And all the time, it's the goddamn birds. *(Pause)* So many things feel a few degrees off-center. So many things.

Simon rolls over to his bookcase, thinks, and reaches for a homemade cassette, which he pops into his deck. The music begins, a gentle, rumbling electric guitar. On the screens, two of the Thrushes dance, while the central four – Cleo, Dora, Eurydice and Electra – comprise a string quartet with spectral instruments that accompanies Simon's spare, plaintive electric tune. Simon lip-syncs to his own words with eyes tightly closed:

Simon: Sleep, sleep, you're always wrong

Come too late and stay too long

Sleep, sleep, you lose your hold

My head is hot, my hands are cold

Why can't your loving arms enfold

This child?

The woods are wide and wild

The things I loved defiled

Why couldn't I be strong?

Sleep, you stay away too long

Sleep, sleep, you grieve my mind

Leave me reeling and crazy blind

Sleep, sleep, you lost your way

Could have come this very day

To guide

A boy boiling up inside

Crazy panic wrapped in crazy pride

Stood and laughed above the man who died

While the traffic moved along and wits
unwind

Sleep, you always grieve my mind

The angel chorus always lies

'Bout how far and fast a man can rise

The cost of every compromise

Sleep, you're such a lowly prize

Sleep, you come because you must

It's the deal we make with dust

Sleep, sleep, I hate your way

You leave me at the break of day

My dreams are just a shadowplay

In air

My strength and my protection are not there

The fire-tongues are lapping and I pray

Sleep, don't leave me at the break of day

Please stay

Sleep, don't leave me at the break of day

The music fades. The Thrushes bow and depart. Simon is alone again.

Simon: I am so tired. I am so sleeplessly tired. In all my life, never have I felt entirely out of options, entirely without a play. There is a chair and a bed and a grave, and an audience full of people shouting for one or another. I can't buy my way out, think my way out, work my way out, pray my way out, beg my way out, drink, drug or fuck my way out, freak my way out, charm my way out. It was always the world that was failing, but this time the bug is eating its way out from inside. It's me that's failing. And everybody cares deeply but impractically, truly but hypothetically. For one single Anne Sullivan I would burn all my disguises. Am I doomed to be one of those ruined, boring cripples... not even old enough for pathos and sympathy? Begging for visits from strangers who are horrified by sickrooms and their teary inhabitants, wailing, clutching like damned souls clambering onto Charon's boat?

I don't even want to die – that's the joke of it -- but I would *settle* for a death, a death that was quiet and did not leave too much mess. I would settle for a couple dozen friends at a pub, a couple of women blubbering just a little, just enough to upset the regulars. My name sprayed on a crosstown bus, scrubbed off in a few weeks. A hundred-dollar scholarship at the local high school to help some picked-on kid buy bass strings or weed or charcoal pencils, because, man, I am heading for the great Who Cares and this train is *running express.* God Damn It, God Damn Me, You and Gene Wilder and Sam Peckinpah and Iggy Pop and Monty Hall and Morris Udall and Ron Popeil and Shirley Chisholm and Kofi Annan and your dry cleaner and the guy who winds Big Ben and all the cocktail waitresses who ever lived and their fucking cross-eyed children! *(Picks up revolver)* Fuck! My life never happens! I want just enough strength to move this twig of curved metal a quarter of an inch. Just a little guts. Jesus, I swear I'll leave a tip for the super and enough to spackle over the bullet hole. Just let me the ever-loving fuck out of this cheap, embarrassing endless lead-out groove of a life. Or convince me otherwise. Talk me into living, you great lachrymose sob-circle of spirit schoolgirls with your fucking yearbook quotes and your roadside tree-trunk memorials festooned with teddy bears and paper hearts. Come on! Save the kid, win valuable prizes, you fucking…

Eddie reappears on his screen once more.

Eddie: That was absolutely putrid. Shameless. We can see that.

Simon: It's a drama-queen magic spell, my man. Never fails. After a speech like that, things have to work out, if only to make me look eternally stupid. I'll be running half-marathons in no time. Reverse psychology for the universe.

Eddie: You don't want out. You want pity. Shithead.

Simon: Look around, asshole. I got nothing.

Eddie: Nothing can be all right. The world is full of guys who make a four-course meal out of nothing.

Simon: If all my bad luck hit me at once, I could be one of those hard-luck stories that goes around the world, grabs you by the throat, gets television producers to build a house full of ramps and trapezes during sweeps week, but I was not lucky enough to have a piano fall on my head or to run my subcompact into the Dallas Cowboys team bus. This disease is too sly. It's like your brother-in-law the company bookkeeper who embezzles $500 a week for 40 years. It quietly drains everything -- money, independence, self-respect, hope, physical power -- so slowly that no one can tell. To the world at large, you're a whiner, siphoning love from the worthy. But if you look down the road while you're pumping your brakes, it's a cliff, man. I can see it. I can feel it. Like a cheater feels a breakup, as a sick taste in my throat, lead in my bones. If there was only a way to hurry things along.

Eddie: Careful what you wish for.

Simon: I never got a thing I wished for. Not a goddamn thing.

Eddie: Didn't you? Are you sure?

Simon: Hey, check this out.

Eddie: Check what out?

Simon reaches awkwardly for his Fender.

Simon: A brick. A brick for your castle. I forgot about it before. We're gonna build it up a few more storeys, straight and strong.

Eddie: I'm touched. Make it a good lie, will you? I can respect a good, durable lie.

Simon: Watch it. I'm a little fucked up. *In vino veritas.*

Simon gathers himself, picks up his Jazzmaster and strums something breathy, Berlin-ish, with barely a melody at all.

Simon: My friend Eddie needs a place to crash

My friend Eddie is a blanket of ash

Unflinchingly cool and unfailingly kind

Could not forgive himself for his poet's mind

Said leave the *songs* to beginners and the drugs to the pros

Didn't know what he needed but he'd measured the dose

Now he's home or somewhere like it

Or at least he's close…

Eddie: Nice. Is that it?

Simon: Yeah.

Eddie: Another concept album? Where does it go from there?

Simon: Go?

Eddie: Mmmmm. Make sure I get to Heaven. Do that for me, will you?

Simon: What?

Eddie: That shit works. It works like a prayer. Didn't you know?

My pal Eddie lived for music and ass

Treated every encore like a Catholic mass

And all he got was a necktie and a patch of grass

When it's time for his sentence, give the boy a pass...

Oh, and that door you're banging on? There's no *inside*. You break it down and find it's a big film set. All that's on the other side is a bigger, more confusing *outside*. That's the punchline, kid.

Eddie disappears.

Simon: Hey, that's not... Eddie? *Eddie?* Where did you go, guy? I'm sorry. I didn't mean to. We could finish that. We could really *make* it something...

The silence reasserts itself.

Simon: The worst part is this. Feeling the wake.

God, how I hate what we're doing. Arguments. Debate. Pros and cons. *"Jimbo, we'll make a list..."* But how can you integrate as components of this oh-so-reasonable process those things that cannot be explained, that fight and claw and resist at any cost reduction into words or clever arguments? Hey. I used to be a good-looking guy. I wore nice clothes. I shaved and washed behind my ears. I've got pictures. I flirted and people *flirted back*. No, really! How do you explain to someone who adjusts household budgets or nursing home income statement line items the "cost" of looking into a sloe, blue eye and wanting beyond all wanting to offer some suitable gift, some *tribute*, and to be able to ask for love in return? How do you amortize the cost of that eye turning to cold glass and electing to see around you and over you and through you? How do you calculate the value of those two arms full of *nothing* -- the nothing that is the end product of a life of living and feeling and giving -- that you bring to a woman as a love-offering? Because it's a seller's market, honey. Free agents *cost*. What is the value of the pat on the arm or the "chin up" or the empty x's and o's one receives after screaming, *howling,* for love and help?

Simon clicks his computer mouse and the screens fill with a seemingly endless succession of dating profiles featuring women, always young, always happy, always expectant.

Simon: Look at them. Just look at them. Where does *I have nothing, can give nothing, have no right or hope of receiving anything* fit in the scheme of pro-life bullet points? How can one quantify the feeling that love, kindness, strength, compassion, are being sucked from you minute by minute, replaced by invisibility and despair? What is the cost of that wild, half-insane tugging that says LOVE ME… I HAVE VALUE… I DO NOT DESERVE TO END MY LIFE

ALONE and shakes you like a jackal shakes a carcass? What emoticons does one affix to that to give it that sly wink, that joking twist, that will keep others from walking away in polite -- *always* polite -- embarrassment? These are real events, you know. They are happening to people *now* and every day, hour, minute. Argue these away. Show me these don't move the golden scales. WHAT CAN YOU GIVE ME THAT IS HARD AND SOLID AND NEGOTIABLE THAT I CAN USE TO BALANCE THESE OUT? What can you give me *today*? What do you say to the man who asks for everything because he *needs everything*? Will you leave him to cut out paper dolls and drink juicy-juice in some state hospital, swimming in scorn, sinking into that mumbling, self-contained twilight of the untouched and unspoken-to? *(He sways, speaks woozily, with a fuck-you lean)* I miss women. I miss breath and skin and the tide of battle. Even the bad stuff. Even the hesitations. The lies.

> *(Sings)* My body's just a cartridge made of callus and skin
>
> To amplify the blast from the explosion within
>
> Skin on the balloon
>
> Deflated too soon
>
> Dress it pretty and make it up nice
>
> So the people can hallucinate their paradise

You should see what this bug does to a man's prick. Most nights there's barely enough to grab for a piss. I'm sick of looking bad. I'm sick of smelling bad. I'm sick of feeling bad. *I want to be clean again.* What can you say? I'm drowning in an ocean of nagging memories, good intentions and bile, a hundred miles from anywhere. Have a go, my choir of knife-tongued Furies. Make it all end. Slice me up. I give you my throat, like Isaac.

We see that the Thrushes have returned, their faces painted white, adorned with painted tear-tracks.

Cleo: The slow advance of all-encasing ice

The slamming of a gate to Paradise

But still, there's soft, affectionate advice.

Dora: Our voices light and giving, like a song

Remind you of the arms where you belong

A haven once again, before too long

Rhoda: These tenets I can offer as your guide:

The good a man may cultivate inside

May be, when shown to others, multiplied

Electra: And one whose life is focused and serene

Spreads solace like a rich ultramarine

It may return in blessings unforeseen

Bryce: In good advice, the guides are not alone

Messages resound inside the bone

And whisper from the feather, leaf and stone

Eurydice: And now, the night prepares to breathe its last

With all the warring arguments amassed

Prepare for gentle footsteps from the past

The Thrushes fade. Simon carries on, as if to negate any suggestion of optimism. He hasn't heard a word they've said.

Simon: And then there are days overcome with petty worries, petty worries made unendurable because they are multiplied by months, years, against a backdrop of physical and financial depletion. A caregiver cancels. A wheelchair malfunctions. Sometimes I use my drugs improperly. I toss them down to deaden things, to send me to an enforced sleep. Such days never really begin. Death practice. String enough together and you can postpone indefinitely any resumption of life. *(Picks up pill bottles)* These over here are good speed to make things fly by faster. And *these*...These used to make me see whole little animated cartoons on the inside of my eyelids. *Where the fuck...?* Every life like mine is a little war against despair. A tiny little chemical war.

We may be saved. Someone may find a breakthrough and shepherd it through what the researchers call the "Valley of Death." They may work for a company not invested in disease-perpetuation. The cure may not be killed by lobbies and politicians. It may come to market. It may be made available. It may be affordable. It may reach you in time. It may work. You may have some useful years, some living *soul*, left that has not been killed by tedium and despair and isolation and impotent rage. Maybe even enough to love something sometime. *This* is what we have. Don't waste it, guys. It must be enough.

I would go on. Yeah, I would. But where would I go? Once you've been visited by the Great Sadness, the world never again feels the same. It's like re-entering a room from which you've made a grand exit because you've forgotten your hat. What would be left to say? What would be left to hold onto?

Philpott again flickers onto his screen, struggling into focus through a haze of snow and interference. The walls of the apartment are suddenly as green with foliage as a Mediterranean glade, the air full of the sounds of ancient music.

Philpott: But when you write your songs, good friend, aren't you reconfirming your grip on life? Isn't this a type of holding on?

Somewhere out there are perfect, mystical combinations of words, notes, gestures, images, and if we train ourselves well, work tirelessly and believe, we may uncover one such. And when we do, the world will change colour and we will unlock some special truth about mankind and be embraced, celebrated and protected as some kind of shaman or elder or, perhaps, wise fool, with special, exalted status. Don't you believe this?

We may not openly admit it, but at the root, all who write, play, shoot, dance, act, compose, really must believe. This is what keeps us going, and the funny thing is, in our urbane, well-read, witty confidence, we throw stones at religion when, in the end, our *quest* -- yes, I'll call it that -- is a religious one. The mystical combinations are like sacred texts or rites, for whom we are dedicated knights or exiled priests.

The only difference between us is how fervently we dare to believe. Are we so timid we search only for the retinue of the ambling, drunken god of wine, or are we true believers looking to unlock the meaning of everything? It's a question of guts in the end: believe a little, fail a little. Gamble everything on the real treasure and lose it all.

All I ever really wanted was a nice little temple in a sylvan glade where I could celebrate the god of small discoveries and happy tears. Not much to ask. At least, I didn't think so.

As we age, we start to see there are an infinite number of ways to be wrong. And one -- *maybe* one -- to be right. And the great caravan of mankind is just a procession of glorious mistakes, glorious and holy mistakes. And we are all called upon to join. You can't fool me. At the end of the day, you're another mad pilgrim, singing his fool head off, looking for the right.

Simon: Ah, but even we who fight the fight must someday give in to the bills and chores and worries. As my nest egg melts away, the tools will vanish, too. The guitars, the Tascam, the amp, the computer. In the end they get it all, the punters and the pushers and the pawnshops. The fools' caravan leaves us behind.

Philpott: Simon, you will always regret the beauty you do not create. What's more, the world, in its way, will regret it also.

Simon trades his electric for the Guild. He tenderly picks up and strums. On various screens reappear Eddie, J.C., and Lawrence.

Lawrence: Fight for it.

J.C.: Let tomorrow care for itself.

Philpott: Nobody can tell your side.

Eddie: You have forever to be dead.

Philpott: Every man has something sacred inside he wants to give to something other than commerce or hatred. If you've found it, follow it. Even a world of plastic trash and tomfoolery needs its shamans, and we never know who they'll be. Maybe even you.

> Beneath the peaks of NothingThere
>
> Are buried thoughts that none can share
>
> Abandoned streets and darkling skies
>
> The frigid light in loveless eyes
>
> A shabby headstone glazed with frost
>
> Delusions of the weary lost
>
> O, leave them buried if you dare
>
> Beneath the peaks of NothingThere!

J.C.: In the beginning was the Word. It's still there. Maybe it just needs a little reverb and some good chord changes.

The stage darkens and Simon, clearly drunk and tired, sits in a small pool of pink light. He is dizzy from following circular arguments that lead nowhere. He has cocooned himself in dark thoughts, and seems ready to ride out the rest of the night with his bourbon, examining fragmentary song ideas like the one he toys with now:

Simon: *(Somberly, bitterly, croons)* You should have known me then

> The bravest holy warrior at the five and ten
>
> The finest courtly love that ever might have been

If you only could have known me then

The time that's gone is gone

And it won't never come again

If you only could have known me then

In a pocket of shadows near Simon's bed, something like a figure stirs. We sense its presence, but we cannot yet see it clearly. Still, we can tell it's important from the way Simon recoils. There is the sense in the room that this is what we have been waiting for; this is what the night's ceremony has ultimately conjured.

Simon: I suspected you would come, probably be the last.

Figure: Why?

Simon: Love. Romantic love. The ultimate anchor tying us to the world. The ultimate weapon of persuasion in the human arsenal. After art and faith and duty and friendship and all that jazz we get hit with.

Figure: That's what you think? I'm romantic love? Don't I represent the failure of love?

Simon: No, not to me. To me, never.

She steps forward into the light and we see Beatrice. She is a slight, slim girl in her late twenties, dressed in a thriftshop print dress, with a wild head of henna-colored hair. She is sweet and sad and her gaunt, pretty face seems always to be struggling toward laughter from beneath a veneer of lingering, inexpressible sadness. It is a face upon which no guile ever settled.

Simon: To me, you always represented the promise of love, Bea. The possibility of love. Any failure was mine, all mine.

There is a long silence.

Simon: You can start arguing any time you like.

I want to tell you some things about love, my love. It was there. It was always there. My God, how it scratched to get out. But it was wrong. It was broken. It never kicked in.

Beatrice: You never said.

Simon: I couldn't. I didn't have the vocabulary. I didn't have the words. I had thousands, but not those particular ones.

Beatrice: Try.

Simon: A little later.

Beatrice: How did it all come to this, Simon?

Simon: I'm tired now. It's hard to learn anymore. When we were together, I had energy.

Beatrice: Together. Were we *together* when we were together?

Simon: For years, I felt I had to be unencumbered, like I was meant for something, something that love would prevent.

Beatrice: Simple fear, disguised as mission. As it usually is.

Simon: So I just kept flinging open doors, shining lights in corners, charging ahead. School, bands, law. But each time, it was never there. It was never the thing. I was never anything. I was always nothing. You have to be *something* to ask someone to bind her life to yours. Don't you? You have to be somebody complete. How many of those do you meet in life? A handful? You have to live, sing, fight a war, give a kid the kiss of life. Write the dictionary. When I look at myself, I see silly putty, an unfinished soap carving. Never brought to fruition. It was always around the corner, always the next thing that was going to do it. You? You were great. Not *going to be*. You were *already* great when I knew you. All the pieces in place.

Beatrice: If only you knew.

Simon: I'm afraid to die *in process*. I want to be known, known and understood.

Beatrice: Nonsense. None of us is known. We are the sum total of pictures and writings and impressions and anecdotes and pranks and manifestoes.

Simon: And mistakes.

Beatrice: And sins and gifts and loves and hates and even abstentions. Billion-piece jigsaws that are never complete. And everyone holds the pieces at a different angle, in a different light. So when we trade them, or look at them, they are changed by the act. We're all kaleidoscopes with unique missing parts. When we ask for love, we're asking for help in putting them together. I would have helped.

Simon: Where does the complete *me* live? Does it exist? I'm not sure. I feel like I've never even seen it.

Beatrice: So?

Simon: So love is like selling a house you've never walked through, a car you've never driven. It's a con. A shell game. It's dishonest, and that's why I could never commit to it.

Beatrice: Oh, how noble! *Idiot!* What scares you so much? What scares you *really?*

Simon: Restitution. Psychic, emotional, spiritual restitution. I can't make it.

Beatrice: Don't you know? We all owe and we never pay. The interest keeps accruing and we keep trying to pay down our debts, but we never do. It's what keeps us bound to each other. It's called *relationship.*

Simon: I could never live with unpaid debts. They felt -- *feel* -- like chains to me. I thought it was freedom I had, but it was just weightlessness. Drift.

Beatrice: Why didn't you tell me these things?

Simon: I never told anyone. I never told myself. Fear. Thirty-one flavors of fear.

Beatrice: Maybe this is a breakthrough.

Simon: It might have counted once.

Beatrice: It always counts.

The lights go down and, suddenly, Beatrice is there, at stage center in a hot light that appears to surround her in flames but not consume her. The screens ignite with images of blooming life.

Beatrice: Let's talk about our world. We have a planet that we are literally burning up. We're choking it, giving it fever, breaking it apart with earthquakes, drowning cities with rising seas like in those old novels you used to read, drying up and poisoning aquifers and reservoirs, forcing peasants to riot and overthrow governments. We are becoming a Third World desert of extreme rich and extreme poor, forcing our kids into limitless foreign wars and lives with missing limbs and scrambled minds, and our lawmakers work a three-day week and accomplish nothing, while the internet enables a few ignorant people to shout down all the wise advice that remains. We are so mesmerized by our own debasement we celebrate it, magnify it, *recycle* it electronically, for entertainment. Our laws aren't enforced. Corporations are horning in on rights that used to be reserved for people. New viruses are incubating in foreign ghettos and we're overdue for a global pandemic. Our antibiotics don't work anymore and companies are too busy engineering better erections to do anything about it. New strains of food owned by conglomerates are replacing the old until eventually they will decide who eats and who doesn't in corporate boardrooms. Poets write poems no one reads. Newspapers are dead so no one looks for truth anymore. And people who study these things say industrial civilization won't survive the century. It's a comfortable, general madness and we all share it and we're all scared. That's why no one is screaming in the street. Who is unaffected to scream *to*? You're on this rollercoaster with the rest of us. We're all heading into that long black tunnel and YOU DON'T GET TO STOP THE RIDE IN THE MIDDLE BECAUSE YOU'RE SCARED. No one is ready. No one is cool. You're in it 'till the bitter end just like all of us. And it *will* be a bitter, bitter end. You ride because you paid the fare and you're going to get your money's worth. Every nickel.

There is a space that seems to be reserved for Simon, but he fails, at first, to speak.

Simon: The ballgame. A nothing-nothing bore.

Beatrice: What?

Simon: Nothing. Look, my life has been over for years. We're just putting last edits on a chapter that will be dropped from the final draft. A superfluous epilogue.

Beatrice: Human life is like human speech. It needs to be spoken up for and defended and fought for hardest when it is at its worst, when it's indefensible. Human life was never happy or fine; it was always a velvet pincushion full of angry stings. Any other assessment is a lie intended to cause you pain. But the human mind is the slipperiest thing on earth. It always finds things to love and savor, no matter what. It's never been defeated yet. Even the urge to write, to sing, to transcend the deepest pain, is a light in the dark. And weighed against the End, the Blackest Black, those small lights shine with the candlepower of white-hot stars. Death always comes soon enough, and, while those lights flare, with even the possibility of love or comfort or transcendence throwing a supernova sparkle over things, it's preferable to night-eternal, which offers not peace but merely a cancellation of all desires, aspirations, achievements. Hang on to the possibilities because you might as well. The chance of joy is infinitely superior to the certainty of nothing. It's the best deal going, and you'll never get a better one.

Simon: I'm beat.

Beatrice: Everyone is tired. Life is a door perpetually closing. We run to catch it but we never do.

Simon: I want to be held and spoken to, quietly. Why did we break up? I never wanted to be married, but I think I would marry you right now. Do you love me, Beatrice?

Beatrice: Enough to save you, yes.

Simon: Enough to stay?

Beatrice: I can make you remember, remember how to feel and to hope.

Simon: Is that enough?

Beatrice: I think it might be. It had better be.

The screens begin to shine with a deep indigo light.

Beatrice: You are here now. You have reached the raw edge of your life, where no one can follow. Now you must find something smothered inside yourself that's trying to cry out. It really is now or never. Nothing is soft. Nobody saves you.

Simon: Too much. Way too much for even you to ask.

Beatrice: Find it.

Simon: Way too much.

Beatrice: So tell me now. Show me all this black lake of emotion you say you have for me. Show me now. Because I'm asking now.

Simon: Don't you believe me? Don't you believe a dying man's declaration?

Beatrice: Tell me. All the words are stupid. It only matters that they hurt.

Simon pauses to collect himself.

Simon: You were my friend, from the time before we forgot how to be happy and loyal. You had magic in you, Beatrice. You taught me. You opened my eyes. You were like a great singing, springing jack-in-the-box with hummingbird's wings, full of glitter and flower petals and itching powder. I never knew a person could live so many different ways, in so many different directions. And you chose me. *Me.* You picked *me* out. You laid everything out at my feet. You cried with me. You gave me surprises. Threw me parties. These were what mattered. And I let it all go with my silence. I should have given you everything. But I didn't. I put it in a 40-page letter -- *huge* fucking tome -- that I never sent, that I carried around in my briefcase for *three months*, always adding some new shit -- *I'm cold, Bea; I'm misunderstood, Bea; my audience ignores me, Bea* -- and I threw it out in a pizza parlor dumpster when I couldn't remember anymore why I started writing it in the first place. I let you go away. And all the time you were asking me *why don't I hear from you? (now, softly)* Why don't I *hear* from you…? I couldn't be fucking bothered. *(Takes out from his bookcase an old 12" of Lydia Lunch and Rowland Howard singing "Some Velvet Morning")* You were Phaedra, who gave me life. And now, this, *this* cheap plastic, is all that's left. You were the turning point. Everything went zigzag and sideways after you -- for me, and for a lot of us. I feel like my youth belonged to another man. Everything I wrote since then is for you, really. I feel like you're the only one who can forgive me, forgive me for my refusal to love. For my thousand various and sundry refusals. You're the one who can give me back the right to live. I can hardly look you in the

264

face. It's too bright. That's the power you have. You have it all, you, you little ageless, untarnished, hair-trigger barroom sprite! You can save this unwanted flesh paperweight, this puff of smoke, if you want to. I can't even bring myself to ask, and I never could. Before you, I am always a child. A petulant little child hiding behind a big *Do Not Disturb* sign as tall as the sky and as wide as the world. And when I let you down, I let the whole world down. I began my 30-year suicide note.

Beatrice: This is your Yes. Your great big Yes. Now sing me something. Something new and sad. Make me miss you again.

The lights return to normal. Beatrice relaxes on the edge of the bed and Simon plays, fumbling at first, a folksy acoustic ballad that sounds as old as toil and sweat, the postscript to his story of jinxed lovers.

Simon: I was a rambler, wild and high

A-looking for a place to die

You held me though I don't know why

There was nothing there to hold

Wasn't that a love, dear soul?

Wasn't that a love?

Wasn't that a love, dear soul?

Wasn't that a love?

You took the ride, you paid the tolls

Covered up my cracks and holes

We were conjoined benighted souls

In orbit to the end

Wasn't that a love, dear friend?

Wasn't that a love?

Wasn't that a love, dear friend?

Wasn't that a love?

Legends live a life that's free

Beyond the scorn and scrutiny

Your headstones and your groveling grace

Just wait for vandals to deface

Your judgment can't control or stain

Two lovedrunk ghosts

In summer rain

Beyond your wrath and dimestore pain

Nothing to excuse, no crimes to explain

The road was dry and full of stones

And wound up to the hill of bones

The women heard my dying moans

'Till all my work was done

'Till evil ate the sun

Wasn't that a love, dear one?

Wasn't that a love?

Wasn't that a love, dear one?

Wasn't that a love?

Beatrice: *(Smiling)* Tell me you just didn't say "a-lookin'."

Simon: I kinda did. Yeah.

Beatrice: Feeling better now?

Simon: I kept waiting for it all to come together. All the variety of threads, the reasons yes, no and maybe. But they don't blend. None of them. They coexist and swim around in the great pool, swooping and diving and moving in parallel, making fantastic patterns, like those we make dragging fine combs through pans of colored oils: intricate, unique, unreproducible. Each perfectly beautiful, perfectly complete and individual. And we stare into them and see what we will. And try and fail to communicate what we see.

He resumes singing.

Simon: What if it was all a lie

Rivers deep and mountains high

First hello to last goodbye

And all that's really real

Is the knife edge that we feel?

What if it's a lie, oh my

What if it's a lie?

No Pearly Gates or

Big Rock Candy Mountain when we die

What if it's a lie oh my

What if it's a lie?

I'll take a spin

I'll cast the die

And see what comes along

Another verse for this poor song

I'll take a spin and cast the die

I'll spin and cast the die.

Beatrice moves closer, still smiling.

She sang the songs and named the names

Grabbed the earth with hands like flames

Called away, but to her shame

She just could not comply

One more prayer to try, Oh Lord

One more prayer to try

Last before she'd say goodbye

One more prayer to try

Beatrice: I would have stayed, if you had just asked.

Simon: The very reason why I couldn't. *(Pause)* I never told you. I never told you.

Beatrice: Find the words. Spend the rest of life on the words. Okay? It's worth it. It's the only thing that is.

She appears behind him, now naked and pale, and tries, with difficulty, to wrap her arms around him. They belong together. The universe seems to want them so. At the crucial instant, Simon turns away. Beatrice, sensing his distance, draws in a short breath and is gone, just gone, in a cloud of powder, like windblown snow, an exorcised ghost.

J.C., Eddie, Philpott and Lawrence reappear, joined on the screens this time by Beatrice and Eurydice.

J.C.: Because you are tasked

Lawrence: Because you are weak

Beatrice: Because you were asked

Philpott: Because you can seek

Eddie: Because you aren't done

You have more things to say

Beatrice: A life is a debt

Every breath helps repay

J.C.: Because life is mystic

Beatrice: Because life is tough

Lawrence: 'Cause death hurts acutely

Eddie: 'Cause more ain't enough

Philpott: Because man's an explorer

Beatrice: Because man is a friend

Eurydice: Existence is yearning

And yearnings won't end

The screens grow almost intolerably bright, then flare out in slowly shrinking points of light, like old television sets being switched off. Only, on one, Eurydice remains. She has a look of consolation.

Eurydice also fades. All is dark, except Simon, illuminated by a single white spot.

Simon: And so, the defense rests. I will go on, for the sum of all reasons, which is no reason at all. And tomorrow, we'll turn it all over one more time. Until our hands and minds and the available light grow weak and we can't turn it over anymore.

There's no lesson. There's no relief. The conversation continues. That'll have to do.

All light fades. It is just Simon, strumming a chiming, elegiac coda like a John Fahey funeral march, lit from stage right by the faint, multicolored play of the neon sign. He resumes what sounds like a continuation of the fragment he had earlier sung to Jessie:

Simon: Her life was supposed to be a shower of gold

> Not a shower of sand too fine to hold

> A satin pillow on a feather bed

> Not a maze of complications sent to fuck up her head.

> But life never ends as what the dreamer believes

> Julie thought as ivory fingers turned to buds and leaves

> The soul just withers while creation grieves

The chord fades in a dying wash of neon sparkles. A spectral voice whispers, seemingly from every corner of the room at once.

Beatrice: Nobody saves you…

The neon flicker very slowly fades to black as the last notes of Simon's guitar die out.

END

For M.M.

Apophenia is an imprint of
www.paraphiliamagazine.com

For information and to purchase other titles:
http://www.paraphiliamagazine.com/books.html